FOREVER OR NEVER

SOPHIE NAASZ

Created with Vellum

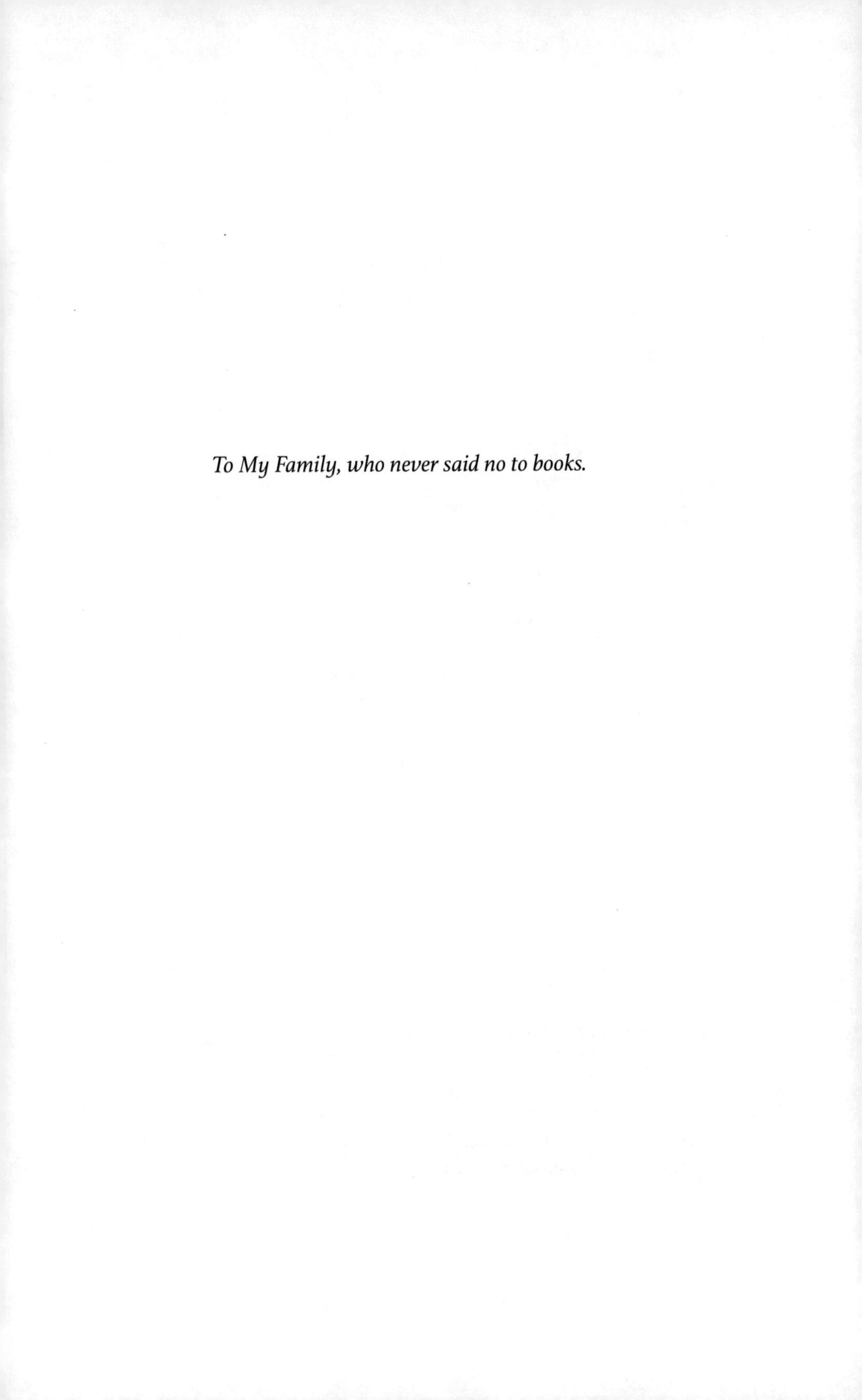

To My Family, who never said no to books.

"I have spread my dreams under your feet; Tread softly because you tread on my dreams."

— W.B. Yeats

PROLOGUE

A sky of emerald eyes winked and yawned, its fiery inhabitants dancing the night away, a tale of splendor that befits its place above the world. And no matter the sadness that seemed to pervade the land they watched by night, forever they danced, beacons of joy, skilled in their every move. One could say they were foolish never looking upon the brethren they claimed to rule, but that was the eye of the blind, for very few who possessed sight saw the purpose of each twirl and each step, the motive put behind a blushing smile, and the thought placed into each laugh; in truth, they ruled well, so well that the dance seemed unintentionally flawless, extravagant and wasteful.

Yet, tonight their dance was altogether the grandest of the centuries, perfectly choreographed to seem wonderful but not too pleasing so to evade the unwanted notice of the blind, yet too perfect so that they may engender the glance of the opened eye.

Down below the dancing stars, in a field swathed by shadows and enveloped with the cold brush of night, a man sat. He was wrinkled, perhaps as old as the land itself, and at first glance, one might think he had been long dead, for centuries even, except for the veracity in the slightest rise of his chest. In truth, such man had been asleep for eight years—a mystery of a life that the townspeople wished not to meddle with—and therefore, they had not set foot within ten feet of the man since the day he had fallen into such a slumber.

The man's even breathing continued as it had for those fateful eight years. There was not a single other movement that would suggest he had awoken, but indeed he had, for right at that moment his eyes were open, an unsettling opal, one not of this world but of something the tongue could not quite embody. The sign of a master seer. The two pale reflecting moons swiveled to the stars reading their flashing dance, for there was no real way to explain how the man looked at the stars other than as if they were precious pieces of literature that were already starting to crumble to ash. His eyes reflected the stars once more before a film of almost glass slid atop them. The seer sighed one last time. He was dead.

It wasn't before another two years that the townspeople found out about his death, for his body had stayed surprisingly intact as if he had died just a second before. Even more odd was a paper, simple as any other, lay beside him—something that had never been there before.

The little girl who had been curious enough to wander within ten feet of the man and found him dead had picked up the paper—she received a scolding for doing so later—and read the last words of the otherworldly man. They had escaped his mouth on his last sigh and magically appeared on the paper, although, he surely did not write them there; "It is of the stars that at the moment I breathe my last, a girl in a thousand years shall breathe her first. Condemned to be a dragon in a world too small to fly in. Blessed with a heart to conquer the night."

And with that last word, the curious tiny girl stirred life into the words, feeding them the element they needed to stretch off the page and whisper into the folds of Time itself. The mother of the curious girl swept her daughter away from the man and batted the sheet of paper to the ground without giving it much of a glance, for, after all, it was just a blank sheet of paper, simple as any other.

1

A gunshot echoes down the narrow alleyway sounding unnervingly like a T-rex's roar—well, like the simulated ones the school tells us were once real. Like I'll ever believe that.

Our history books are filled with pictures of millions of species that once roamed the land: birds with rainbow feathers, seals with long drooping noses.

And of course, every single one of them was slaughtered into extinction by human beings.

I sigh at the thought.

What a lovely species we humans are!

The roar sounds again. Judging by the number of echoes it makes as it ricochets off the shabby buildings around me, I calculate that my pursuers are about two minutes away. I have time.

I sit and bite the dust encrusted sandwich that got me into this mess, and dirt, is it worth it. The lettuce is a bit dry, and the tomatoes are really just globs made from strands of DNA that scientists put together and colored red in hopes of imitating the tomatoes seen in pre-A.R.T. (Advanced Reality and Tech) pictures.

I let out a snort.

The engineer who gave our era that name must have had a great sense of sarcasm, naming our completely unimaginative world after an extinct profession that required so much creativity. It's either that, or he was just a very hopeful guy. I'd bet on the former.

My Lynk's countdown warns me that my two minutes are almost up, and sure enough, in a second, the slaps of polished shoes on the chemical-filled earth, dried to the point of cracking, fill my ears.

Reluctantly, I finish the little bit of heaven I was savoring and stuff the rest of the sandwich into my mouth. I'd rather eat it faster than take the risk of losing it to my pursuers.

As the group of kids grows seconds away, I get up, wipe off the crumbs on my beat-up jeans, and eye the nearest building's wall.

It's an ugly gray cement, but it has holes and hollows, exactly the kind of wall I like. Adrenaline starts rushing through my veins at the sight. I'd take an ugly and riddled wall any day if the other option was a smooth-walled palace.

In truth though, a perfectly smooth wall is not a challenge for me, thanks to the eighteen years I've spent living in this crazy city. But, the fact is, just because I can, doesn't mean I *want* to.

I'm on the roof just as the group of kids rounds the corner. The boys, who would argue they're men, but are still showing signs of being right in the middle of adolescence, are huffing and puffing as if there are some little pigs' houses in need of blowing down.

I bite down on my lip to keep myself from laughing at their "tough" facade. For dirt's sake, the lead kid is holding his gun as if it's a wild animal he doesn't know how to tame. I bet he shot it earlier on accident.

Drinking in their appearance, I draw the conclusion that these boys are definitely not street kids. It's likely that they're just rich kids who snuck away from their parents, thinking that this side of the city would be just a lovely and perfectly safe place to visit.

As if!

The funny thing is that this is not the first time I've seen rich kids sneak into the city. Sometimes they just get robbed, other times, they're not so lucky.

Just being in the presence of such ignorance used to make me blaze with anger, but now I just let apathy slide, chillingly, through me, freezing the ire until it shatters into dust and blows away.

Until I am as imperturbable as the wind.

I stay quiet. Act rationally and purposefully. And when they come strutting around dangerous streets, like fat fluffy pigeons disguised as common sparrows, I laugh mercilessly as their feathers get ruffled, amused that they're actually surprised—watching like a hawk who waits for his prey to fatten as much as possible before swiftly taking his due.

I'll steal a sandwich, some coins, a fine pair of shoes straight off their feet. I'll act tough, fool with them for a bit...but I never beat them up, I only do what is necessary to scare them from coming back...to spare them from a worse fate.

Sure, I hate the rich sometimes and how difficult they make our lives on this half of the city, but I also know that it's not the kids' fault...so I try in my own way to be half-nice to them.

As the lead boy looks up, finally straightening from panting and wheezing like an old overworked donkey, I know my assumptions about his identity are correct by the haughty gaze he levels on the buildings around him.

Kids born and raised in these parts would look at these dirty buildings and weathered roofs as weapons, hiding places, and escapes. He simply looks at them as if they made a mistake by coming too close.

I don't have time to deal with him and his friends today.

My sister's sallow face, as white as ashes are black, rises in my mind: Her eyes rheumy, her chest weakly rising, the movement so faint it's barely discernible. She lies immobile, a fraying string away from death.

I came out here for her, and I must not get distracted any more than I already have.

Pushing the image away before I'm lost to grief, I take hold of the pain, molding and bending it into a cold sharp, dagger, like how an ironsmith works metal.

Sakura needs a cure, and if I don't find one soon, Death will come for her, a gleaming blade in hand and a smirk on his lips.

Slowly turning around on the roof—away from my desire to scare away the boy below me—I'm about to move forward when I hear a small rock roll off the roof. I curse quietly. My attempt at silently slipping away without a confrontation foiled by just one small slip.

Now, I've basically uncovered my location for their sole benefit. I might as well invite them to tea while I'm at it.

Turning to witness my own demise, I watch as the rock falls. It has the grace to hit the leader right square on the forehead. I curse again.

I guess I got my wish of confronting him.

The chestnut-haired boy spins around and immediately sees me, his eyes narrowing to two twin pots of foolish fire.

Combined, the serious stare and the diamond-shaped red mark on his head from the rock, make a picture so absurd that I cannot even attempt to hold in my laugh, and it bolts out of my throat, pulling a snort from my nose with it.

The boy's nose scrunches at the sound like I've seen genetically mutated pigs do as they search for their favorite scraps in the slop. But what's even worse is the look of murder on his face. I almost let out another hiccup of laughter at how easily this boy is enraged, but I quickly reign it in. I may be reckless, but I don't have a death wish.

"Come down and bow to me, you little urchin," the child says, with a voice impressively snobby for such a young age. His demand is no surprise, *all*—well except the select few—rich people think they're kings or something. I'm tired of it.

"Well then king, as a tribute I shall chop off your head." I do a sloppy over-exaggerated bow followed by a sharp swipe, the macabre movement a person would make using a scythe to chop a head off. The boy's eyes widen at my tenacity, but in his defense, he recovers pretty fast—well, for a *rich* kid.

"It's seven to one. Stop the back talk, and admit defeat. Perhaps then, I may be merciful."

I suddenly have a great urge to play with this kid who seems so sure of himself.

"King, but do you not realize that I am the gingerbread man?"

"Don't call me king!" the boy tries to act as if he is in charge, but the fear in his eyes tells another story. He knows he's playing a game that he doesn't know the rules to.

His fear only makes me bolder.

I jump from foot to foot, the movement expending some of the adrenaline rushing through me, "Tell me, you do know the story of the gingerbread man, don't you?" It's a pre-A.R.T. story, but its popularity has spread throughout this era, too.

"Of course, I do," he snaps, trying to sound confident in front of his friends, but he honestly and truthfully doesn't know what I'm getting at.

"Well, then you must know what his slogan is. Mind to tell me?" Playing with this pigeon makes me feel like a hawk again, and I soak up the feeling. Around these parts, it's very rare that I find that I'm the big guy in face-offs.

"Yes, I know it! He always says 'run, run as fast as you can, you'll never catch me-"

"I'm the gingerbread man," I finish as I race away across the roof and jump onto the next building's top floor window sill before the boy can even stop stuttering the next word of the slogan.

I crouch there, chuckling softly—pigeon feathers are just too easy to ruffle. Sighing, I start to adjust my footing on the window sill, the glass of the half-broken window digging into my back when a hand comes around my mouth and a fist slams into my ribs. Pools of blackness drown out my sight.

2

I stumble backward through the window and into the building, struggling to take a deep breath in through my nose to clear my vision.

The guy—luckily, he's by himself—is probably 5'11", judging by his stance, and is well-muscled, with that force he put behind his punch. My ribs ache, but luckily the guy wasn't trying to hurt me, he was probably just acting upon reflex.

The fact that he didn't knock me out, brings me to two conclusions: he doesn't want to sell me in the market, or two, he's just plain old stupid. I'm hoping for the latter—if he doesn't want me for the market, then there's little chance he'll care to keep me alive.

Breathing in, I send my skull flying back into his nose, already whipping around to face him as he stumbles in shock. I don't give him time to recover before landing two sharp jabs to his abdomen, followed by a kick. Unfortunately, he regains enough consciousness, and ducks as my foot sails over his head—although barely. I manage to land another blow before he assumes a fighting stance.

"Dirt," I curse under my breath. He actually looks like he knows how to fight. Spinning around, he sends out his fists in neat and controlled jabs, each step he takes forming a routine, and that routine forming a lethal kind of dance.

A beautiful mask of concentration falls over his face as he works, and his agility wraps around his body like a costume of elegance.

He is light and lithe, a leaf twirling in the breeze, moving swiftly but without rush.

I soak in his control with a touch of admiration, but my attention serves another purpose. He favors his right arm, more frequently starting attacks with his left side, leaving his right neck and shoulder unprotected.

A small smile lifts the corners of my mouth.

This guy is good, but I'm better.

My back arches as I do a flip in the air, and as gravity clasps me in its tumultuous grasp, I send out a graceful jab right for his neck, which is adorned with a small silver chain. He crumples like a rag doll and sinks to the floor unconscious.

Slowly, I walk toward him. Caution stilling the energy in my veins as I approach his prone body.

Once I confirm that he is not awake, I let my eyes unfocus, collecting information.

His hair is a dark brown, shaggy, with the ends not exactly the same length. But the color and cut together only add on to his charming image. Like all the heroes in pre-A.R.T. stories, he has a strong, chiseled jaw with stubble daring to grace upon it. His skin is the color of honey as if he has spent days soaking in the sun, and his arms are gracefully lined with muscles.

Honestly, he's the perfect definition of "handsome" if there ever was one, but with all the modifications people are getting these days, I've learned not to trust a pretty face.

Oddly though, I don't see a flashing blue light glowing behind his ear, the sign of an online Lynk.

That's weird...it's probably offline.

Only people who are extremely against A.R.T. tech don't have a Lynk installed--after all, they are free nowadays. Well, it's those crazy people and seers; in stories, seers never have tech, because it supposedly blocks their true sight. But, he's definitely not a seer, as the last one died about a thousand years ago.

I, personally, could never go without my Lynk. People adore the thousands of apps coded into each and every Lynk called LxApps. They range from being able to change the pigmentation of one's hair, to creating a virtual reality world that is rumored to be so lifelike that people lose themselves in it, forgetting that they're not in the real world.

The man who made the first Lynk actually died last Sunday and the memorial procession lasted two days long. The streets were crowded, and some die-hard fans were actually weeping. I mean, I love my Lynk, and I'm grateful to the guy who made it, but it's not like I actually mourn him. For dirt's sake, the guy lived to one hundred and eighty-six—most people in these parts don't even live to see seventy. All I'm saying is that his family should just be grateful that he lived such a long life.

After I had bowed to his image on a Jumbo screen that day—his coffin was not allowed to be displayed in front of citizens in fear that those same crazy fans who were weeping might try to steal the body —I had taken advantage of the crowds, slipping in between the sweaty masses and slipping out with a few pouches of coins. It wasn't a lot to them, but to a street kid like me, it was the difference between actually eating for a month or starving

The man was a genius during his life, but he really gained my support in death—for giving me the chance to snatch some coins.

I know how dangerous some of the apps he wrote can be, so I only have the basics: a healing program that can heal a scratch or even a broken bone, a comm-system, an app to enhance my eyes—when I was seven, I lost my glasses in a fight and the outcome wasn't so pretty, so now, I always just keep the eye-enhancing app on.

The last app I have is called a coding canvas, and to me, it is by far the most important app I'll ever have. Every serious coder has a coding canvas. It's basically a blank slate that comes up in my vision when I call on it and connects to my thoughts, so I can code just by thinking about it. When I was eight, I used the canvas to code my own app that allows me to see all the coding in the world around me. If someone's hair is tinted by one of their LxApps, I can see the code hovering around their head that the Lynk formed to change their hair. I can even see the strand of code that slightly altered the color of the wood that makes up the room I'm standing in right now.

I've never turned the app off since the day I coded it, and the sight of the code hovering near the wooden walls comforts me, like how a child's blanket might offer solace. In a lot of ways, I guess the code has become some sort of a guide or parent to me—especially since my real parents died when I was eight.

Ever since they passed away, I dove into the world of zeros and ones anytime the grief became too hard to bear. And anytime my sister's sickness sent her into unconsciousness, I dragged myself up the walls of these alleys, strengthening my muscles, sharpening my rage. I grew stronger as a result, but I left my childhood behind.

I turn around and look at my reflection in what's left of the broken window. A short girl, approximately 5'3", stares back at me. Her long black hair is tied up in a messy knot, the untucked strands outlining her heart-shaped face, and her frame is skinny, built up only by hard muscle and not an ounce of fat. The scratches and bruises that litter her arms and legs tell of a hard life, and the scar that runs down her cheek and over the left corner of her lip screams of past pain. And yet, the significant thing about the girl is not her dirt-laden clothes or scarred arms, but the two laughing doe-shaped brown eyes on her hardened Asian face and the slight lines right above the corners of her mouth that have been etched by dozens of smiles.

In a city like this, the streets and people kill almost all joy and laughter, and yet the girl who looks back at me has managed to tuck away and withhold some happiness from the cold-hearted thieves of this city. I wish I could feel that love that seems evident in the reflection, but it disappeared when my sister grew ill again. Now, all I can do is place on a veneer of those memories and hope no one notices the difference.

I flash a cold smile at my reflection, hoping to pull some joy from deep within myself, but the window just mirrors back the image of a girl, looking silly as she tries to smile when she clearly is trying to hide a deeply set grimace.

I turn away from my reflection with a bitter sigh. I always used to praise myself for being unbreakable, the girl who found love in a loveless world, but look at me now.

I'm about to leave and head to the market—I don't really care what happens to the guy lying on the floor, as long as he's not bothering me—when I detect something amiss in the corner of my vision.

My eyes fly to the code floating around me, hugging each modified object in the room. I see the wood wall's tinted coloring, the fragrance enhancement on the little plant in the corner, but what stops me short, is that no code, not even *one* line, hangs over the guy on the ground. Even a person with no modifications would have a line or two, telling about his Lynk, but this guy has none. My body stills and my breath hitches. This guy doesn't look like some crazy, non-tech fanatic. No, in fact, he looks like any normal guy—except he has no Lynk.

I guess someone could have cut his out and stolen it, but I don't see a scar behind his ear when I bend down beside him. The hairs on my neck stand up straight, and my gut churns with unease. Something's wrong, and I can't afford to get mixed up with it.

I leave the building quickly, quietly, like a ghost drifting through a world it once knew.

THE CITY SMELLS like an old cookbook, each building and market stand like a page clinging to all the fragrances and spices that happened to fall as it lay open on the counter. And yet, at the same time, the smells clack and clash like soldiers on a battlefield while money rains down from their war like blood.

If a place could ever be called chaotic, I would argue that it's definitely here. People are pushing and shoving through the tightly knit crowd as if their Lynks are going to be taken away if they don't smack people hard enough.

The guy in front of me hollers at a merchant, bickering about the high price of the sweet smelling *pao douce* buns, while a speedy little kid, camouflaged by the dense crowd, runs behind him, cuts off the man's money pouch, and zips through the crowd like a minnow swimming among sharks. The child glances at me before he disappears, his eyes widening as he realizes I know what he did. I just shrug and wink at him. Who am I to judge?

The man finally stops arguing, grumbling about high prices, and reluctantly, deciding to buy the sweet buns, he reaches for his money pouch—the pouch that is no longer there. I watch his face register shock and then slowly turn purple in anger, one shade slowly giving way to a darker one, just how a plum ripens as it grows. When it stops darkening, his face has become a fully mature, overgrown eggplant. Stuttering and spitting, he turns toward the nearest person, who happens to be his good old friend the merchant, and starts arguing, as is human nature.

I chuckle at the predictability of humanity. We are like the broken record spinning on a turntable, playing the same ugly note again and again, and yet never realizing just how horrible the sound is. Yet, if the record were to be restarted, the needle replaced, and the volume turned up, the song would start to play an innocent tune, and then "screech!" the terrible note would shriek again. It doesn't matter the song or how lovely the turntable is, every single time, the horrible jarring note will persistently ring out. It's inevitable. I've learned to stop listening to the song—that's the only way to stop hearing the faults of humanity.

The fever of the crowd leaves me, like a blanket falling off my shoulders as I walk through the grand wooden doors that have no code floating around them—they're pure wood. The faded red wooden sign hangs over the door, the word *Apothecary* written in swirling golden letters like how a magician plays with her wand.

The door closes with the sound of clinking chimes, and I glance up fondly at the ceiling that holds rows and rows of plants. The herbs swing from the rafters, climb up the beams, and some have even wrapped themselves around the bookcases, like little bodyguards for the ancient tomes.

The store is tiny, probably only 250 square feet in total, but the high ceiling makes up for the small floor space, allowing twelve ten-foot-tall bookshelves overflowing with books and a large black table filled with herbs, a stove, and vials upon vials of medicines, to comfortably fit along the walls. Two rolling ladders are stored in a corner of the room in case the highest shelves have to be reached, but what fills me with awe every time I come in here, is the number of books. In addition to hundreds of books on wellness, health, remedies, and herbs, there are dystopian novels, books about folktales, nonfiction magazines, comics, action books, bibles, dusty old tomes that have titles too faded to read, and every other kind of book possible. Although, the store owner is an apothecary, his passion is reading, and so the result is that even after browsing the shelves for nearly four years, I have maybe opened only two percent of the books in this shop, and I love it. There is always another story waiting to be found.

"Konnichiwa Kayda Kawano!"

"Nē Fumihiko!" I turn around and greet an old man with a jovial face; he has wrinkle lines from laughing, and two golden-brown eyes that sparkle in the rays of sun shining through the window like a crowd of daffodils. The sight of him instantly calms my beating heart, and if any fear lingered with me from meeting the Lynk-less guy, the books that tower on the shelves around me manage to smooth it all away. If I were to call any place home, it would be here.

Fumihiko has been in my life ever since I was very little; he was a dear friend to my mother, both of them bonding quickly over their love for books, tea, and pre-A.R.T Asian culture; After the death of my parents, Fumihiko stepped in and cared for us as much as he could, keeping us clothed and fed for the most part.

"I need-"

"I know what you need," Fumihiko interrupts, his voice a gentle bay of reassurance and comfort, as he holds out a little wrapped parcel in my direction without looking up from his book.

He reads like he requires the words to live, and in a way, I get it. Although, I've never been an avid reader—unless it's a pre-A.R.T. fairytale—I can see how the letters on each page could almost be like the numbers in any line of code that all hackers seek, the difference being that letters normally tell a story, whereas my code hacks into websites, stealing me forbidden information.

I guess everyone has their thing.

Unwrapping the parcel, I call out, my voice muddled with disappointment "But this is only a few poppy seeds, hyssop, and a comb of honey. Surely you've found something else by now?" I walk up to his desk ready to plead my case, ready to argue, if there's even a chance he's holding something back.

"I didn't find anything, Kayda." He's still not meeting my eyes.

"Did you look in all the books. You could not have looked in *all* the books"

"I did."

"No, you couldn't have possibly read them all. Here," I pull off a book from the shelf behind me and place it on his desk with a loud thump. The title reads *An Antidote for Every Ailment*, "look at this one."

"Kay-"

"Oh look, here's another one, *One Hundred Illnesses, One Hundred Cures*!"

"Kayda..."

"Look, I don't think you've read this one, or this one, or even this one." I pile the books higher and higher forming a sizable tower on top of his desk, my shaking arms making sloppy work of it.

"Kayda."

"No, there's got to be a book here. Even if there is only one tome in all of these musty shelves, I'll find it. Just point me in the right direction. I'll go right now."

"Kayda, there is no cure."

"Of course, there is. Don't fool around with me, Fumihiko," I say sternly, looking behind his back, on his desk, anywhere a book may be, but I don't see one, at least not any book that would help me.

"It's not here, Kayda. It's nowhere."

"Stop it!" I shout, my words trembling in fury and outrage, "There is a cure, I *know* it."

"No, there isn't. I love you and your sister very much, and if I could, I would raise the sky for you, but it's time you face the truth. I haven't found a remedy for your sister's illness, and I'm never going to find one. I'm so sorry."

The words, the sympathy in his voice—that same animated, water-smoothed voice that soothed me as a kid— reminds me of the people who tried to comfort me at my mother and father's funeral. They would say "I'm terribly sorry for your loss," or "I know how you feel, but it will be okay," while on the inside, I was crumbling to dust, an eight-year-old unable to comprehend why people had to die.

All I knew for sure was that they *didn't* understand. They didn't *know* how it felt for your heart to cave in, your lungs to collapse, your only anchor in this horrible world to float away, free from its moorings.

They didn't *know* how it felt to drown in a world of air, each breath harsh, taunting me with the life that it ran through my veins, life that I didn't want if I couldn't share it with my parents. My whole world crumbled that day, and I was left, an eight-year-old, in a world she despised, a world she only stayed in for her sister. I may have lived, unlike my parents, but some vital part of me died with them, and I never got it back.

Now, as I look at Fumihiko, the memories of that day—memories I have hidden behind walls and barriers, fences of iron and posts of steel—come surging towards the surface, and I feel vulnerable, a feeling I swore to my eight-year-old self I would never feel again. I can't take this.

I thought that *someone* understood the pain, the loneliness, and now realizing how wrong I was, the little girl inside me crumples to the ground like a marionette puppet whose strings have been cut. I opened my heart, and now Fumihiko has stabbed me where it hurts the hardest.

"You're just like the rest of them. You give up when it doesn't benefit you!"

"No, Kayda, you know that's not tru-"

"Stop. I don't care what you have to say. You're dead to me." I spin around and storm through the wooden door, my first tears dropping, as hot as embers of a dying fire on my cheeks, as I weave through the crowd. I glance one last time at the jaunty storefront behind me: the wooden sign with swirling red letters, the maze of leaves that peak through the windows. I soak it all in because I know as certain as a seer knows the future that the apothecary, my home for the last twelve years, will disappear behind me like a mountain vanishing in mist, and I may never walk this path again.

3

I'm running through the crowds, my tears falling as I try to shove through the bodies that are positioned too close. Before, the market was bustling with energy, frantic and sweet, but now, I feel like the people are all executioners, trying to grab onto me, trying to pull me away from this life. The too strong smells only make it worse, snaking themselves around me, like ropes trying to bind my wrists. I can't breathe. Merchants are still calling out their wares and goods, but the fake smiles that are on their faces slowly morph into big-toothed growls. The world is trying to capture me, and I can't run fast enough. I can't escape.

My vision starts to blur, the people around me, now just pinpricks of light in a distant world, sound so far away, and I feel like a big hand is squeezing my throat, slowly growing tighter and tighter, causing black spots to coat the world when—I break through the last barrier of people ringing around the market.

My headache immediately relents, the consequential fist of fear at my throat already loosening its perilous grip, and I stumble into the first alleyway I see, slumping to the floor like an injured soldier. Memories grab at me like ghosts, tugging at my mind, trying to get into the recesses of my head. I try so hard to block them out, to build a wall where my other one crumbled and fell, but exhaustion renders me weak, and like a wolf-trapped hare, I can't do anything but grit my teeth as the memory takes a hold of my mind.

"Do you want to hear a story?" she says, leaning over me, the curtain of her black velvety hair tickling my nose, and her scent, like jasmine and honey, wraps around me in a warm embrace, more comforting than any blanket could ever be. She's leaning over me, a teasing smile on her face, her soft brown eyes, sparkling with mirth.

"Yes, yes! I want to hear a story!" my eight-year-old self replies giggling, clearly enticed by the prospect of a tale.

"I'm not quite convinced, maybe I'll come back tomorrow." She feigns getting up and walking to the door.

"No, no," I squeal, "I want a story, please*!"*

It's a game we always used to play: my mom faking that she would leave, and me shrieking for her to stay. It always made the story more exciting somehow when she started to tell it.

"All right then, I shall tell you the tale of Aladdin.*" I settle into her lap, curling up in her arms, finding just the right position. Surrounded by the warmth of her, I feel like a bird flying on a fine morning. I feel* free.

"Buried under the red shifting sands, hidden deep within the dunes of flaked sun, there was a lamp, gold as glory."

"And bright as greed," I say giggling.

"Yes, Kayda, that's right. It was gold as glory and bright as greed, and there were little pictures engraved around the top of the lamp. They were sketches of lions fighting Death and great big birds soaking the world in life. And when one looked at the lamp, its beauty was so profound-" I chuckle at the strange word, "that at once, tears would streak the viewer's face. Yet, very few ever saw the lamp, for it was cradled in the desert's arms, deeply hidden in the sands of the Earth. And so, nobody ever knew for sure if the lamp contained the great power it was rumored to hold. Many had gone looking for it, seeking the three wishes that the lamp would grant. And yet none came back with it in their possession because—you see—only a person who did not want the lamp for themselves could find it. And so, this

is where the story of Aladdin begins, with a prince destined to find a genie in a gold lamp, a prince madly in love-"

The memory is interrupted by another.

"-love is peace. Now, to read an excerpt from the Bible, the Romans, 8:35-39,'Who shall separate us from the love of Christ? Shall trouble or hardship or persecution or famine or nakedness or danger or sword? As it is written: "For your sake, we face death all day long; we are considered as sheep to be slaughtered." No, in all these things we are more than conquerors through him who loved us. For I am convinced that neither death nor life, neither angels nor demons, neither the present nor the future, nor any powers, neither height nor depth, nor anything else in all creation, will be able to separate us from the love of God that is in Christ Jesus our Lord.'" The priest's voice is monotonous. The words he drones on and on don't mean anything to me. They don't tell about my mother's voice, smooth and strong, filled with hints of mystery and hope. They don't tell about my father's always mussed up hair, or the banana splits he would make me whenever I was sad. They don't tell about a family broken in half by death. They're just words after all. They can't even describe the pain welling up inside of me. I suddenly get up, no longer able to sit in this imitation of a funeral and run through the church's doors, my short, stubby eight-year-old legs pumping hard. I run out of my parents' funeral service, past all the pews of people who are trying to appear sad, people who never even knew my parents—at least not really. I run from the priest's words, words he says just so he can get a check in the mail. I run even as my lungs start to burn, as my leg muscles start to cramp. I run and run and run until the scent of death leaves my nose, and then I sit in an alley, tears running down my cheeks and mourn my parents the right way, by telling a story.

THE MEMORIES LEAVE me like a mist slowly burning in the sun's rays, and I'm left alone, once again, sitting in the alley outside of the marketplace. A tear runs down my cheek, a silvery path of grief, and as I go to wipe it away, I realize that my hand is clenched so hard in a fist that my knuckles have turned white. I slowly uncurl my fingers, and smudge away the tear. The memory of my mom has uprooted something deep within me, something dangerous, and I don't know how to tie it back down.

⚬

THE JOG back to the house is a blur, the buildings passing by like the shadows of hummingbirds, dark silhouettes, moving by too fast to dwell on. I finally take the turn where *Li Jin's*, a Chinese restaurant, stooping and unkempt, huddles against an old, crumbling museum that is slowly becoming history itself. It's a turn I've taken countless times, one I've walked in joy and one I've walked in sorrow. I let out a sigh, this is the turn that leads to our street.

The road is cracked and dry, weeds sprouting out through the middle of it—a car couldn't have driven across it even if it had four-wheel drive. Lining the dark path are heaps of trash, stacks of forgotten CDs, and take-out boxes. Here, the shacks are toppling over, their owners not even realizing the downfall of their own structures. It's a mess and it's ugly, but it's home.

I hike around the foul-smelling piles, jump over the biggest cracks, and in less than a minute, I'm greeted by a cute, little cottage, the first building that's not a shack and that's not tilted. The windows are tinted, so nobody can see in, and the door has two bolts, but otherwise, the cottage looks normal: a light blue color, with a white door.

The cost of having a nice-looking house is that I had to pile even more trash on the already polluted street in front of our house, so nobody would notice it was any different from the house next door. But just in case, I also rigged two old beaten up radios to act as security alarms. If someone breaks past the two bolts on the front door and passes my trigger line, a pre-A.R.T. song will start to blast through the radios, and a signal will be sent straight to my Lynk. I always thought about how cool it would be to face off an intruder with a song playing in the background, like one of those professional wrestlers on TV showing off to their theme song. But I've come to realize that anybody who got through two metal bolts would *definitely* not be intimidated by a skinny girl like me standing in the hallway with music at her back. Actually, they'd probably just laugh.

I unlock the first bolt with a press of my finger to the plant that sits on the porch—it's not a real plant, just a plastic thing I've connected to the bolt and coded to read Sakura's fingerprint and my own. The next lock is a bit trickier. I've rigged it to scan my brain waves, but in order for the tech to recognize that it's me, I have to think about the day my sister grew ill, a memory that provokes enough emotional response for the scanners to recognize that it's me. A slight click issues before the second bolt gives out, and then I'm in.

Our little house—if it can be called that—is drastically nicer than any of the other houses on the street, but still, it's quite modest. In other words, it's nothing like what those rich pigeons roost in. Our cottage has two floors, but the second floor used to be occupied by our parents so we kind of steer clear of it and the bad memories it arouses. My bedroom is the room to the right of the entryway, and my sister's room is only a little bit farther down. Our house is a bit crazy but in a good, homey kind of way.

Each of the rooms has been painted their own color at my mother's insistence, and each one is startlingly unique. The walls of my room, for example, are a swirl of gold, red, and orange, just like the sands of the desert that my mom described to me while reciting the pre-A.R.T story, *Aladdin.* I had always been so intrigued by that story, especially by the land of golden dunes it describes, so on my fifth birthday, my mom had painted my room just as I imagine what a desert would look like. Even to this day, I think it's beautiful. My sister's room is a soft lilac, swirled with a darker shade of magenta, and even though I don't like the color purple, the swirls are nonetheless bewitching.

But if any room in the house was to be called a masterpiece, it would be where my parents used to sleep. Their room is not simply one color. Instead, my mother painted scenes from pre-A.R.T stories all over the walls in breathtaking colors. *Aladdin* was all reds and golds, but the *Sleeping Beauty* section of the wall was all deep purples and moody blues. I used to sit in my mother's room for hours, soaking in each and every detail, and admiring all the scenes shown on the walls. Sometimes, I still do, but it hurts to look at the paintings she had created without being able to hear her voice narrate them as well.

"Sakura, are you awake?" I plop the little bag of food I stole on the way to the apothecary on the countertop, but I keep the bundle that contains Sakura's medicine under my arm.

"Sakura, I brought you some food and medicine." No response. She's probably asleep. I tip toe into her room. The air is stale and heavy. Everything smells of sickness, but I don't care. I walk up to the wooden bed and glance at the frail figure curled up in a small ball on top. I put my hand on Sakura's forehead. The waves of heat that greet my hand confirm my suspicions: her fever hasn't broken. She coughs weakly, and her breaths are labored, each inhale strained, like the sound of a wounded soldier slowly dying on the battlefield. The sound is no good sign, and I cringe.

This is the longest she has ever had a fever, and I don't know how to help her. I open the little parcel that Fumihiko gave me, already feeling guilty about our fight. I *do* know that he loves us, but I don't agree with him in his certainty that there is no cure, and if he's not willing to help me, then it's for the best that I left him behind. I sigh; why must everything be a choice between one thing and another? Why can't I sometimes get both? The world provides me with so many questions, and yet almost every single one is left unanswered, repeated back to me, like echoes in a canyon.

I leave her room and prepare a simple syrup with the hyssop and honey. Together, they should soothe her throat and stop her cough, and with the poppy seeds I sprinkle into the mixture, the pain in her chest and lungs might fade slightly, but it's far from an antidote.

I return to her room and gently nudge her. She doesn't stir. I try again, poking her a little harder, but still, she doesn't awaken. My heart starts to speed up, its beats echoing in my chest, making a wild song in my eardrums.

"Sakura...," I whisper my voice weak from nerves. At first, there's no response, but then, her eyes flutter the tiniest bit, and my heart nearly does a somersault in relief.

"I need you to drink this," I say, tilting the syrup into her mouth. She doesn't nod or reply but she manages to swallow, and that's all I need. I sit and caress her forehead until I know she's no longer awake, and then, I dare to glance down at her. Sallow ivory skin stands out against the tangles of her midnight hair that spread out in a halo on her pillow, and sweat beads her forehead, even as she shivers under the ten layers of covers that I've piled on top of her. I can't help it; a cry escapes my mouth.

The name "Sakura" means "cherry blossoms", and from the moment she was born, Sakura *was* like a cherry blossom. Her body is dainty and graceful, and when she moves, it's as if she's floating, just how a blossom falls to the ground. Rosy cheeks and a heart-shaped face make her look innocent and sweet. Her perfectly shaped lips are consistently a newly-budded, rose pink, and her large eyes are blessed with thick lashes. I once was jealous of her beauty, so grand next to my unruly hair and serious look. Where I'm all angles, she's curves, and it lends her a natural grace.

Yet, the best part about Sakura is not her looks but her character. She's funny, with a flair for dramatics, and her attitude is as fierce as her face is pretty. Sakura makes me laugh like there's no tomorrow, and ever since she has fallen ill, I haven't laughed nearly as much. Just looking at her hurts, and the difference between how she looked five years ago and how she looks today, is like the difference between night and day.

A single tear runs down my cheek, a perfect droplet containing all my anguish, fear, and hope; that's all I'll allow. I have to stay strong for her because if I don't believe, then there's no one else to take care of her, no one else to carry hope for her, no one else who will love her. She's only got me. I curl up next to her and fall asleep.

I wake up to weak sunlight, and with a look at the foggy windows,

I know that it's probably around six in the morning. I'm about to make breakfast when I look down at Sakura. If anything, her fever has only gotten worse, and suddenly I wish there were more people waiting around her bed, praying for her to get better. Abruptly, I'm reminded of what I thought about last night, that she *only* has me.

That one thought threatens to crumple me. A girl like Sakura should be popular, with hundreds of friends and parties every weekend. Even around these parts, you'd be surprised with how social people are. And the loneliness in her life is all my fault. My mind goes to the story of Aladdin, dreaming, fantasizing. What I could do with a wish right now! I could ask for Sakura's sickness to be healed, for medicine, for help. I wouldn't waste it like the foolish men in the story, asking for riches and fame. Dirt, I could still save her if only I could be granted a wish. But Aladdin's just a story, and wish-granting genies don't exist. The reality is that Sakura is dying and I can't do anything about it.

The guilt, the pain, the fear, wells up inside of me, threatening to bubble over, and so I do the only thing I know how to do, the only thing I've always done when my sister's situation has gotten perilous. I run.

I'm out the door in a second, dashing through the familiar alleys. The shapes of the buildings blowing past me are the only comfort I can find these days. I don't know if I'm trying to run away from this world, or if I just need a break. All I know is that it feels right for my feet to hit the hard-packed earth again and again, guiding me through the maze of these dirty streets. I've never felt so free as when I'm running.

After a few minutes, my wild gallop has calmed into a steadily paced sprint. I'm dashing through the buildings, the network of clotheslines hanging above, forming a sort of net or cage above the city, keeping angels from flying to our help. Most of the buildings have worn down edges as if some giant came by and ran his fingers along the roofline.

I come around a corner and see the lake that's in the center of the city, blue and glistening. On the other side, stand skyscrapers and mansions, big yards with grass shimmering like tiny emeralds: an abundance of wealth glimmering just beyond my side of the city. But at the right end of the lake glowers the police headquarters, the execution square glaring at its left: a reminder that even though our worlds are connected, pigeons and street rats don't mix well together.

So, although only a lake divides one side from the other, it's almost like we're two different races of people, living on two separate planets, only able to see each other if we look through a telescope.

As I'm running, I catch a glimpse of the twenty-eight-foot wall that surrounds the city. Its gray stone is ominous even in the late afternoon sunlight. There are no doors in the wall, nor are there any exits from the city. In other words, no one comes in or goes out; that's how it's been since I was a kid, since my mom was a kid, and even since her mom was a kid. That's just how it is. Of course, there have been rumors that there are cities beyond ours, or that we're test subjects in a big science experiment, but I don't believe any of them. All I know is that no one in our city's history has ever gone past the walls—well, anyone that is *alive*. All executions take place on the wall, and every time, the body is pushed over the wall into the unknown. Just seeing the wall now sends a shiver racing down my spine. Something's wrong with that wall, and I don't think I want to know what.

I'm running so fast, my thoughts occupied by the wall, that I don't see the guy until he slams into me. We collide, and I hit the red bricks of the building behind me hard enough to knock the air out of my lungs, and yet I'm already sizing the guy up. He's probably 5'11", and judging by the weight that smashed into me when I hit the wall, I'd say he was about 165 pounds, wait...the guy confirms my suspicions as he turns around with a smirk on his face.

"For dirt's sake, it's got to be *you* again?" I glare at him, my annoyance flaring, but as I stare at his face, I realize that his eyes are a light green flecked with little pieces of gold, something I hadn't noticed the first time I met him—probably because he was unconscious for most of our last meeting.

"Hey, darling, I'd love to talk and all, but I didn't slam you into a wall for nothing. There are peo-"

"Darling!? I am not your darling!"

"Whatever you say, little dragon, but you've got to be quiet now." He puts a hand over my mouth and pushes me further into the space between two buildings. I'm about to bite his hand when he raises an eyebrow at me. He slowly lifts his hand from my mouth, putting his index finger up to his lips. I keep quiet, only because I'm smart enough to know that he's being chased and is hiding, although I do have the urge to shout to his pursuers just to annoy him. Sure enough, a group of enraged pigeons run in our direction but race right past our hiding place, totally oblivious to our presence. I snort.

"What?"

"What do you mean *what*?" I retort.

"I mean why'd you laugh when you saw a horde of angry people barreling down the street you're hiding in."

"You know they could never really hurt you." I look him up and down, "Well, let me rephrase that, they could never hurt *me.* They're just pigeons after all."

Now it's his turn to laugh. "*Pigeons,* is that what you call them? Seriously?"

I turn and look at him, *really* look at him. The last time I met him, I knocked him out, and all I noticed was the lack of code floating around him. Now though, I see that his posture is neither rigid like the wealthy, nor slightly crouched like the poor. No, he holds himself differently than anyone I've ever met. In a way, if it's possible in a world that no one comes or goes, he seems almost foreign.

"I don't think you should be making fun of the person who knocked you out in ten seconds."

"Ouch, the little dragon breathes fire too."

"How do you know my name?"

"I never said your name."

"Quit playing with me. You call me little dragon, and that's the nickname my mom gave me years ago. So, answer my question, or I'll knock you out again." I raise my fist, so he knows I'm not bluffing.

"Okay, okay, what if I said that a little birdy told me I would meet a pretty girl whose nickname was dragon, and you happened to be the first pretty girl I knocked into?"

"Flattery won't help," I say folding my arms. This guy is as arrogant as any pigeon.

"I'm not flattering, I'm flirting, there's a difference. An old gentleman flatters, but when a young handsome guy like myself gives out compliments, there's only one word for that: flirting, a skill I happen to excel at. "

"Yeah, yeah, well take your flirting or whatever you call it to another alley before I punch your pretty little face and give you an ugly black eye. Try your so-called skill with that."

"Are you sure you want me to leave?" He feigns a pout.

"Honestly, has anyone ever told you how annoying you are?"

"That's how it always starts," he says and winks, "See you around, little dragon." He turns and vanishes into the shadows in a way that makes magic seem real, leaving me to ponder over the conversation and the reason why I chose to talk to him, instead of fight him. People, as I have learned, always have their own motivations for doing things; it's never just for the good of others. The kind people in this city are few and far between, like shooting stars fallen from the sky and trapped in these dirty streets, scattered so far from one another. And so, a long time ago, I came to the conclusion that I didn't like humans and would be better off without their company, save, of course, my sister. I never had a problem with upholding that decision, well, until today.

4

The lines of code jump before me like puppies fighting over who gets to go for a walk. I grab them with a thought, fitting them together like pieces of a puzzle, and slowly, the chaos in my vision dwindles down to neat piles of code. I twist together the first two groups, altering a few lines of their code as I go. Then, I grab the next pile and unspool the lines, like a bundle of wool. I'm searching for a single line, a tiny fault.

The numbers are all in order, until—there, a small inconsistency, my door in, the perfect place to stage a hack. I prod at the numbers a little, loosening up the line. The best thing about a coding canvas is that it stores all past coding, which saves so much time. I grab a little bundle of code that I wrote last week. To an untrained eye, it would probably look like a blur of numbers floating above my hand, but I see what it really is: a key. I shove the key around the small fault in the code. At first, it looks like nothing's happening, but in exactly ten seconds, the little imperfect number turns red, indicating I've accessed it. All the numbers surrounding it turn red too, an army slowly kneeling to me. I quickly attach the red pile of code to the last few groups hovering in my vision.

My code works fast, working through the lines of numbers,

cracking them open like pistachios and leaving the nut for me to eat. When my bug has finished its job, I look on in satisfaction at the red walls of code in front of me, code that I can now bend in any way I please. I feel like a performer bowing on stage to a standing ovation. Dirt, I feel like a queen!

When I was young, I learned to hack by sheer will. I would force the numbers around and build them in formations like defense towers. I would hide in my castles of numbers for hours, trying out the simplest of codes, tweaking them a bit, so that they became stronger. In a matter of days, my brute way of coding evolved into a well-timed dance. Numbers streamed together to form lines, and lines formed groups of lethal hacks that could take down any firewall. I became a hacker, and I rose through the ranks, my hacks becoming stronger and fiercer. Soon, I took hacking jobs, and not long after, I was in demand.

All over the city, people started to recognize the hacker, *Dragon,* my username. I became some sort of a legend. Rumor has it that I breached the city's bank and stole thousands of kimas—the currency around here—from the rich, or that I managed to find what lay beyond the wall. Neither I've done, although, the first does sound like something I would do. And so, as my reputation grew larger, more job offers started popping up, and more frequently, Sakura and I weren't hungry when we went to bed. All was well until Sakura grew sick. I had to start taking care of her more, which meant less time taking job offers. After a week, we started going to bed hungry again. And yet, every once and a while, I'll take another job, and so, to this day, the *Dragon* remains the best hacker in the city, but no one knows it's me, not even my sister.

I snap my attention back to the code hovering around me, and I rearrange the lines of numbers, like putting a story in the right order. Suddenly, the numbers turn to letters. Just what I was hoping for. Information begins to scrawl frantically across my vision. This is so much easier than trying to talk to people. So much better than trying to carry a conversation with that guy who slammed me into an alley two days ago. I push the memory away, trying to focus on the task at hand.

Name: Johnathan Shirliwig

I can't help myself, an obnoxiously loud laugh falls from my lips. Jonathan Shirliwig, *that's* the pigeon's name. Hacking into the personal account of that guy I teased with the gingerbread story was too easy, something I could perform in my sleep. Thinking back to our first encounter, he *did* look really funny with that red mark on his forehead, but who would have known he had such a funny name, too. I look at the other information his account holds. I need something good, something that would teach him a lesson. Just because I didn't punch him in the alley, doesn't mean that I wasn't planning on seeking revenge. Maybe I was just waiting for the right time.

Height: 5' 10"

Weight: 190

So, the guy's a little bit chubby. I wonder if that information would be enough to embarrass him in front of his friends. I decide to look for something better. I sort through the information, looking at school records, the summer camps he participated in, until I see medical records. Medical records always hide the most embarrassing information, like if someone wears a wig because their hair is falling out, or if a person used their Lynk to grow two inches, because the law states that a doctor has to approve of any unnatural changes to one's body. I'm reading through his information when, *bingo,* I spot the perfect little piece of information.

"A surgery to remove the abnormal growth would be ineffective, for it is located on the lower region of the back. The patient will have to keep the skin inconsistency."

In other words, this guy has a mole, and on his lower back! I drop to the floor with an incredulous smile at my luck, overcome with giggles. For a second, I feel like a normal eighteen-year-old planning revenge against one of her peers, sipping his secrets like a can of coke.

I change the sentence back into code with a swish of my hand and send it out to all the kid's contacts, information that also happens to be on his personal account. Satisfied, I wipe the canvas of code clear, I don't need the kid's information for what I'm about to do next.

I set up a system check, throwing all the worst bugs and hacks that I could possibly make, at my house's security system. Doing this every week ensures that the radio security alarm is still working, and every week, without fail, the system successfully deflects each and every virus I throw at it. Nothing bad about being cautious. As the check starts its work— it normally takes about an hour—I get up and go check on Sakura.

Since giving her the hyssop, she's gotten better, and fortunately, her fever broke yesterday, but she's still as weak as a newly born lamb. I grab a wet washcloth and slowly wipe it across her forehead, hoping to lower her temperature a little bit more. All I get in response is a feeble sigh of relief, but my heart speeds up, nevertheless, at the sound of it. I settle down on the bed next to her, curling around her like how Mom used to, and I start to tell a story.

"There once was a town where the rich had it all, and yet, the poor still could laugh. They shared their love with other families who needed it and enriched the air with the spices of cooking. And, dirt, was their music good! On the streets, musicians played saxophones, and from the rooftops rang the high, clear notes of trumpets."

I feign playing the saxophone and trumpet just like my mother used to, even though Sakura's eyes are closed.

"The notes danced in the air all through the daytime and all through the night, painting the townspeople's lives in joyful tunes. And although most of the more modest people in the town were kind spirits, there was a man who was known specifically for his loving heart. So, on the day he died, many mourned his loss, but none as much as his little daughter. On that day, her beautiful brown eyes were overflowing with relentless tears and her shiny ringlets were in tangles. Not even the rich, blonde girl, her best friend, could ease her pain. And, yet as the years passed, she hardened her grief into a fierce burning goal, to open a restaurant, which was the wish of her father."

I look down at Sakura before continuing.

"She was a hardworking girl who forced her way through life's troubles

with a wide smile and a bell-like laugh. One day, while she was wishing on a star while waiting tables, a frog jumped up right next to her and promptly asked to be kissed. Alarmed by a talking frog, the girl shrieked and ran away, but as fate had written, she ended up kissing the mucusy creature. Inevitably, she turned into a frog, too."

Looking in the corner of my eye, I see the timer for my system check, which reads fifteen minutes. I have to wrap it up.

"Through swamps, bayous, forests, and foreign lands, she traveled with the frog who claimed he was a cursed prince, and against her every motive, she found herself falling in love with the slimy being. Despite being an amphibian, he proved to be caring, funny, and understanding. So, when hope started to fly away, love took root, pushing the two creatures together. Their love sprouted, unblemished and pure, and at once, the curse broke under the force of their love. And so, a hardworking peasant girl and a charming prince made history when they opened up an amazing restaurant. From that day on, the music changed into a beat of hope, a beat of love," I finish using the same line my mom always ended with.

I'm walking to my room and logging into my coding canvas just as my Lynk notifies me that I've received a message. I leave the coding canvas and go to my public comm-system specifically for the *Dragon* —I have another system that only my sister knows the number to—expecting a message about a possible hacking job, but instead it reads:

"Hey, little dragon."

Ugh, it's that guy again. Wait, but if he's messaging me on this account...Dirt, he's figured out that I'm the *Dragon*. Maybe, if I act like I don't know who he is, he might get confused and leave me alone.

"Who are you? Do you have a job offer?"

"Kayda, I know it's you."

Dirt, this guy is not going to leave me alone.

"Fine, if it's me, Kayda, then what do you want?"

"I want you to come to dinner with me."

"If you don't give me a serious reply, I'm going to end this comm-link."

"Fine, fine. I have a job offer."

"The guy can actually speak without flirting," I reply dead-panning.

"Ouch, her fire strikes once again."

"Get to the point. Remember, I can still end the link."

"I don't give instructions over text. Find me in the alleyway at sunset where we met last time, and I'll give you the job description."

"I'm not coming."

"Suit yourself, little dragon, but I'll be there in case you change your mind."

My Lynk issues a beep, notifying me that my security check has just finished its work, and I'm about to close the comm, when one more message pops up on the screen.

"By the way, the name's Jax."

5

For some wild reason, I can't get him out of my head. The name "Jax" keeps popping up in my thoughts, like some weird fever running through my body. I need a remedy. I didn't ask for a friend. In fact, I'm probably better off without one. I have a history with the people I care about getting harmed.

Once, when I was nine, I brought home a stray dog. He was a scruffy mutt, with a tangle of brown hair on his back and triangles of black on his pointy ears. His feet were all scuffed up, and fleas had definitely taken up residence in the knots of his fur. I didn't care. I brought him home, my excitement bursting from my lips in bouts of laughter. I washed his fur and detangled all the dirty coils. I even clipped his nails! In just an hour, I became so attached to him, that I decided to name him—every street kid knows not to go as far as naming—but I couldn't stand to just simply call him "dog." So, he became "Doc," named after the only dwarf in Snow White that didn't have an adjective for a first name. That night, my sister and I stayed up late teaching him tricks, making him treats, and telling him all the best stories. We ended up falling asleep on top of each other in a big pile. I think that might have been the best night I've had since my parents died.

The next morning, I let him out alone to pee as it was raining, but when I came back to let him in, someone was hauling his dead body away, most likely to eat him. I ran and jumped at the man, clinging to his frail frame, clawing at his dry skin, anything that would cause him pain. I might have been small, but I was angry. I screamed and screamed at him to bring Doc back to me although I knew he couldn't, well not in the way that I wished. That day I almost killed a man.

The only thing that stopped me was my sister's small hand gently tugging on my shirt. I let the man go and crumpled into my sister's arms, crying as rain soaked through my clothes, the cold droplets mixing with my salty tears. I cried until my tears dried up and the rain stopped pouring down. And then, my sister and I buried Doc and planted a few daisy seeds in the ground with him. When spring came, they bloomed, and that was the end of Doc in our lives.

Since then, I've never saved another stray, although multiple have come up to me begging for food, and I've never named another animal, or plant for that matter. In my opinion, the pain that comes with losing something is not worth being able to call that "something" a cool name. You see, naming an object or a person gives them a certain amount of importance. I totally understand that it's a natural response for the human brain to attach itself to a name, but I just don't get *why* Jax had to tell me his name. He probably knew that it would get into my head and just wanted to annoy me. Ugh, I wish I never saw that last message.

I'm tidying my room, giving my hands something to do in an attempt to distract myself. I bend over grabbing the blanket that's slipped off of my bed, the blanket that my mom knit for me. Not unlike her room, the blanket's threads depict countless pre-A.R.T. stories. I run my hand over the section that portrays *The Princess and the Frog,* recalling when I told the story to my sister, but inevitably my hand slides over to the red and gold section of *Aladdin*.

Aladdin in some ways has always described how I feel, like a lamp filled with unimaginable power buried under unrelenting sands, and for some reason, the feel of the threaded sand beneath my fingers makes me feel impulsive, brave, and strong. I'm tired of being forgotten, tired of waiting for Prince Ali to come and find me. I want to raise from the sands myself and break out of the golden lamp with the little pictures scrawled around its top. For once I want to be free.

I know that excuses aren't going to stop me now, so for once, I do what I want.

"Sakura, I'm going out. I'll be back in an hour or two." Not waiting for a response, I walk out into the early evening air, the cold feeling frisky and untamed against my skin. I dash into the shadows, blending in with the heaps of trash piled on the sides of the road, and quietly, like a lost waif, I glide through the streets. This city could be called a maze of ramshackle buildings and dilapidated towers, but if it is a maze, then I am the minotaur in the middle, the keeper of all the twists and turns.

I arrive an alley away from the meeting spot and scan the buildings nearest to me. The one in front of me is made from wood that seems to be bloated with water and would, no doubt, crumble to the touch. It's no good. I turn to the building adjacent from the meeting spot inspecting the worn-down concrete of its walls, the possible footholds and grips. This one's perfect. I grab the first handhold I see, clinging to the wall with only my right hand. I haven't climbed since that day with Jonathan Shirliwig, and my limbs are practically shaking with adrenaline, but I don't care. It feels *so* good. The muscles in my arms strain as I grab handhold after handhold. This climb is a piece of cake for a spider like me, and I relish every moment of it.

I'm standing on top of the building in less than five minutes, not a drop of sweat on my forehead. I wish the building was fifty stories high so I could climb until my muscles wear out and this world becomes a distant memory, but skyscrapers are only found in the rich portion of this city. One day, I'm going to walk into their half of the city and scale the tallest building I see, just because I can. But that day is not today.

Floating across the building's flat roof, I cling to the shadows like a child holding onto her mother. When I reach the edge of the roof that overlooks the meeting spot, I stop, crouched behind an old electrical unit. Disappointment flares inside me. He's not even here yet. In truth, it *is* really early still. He'll probably come just as the sun sets. Settling in, I sigh, it's going to be a long night.

I sit for an hour, reciting pre-A.R.T. poems in my head. I'm finishing the first part of Maya Angelou's "Still I Rise" whispering the words into the air, just as the last ray of sun seeps from the sky. I look over the edge of the building and see Jax standing in the alleyway. He's right on time. My limbs are stiff, and I would love to walk around, but I force my body to stay right where it is. I'm not meeting him now. If I went down there, I'd look like some eager child showing up for a play date. No, I'm going to make him wait.

I sit patiently as the city's lights start dwindling out, making room for the stars in the indigo sky. All the buildings seem so vulnerable at this time of night, curled up and sleeping with their bellies exposed to anyone walking by. If I had to describe the scene in one word, I'd say it was peaceful.

In the day, the streets are always so crowded even if it doesn't look like it. In every building, someone's always watching the street, listening to what's happening below them. This city offers no privacy. People are always just around the corner, fighting, screaming, or just watching.

Without all the hidden eyes following my back, or the sounds of gunshots echoing in the streets, I'm almost able to pretend that this is a night in one of my mom's stories. If I squint a little, the buildings don't look as dilapidated. And if I hold my breath, I don't smell the scent of death that always seems to taint the air. For a moment it could look like a beautiful starry night. But yet again, people see what they want to see.

I widen my eyes, once again looking over a beaten-down city. It's best not to lie to oneself. That's how people get lost.

It's now about an hour and a half after sunset, and Jax shifts for the first time all night. He stretches, looking around one last time, and with a sigh, he starts to walk down the alleyway. It's time. I pat my right thigh, left arm, and back, checking that all the knives I strapped on that morning are still there. Assured that they are all in their places, I race across the roof as light as a feather, not even disturbing the littlest of pebbles and jump quietly on to the window sill of the floor below me. I look to see where Jax is, expecting him to be on the street next to the building I'm crouching on, but he's already almost at the mouth of the narrow street. Dirt, he walks fast. Now, I'm going to have to work harder.

I take a quick scan of my surroundings before seeing a crumbled terrace on the building that marks the end of the alleyway. It's not too far away. I jump to the next building and shimmy on to the roof before I start running. I don't give myself time to think before I jump across the alley, soaring for a second like a bird in the sky. In that moment, every one of my thoughts scatters, and all that matters are the thumping of my heart and the feel of the wind tugging at my clothes. It ends too fast. My feet hit the terrace scrambling for purchase, and I brace my knees to absorb the impact. Other than the symphony of joy singing through my veins, I make no sound as I land.

I don't stop to appreciate my skill, but instead, I slither down the wall clinging to the shadows. In a matter of seconds, I'm on the ground, unscathed and pulsing with adrenaline. I love this.

Jax walks forward a step, and I slip the knife from my forearm. He's now directly in front of my hiding place. That's my cue.

"Hey Jax," I whisper against his neck, the blade of my knife pressing right against his jugular, about a half-inch above the silver chain I noticed he wore the first time I met him. I feel his muscles tighten in response, but that's it. He must have gotten into quite a few fights in the past.

"Way to make an entrance, little dragon, but I do have to say that I was expecting more fire. Perhaps next time you should walk in juggling flamethrowers." His throat bobs as he speaks, his flesh coming dangerously close to splitting against the sharp edge of my blade.

"I'll think about the suggestion."

"So, you *do* listen to what I'm saying. Good, because I'm going to need to persuade you in a second."

"I don't need to be persuaded, it's simple: if the offer's good I accept it, if it's bad then I leave, that's it. Now, tell me what you want me to do."

"I'll explain all the details once you remove the blade from my throat."

I glare at him.

"*Please.*"

Reluctantly, I retract my weapon, but I don't put it away. Not yet. Just because I don't hate him doesn't mean I trust him. Trust is an immaculately forged blade, perfected for years. It doesn't just come with the flick of a hand. It takes time.

"Start speaking."

"You don't have to be so rude."

"I'm only rude because you're so annoying." Oops, I didn't mean to let that slip. My cheeks turn rosy, and I turn my head slightly away from him, grateful for the shadows that come with this hour. Now he knows that his little taunts actually affect me.

"Why thank you, Kayda, you're always so kind." He lets out a bark of laughter, so unlike mine. It's rich and melodious.

I can't help myself.

I lean ever so slightly closer to him, intoxicated by the sound of his laughter, wishing to hear it ring out one more time.

His voice changes, growing more passionate as he whispers, "Haven't you ever wished to teach the rich a lesson, but didn't want to draw attention to yourself? Don't you want them to pay for what they do to us?"

"Giving a grand speech on my hopes and wants isn't what I'd call 'explaining the details.' Perhaps you can take a suggestion from me and cut to the chase."

He ignores me.

"Don't you ever think about what would've happened if your sister had been properly fed and cared for before she caught that illness?" He says it so casually, but that last line makes my anger flare as high as the twenty-eight-foot wall that surrounds this city. Any comfort I was starting to feel in his presence flies away as fast as a bullet shoots out from a gun. He just made a *really* big mistake.

"How do you know about my sister?" I'm on him in a second, clutching his shirt in my fist. Nobody threatens my sister without consequences.

"Remember, I told you before-"

"Yah, yah, a little birdy told you. I don't care where you're getting the information but if you dare-"

"I know, I know, you'll knock me out."

"No, if you touch my sister, I'll kill you," I growl, drawing out the last three words. I give him the full heat of my stare, the anger, and the murder swirling around in it as evident as the sun during day. I let him take in the weight of my words, the truth in them. I'm not kidding, and I make sure he knows it before I release his shirt. I would do anything for my sister.

"Get to the point now, or I'm really leaving. And I assure you, if I walk away, the next time I see you, I won't be as kind." Before I can turn to leave he starts talking, his voice lacking the levity it held just a moment ago. Good, I've managed to intimidate him.

"I'm going to start a rebellion."

I laugh, the note ringing hollow, echoing down the alleyway, cruelly loud in the silence. It's exactly the opposite of the laugh he let out earlier. Where his was comforting, mine is eerie. I let each and every echo finish before I speak again.

"Everybody swears that they're going to start a rebellion: the peasants on the street declare it, and the merchants in the marketplace practically yell it out to their customers. Yet, not one of them has ever done so. What makes you think I'm going to trust that you're any different from them?"

"Again, I'll remind you that I have a source for information, and as you know, information can be very helpful in this world. If you're not convinced, the fact that I've stayed alive this long without ruining my pretty little face should satisfy your worries. I assure you, I'm not like the rest of the people in this city. When I make a promise, I always keep it."

"You don't fight well enough," I say bluntly, crossing my arms.

"That's not a fair statement. You've only seen me fight when I was up against you, and you're like a machine."

Did he actually just *compliment* me?

"Is that what you want me for, to *fight* like your bodyguard or something?" I say angrily.

"Well, your fighting skills will come in handy, but I also need you as the *Dragon.*"

So, the guy doesn't know I'm a spider. The relief washes over me fast and comforting. At least Jax doesn't know *everything.*

"But, I still don't get what makes you think you can do something that experienced spies and soldiers probably can't even do. These people we're going up against, they have money, they have resources, and compared to them, we're just a bunch of rats with dreams."

"And that's exactly why I think we can win. They may have money and resources, but we have dreams, we have hope, we have motivation. Victory doesn't come with troops who wear matching pristine uniforms. No, it comes with the group of soldiers who wear muddied and ripped clothes; soldiers who carry hope even though they've been trodden on again and again. Kayda, don't you want to live in a world where you don't have to worry about going hungry? Don't you still dream?"

I still at his words, my mind at war with itself. The thing is, I don't know if I have a dream anymore. I once just wished for a life where Sakura wasn't sick, but even then, life would still be the same, we'd still go hungry, we'd still have to skip school in favor of finding work. We live the lives of orphans in an overcrowded city, and that's never going to change. I don't even know what I want anymore. For once, in this city of myriad twists and endless alleys, I feel lost.

"This is not a war to be fought by trained spies, agents, and soldiers. This is a war for the common people; the thieves, the criminals, the merchants who bellow out their goods from dawn to dusk. This is a fight for righteousness, and only people who've been oppressed and beaten down too many times to count know what that really means." His voice holds so much fervor that I'm taken aback.

"You're practically trying to accomplish the impossible."

"If I don't go for the impossible, then who else will?" He says the sentence quietly, seriously, as if it's what he was born to say. This guy's good and not just with words. For Dirt's sake he planned this all out —revealing that he knew who I was, which is good leverage against me, and offering a chance at revenge, a chance almost too tempting not to take—as if he was just organizing a child's birthday party. Behind his pretty face, this guy is a mastermind.

"Kayda, you have to understand. This world is unfair, and I want to change that, but I need help."

I'm quiet for a moment, but then I ask him, "Do you really think you can make a difference?"

"I know I can," he responds in a second, not even having to think about the answer.

"Please just think about it. Don't you want to get revenge? To stop the suffering of people like us, to stop more people from falling ill." His voice softens on the last few words, and I don't have it in me to feel any more anger towards him or the meaning that he implied with those last few words. No matter how annoyed I want to be at him for being so foolish, for thinking that he could change this world, some part of me is warmed by the hope that he has managed to hold on to. He reminds me of myself in some ways. Well, my old self. The girl who used to smile and laugh. The girl who found love in a loveless world. Suddenly, I'm struck with want to become that girl again.

The reckless feeling that made me come here and meet Jax wraps its arms around me in a tight embrace, poking the embers that rest in my soul, stirring them up until they become flames. I don't want another girl to lose her childhood because she doesn't have enough food to eat or to have to ignore the calls of other children inviting her to play just because this world is too dangerous for love to survive. I don't want another girl to turn out like me.

I've always ignored the feeling of "want," I've pushed it down in favor of doing what I needed. When I go to the market to buy food, I consistently get just enough to survive a week, no less, no more. I ignore the cravings that come with smelling *pao douce* buns and meat pies, always saving my money for the necessities. So, now, as I try to tug on those flames of want, it's hard to fight away the instinct to stop, to think it over, to walk away. And I almost do. But when I think about Sakura's sick face and the life she could've had if only I was able to obtain a remedy, the flames rise higher, any restraint I managed to hold with me before bursting into brilliant fireworks. The locks that I shackled around myself when my parents died, start to fall away, clinking to the ground. I finally realize what the feeling was that was let loose when I got lost in that memory of my mother. It was hope.

That very shred of hope, unfamiliar and yet not unwelcome, rises inside me, and once again, I'm like a genie stuck in a golden lamp, straining at the desert that covers me, fighting against the red, shifting sands, lifting up the dunes of flaked sun. But unlike the story, I rise like Maya Angelou, up, and up, the surface ever nearer, until the sun beats down on the engraved pictures of lions fighting Death and birds washing the world in life ringing my golden top.

"I'm in," I whisper, the words sounding like a prophecy.

"That just made us a team." And with those six words, Jax lifts the top off of the golden lamp, letting me out of the astonishingly beautiful cage. Finally, I'm free.

6

"*Are you in?*"

The message flies into my vision received through my Lynk. It's Leum. He's our new recruit. Jax found him on the streets fighting off a group of pigeons, and when Jax offered a place in our rebellion to him, the kid took it without a moment to think. It turns out, he has access to a lot of equipment that proves very useful to us, equipment that must only come from the rich. The assumption is obvious, but still, I never outright ask where the stuff comes from or how he comes to obtain it. Leum gets it, he brings it to me, and that's all I care about.

It's only been a week since I agreed to help Jax, but we've already gotten so much done. A few days ago, I set up a secret comm-system for the three of us, the one Leum just used to message me. We've also mapped out the whole city. It took us a few hours of roaming around at midnight through the deserted streets, but now, we've got a rough idea of where each and every building is located. Now, each one of us can travel around the city, even the rich sector, without fearing becoming lost.

For once in my life, I feel like part of a team, and the rush of it, the excitement of feeling part of a whole, almost makes me regret never playing with the other children when I was younger. *Almost*. It's as if my whole life has been split into two halves: before I said "yes" to Jax and after. It's kind of like how eating chocolate for the first time changes someone's whole outlook on food. One taste of hope and I'm hooked.

"Yep, I'm in."

Right now, I'm hacking into the network that holds everyone's personal security information. It's sort of what I did to find information on Jonathan Shirliwig, except on a grander scale. Instead of stealing information from one account, we're going to sort through all the profiles looking for three main factors that will make them the perfect target: one, the person must have money and *a lot* of it, two, the person is young, therefore more gullible and ill-prepared, and three, he has to live in an apartment building.

Apartment buildings are so much easier to break into than houses. Those big mansions on the rich side of the city always have bodyguards standing at the doors and security cameras lining each wall. In an apartment building, people forget about the possibility of even being broken into. Because so many people live together in one building, people start to get lazy, thinking along the lines of "numbers equal power," whereas, in truth, it simply makes them easier targets. For criminals, it means less security and less to hide.

In a crowded building, what difference does one more person make? None. And that's exactly what our plan is going to take advantage of. We'll steal a large sum of money, which will be used to support our rebellion, and then we'll disappear before anyone realizes what we've done. The details can be figured out later. Now, it's time to find our candidate.

"Kayda, it's going to take us years to search through all these profiles. Do you think you could whip up a batch of code that could do the job in a minute?" Jax has joined the group chat. How sweet.

"Yes, sir." Although he can't see me, I send a mock salute in the direction of the screen before I dive into the world of numbers. The group comm-system no longer shows up in my vision. All I see are white walls that go on forever. A land of nothingness. A place of infinite possibilities. I sigh in pleasure as I enter the coding canvas app.

I take a quick look at my history in this app, at all the bugs, viruses, and data attacks I've built up over the years. The sight makes my chest swell with pride. There's so many, it's practically an army. And yet none of them quite fit what I'm looking for. I need something that will harness all the data and then sort through it, capable of pinpointing certain people with the three qualities we're looking for. I don't have anything already coded that will do exactly that, but maybe if I combine some old programming with a few new lines of code...it might just work.

I grab a netting virus, which should trap the data, and meld it together with one of my more brilliant inventions, which I call *The Creature*. It's a piece of code that basically chews up data and spits it out in a large jumble. It's kind of like a paper shredder for code.

Now's the hard part. I start writing lines of code, my fingers flying over the keys on my computer, the lines appearing in the coding canvas. A pattern starts to form: number...letter...bracket...number... space...underscore...number...number...number. And that sequence starts to align with the beats of my heart. Like drums, those beats lay out the base for a ballad, and soon my coding flies to the rhythm like a dancer swept up in song. I'm rushed into the thrill of it, lost in the pounding melody of the code. The world is gone, and I'm left dancing a waltz with numbers.

They fly around me, moving and swaying to each thump of my heart. Tall eights dance with sixes, as fives bend over, sweeping young beautiful twos off their feet. If someone were to call my name right now, I wouldn't even be aware of it. I can't take my eyes off the screen. It's the most beautiful dance I have ever seen. And here I am, standing in the middle of the commotion, the composer, orchestrating each step with a motion of my hands and a point of my finger.

This is what I call coding.

The song starts to slow down, the wild pace of it giving way to a somber march. The nines bow to their partners, and the sixes kiss the hands of fours in goodbye. The numbers resume their still positions, the song finally coming to an end. Reluctantly, I let go of the last vestiges of the song that cling to my mind. Immediately, I'm transported back into reality.

The coding canvas is no longer a world of white everlasting nothing, but instead, it's filled with lines and lines of code. Carefully, I add this new combination of numbers and letters to the net and *The Creature.* Scanning quickly over my work, the corners of my mouth slightly lift in satisfaction. This new monster of a virus should catch the data as the net does, scan through it with the viciousness of *The Creature,* and select the best candidate. Where it would take us days to look through all the profiles, this monster of code will do it in ten seconds. It's, hands down, the most beautiful piece of coding I've ever written. Even more beautiful than my infamous *Creature.*

"I finished writing a virus big enough to handle the job, and I'm putting it in the system now," I notify the group, sending the message with a mere thought.

"That was fast. How long did that take you to write, a minute?" Jax replies nearly a second after I send the message. I guess he feels a bit restless, not being able to help out even a bit. I don't think he could write a line of code to save his life.

"Actually 38 seconds, to be exact. What else would you expect from the *Dragon?*" Writing my hacker name reminds me of when Jax first told Leum who I was in the coding world. His reaction was priceless. First, he entered shock, shaking his head to and fro. It was actually quite funny, and I had to work hard to hold in the obnoxious snort that threatened to erupt. Then as his mind wrapped around the fact that I, indeed, was the *Dragon,* his cheeks grew warm, and his eyes brightened becoming two little twinkling stars. He asked for my signature, and as flustered as I was, realizing that I actually had a *fan,* I quickly jotted the word *Dragon* onto a piece of paper.

Never before, had I been asked to write out the word "dragon," because nobody ever knew to ask me. The signature was not even pretty. It was, in all honesty, just a scribble of graphite that could possibly be seen as the word "dragon." Feeling very uncomfortable, I gave it to Leum while Jax laughed the whole time. But when Leum clutched it to his chest as if it was a priceless masterpiece, I couldn't even hold in my laugh, breaking down in high pitched giggles.

"It looks like you already have a die-hard fan," Jax had bellowed out with a whoop. And finally realizing how he must have been fawning over the little slip of paper in his hand, Leum's cheeks heated, turning a rosy pink. It just made me giggle harder. And because Jax and I were already laughing our heads off, it was hard for Leum to resist the levity of the moment. Soon, he started chuckling too, but I noticed that it was not until after he tucked the little piece of paper safely into a pocket in his worn-out jacket, that he let himself relax. I realized then that the guy really did admire me. And the thought had made me swell with pride. At that moment, it really hit me that although though my sister is sick and we're orphans, I can still be a role model to someone else in this sad world.

The moment only brightened after that realization, and for a good five minutes, we just sat on the dirty streets in an abandoned alleyway guffawing like drunken sailors with stupid smiles on our faces. Just the thought of it makes me grin now.

I look into the corner of my eye just as the timer flashes red, signaling its end.

"Who's ready to choose our victim?"

"I can't wait," Jax replies, and I can picture the look of anticipation that he must be wearing. I, myself, feel like I'm riding a roller coaster, still ticking up to the top, and I know when I get to the pinnacle of the ride there's no way to go but down.

I open my data storage where the information of the candidates should have been sent when the hack finished. Three profiles show up.

Tim Reiley

Age: 37

Address: room 1081 in Skyhigh Tower

Income per year: 8,322 kimas

. . .

So, this guy definitely fits the rich part of the qualification, but he's a bit too old. I choose the next profile.

Margaret Avocine

Age: 15
Address: penthouse 2023 in Zkyscraper
Income per year: 7,560 kimas

She's really young and rich but also lives in a penthouse, which means there's more security than in a normal apartment. For us, more security can only be bad. I cross my fingers as I pull up the last candidate's profile.

Mark Valtin

Age:22
Address: room 1009 Skyhigh Tower
Income per year: 7,200 kimas

This guy is young, lives in an apartment, and is rich. In all ways that matter to us, this guy is Mr. Perfect. It'll be a piece of cake to steal from him. Someone else might feel bad about choosing a person to steal thousands of kimas from, but I don't. I feel excited.

"I'm sending you the best candidate. I think I found Mr. Perfect."

"Hey, hey, hey. Hold on there. I didn't realize I had competition here. Don't give up on me just yet! I thought you were starting to like me. I mean, think about it; I'm handsome and great with words. Aren't I your Mr. Perfect?"

"You're arrogant, and short, and really not *that* good-looking." The last part might be a slight lie—Jax actually is handsome—but it's not like I'm going to tell him that. For dirt's sake, his arrogance would probably double if he knew I thought that.

"Short! I'm 5'11!"

"Yep, for a guy around here, you're short. Anyway, I meant that the man was the perfect person for us to steal from: he's young, lives in an apartment, and is rich."

"Oh good, I thought I was going to have to give you a speech on all my amazing qualities."

"You* are *short. I'm 6' 4" and I'm sixteen—three years younger than you." The response is a little delayed, but the bolded letters, which signify that Leum sent the message, make me giggle. So, I don't just have a fan, I have a partner in terrorizing Jax. This just got a whole lot more interesting.

"You're siding with Kayda, really! I thought you liked me :("

"Kayda has better comebacks."

"Accept it, Jax, you're not as cool as you think. Why? Because a girl who's about eight inches shorter than you managed to knock you out in ten seconds. " I send the message with a smirk on my lips, imagining the face that Jax will make when he reads it.

"Aww, not that again, " Jax sends back.

"She's also about seventy pounds lighter than you," Leum adds helpfully.

"You guys wound me, " Jax replies.

"That's the point."

"Guys, you know I'd love to fool around with the two of you all day, but I've got a life even if you two don't, " I say thinking about the medicine I've got to make for Sakura.

"Hey :(I thought you were on my team," Leum replies.

"You should have sided with me, Leum: a dragon can't control its fire."

"If you two don't stop acting like three-year-olds arguing about who gets to eat the cheerios first, then you'll really feel the heat of my fire. So, take my advice and look at the candidate I chose. Leum, stock up on equipment you think we might need. And Jax, do your thing, make up a plan that would scare the dirt right out of this city. We've got some money to steal. Meet me in the normal spot two hours before dawn. Don't be late."

"Yes, Mom," Jax answers sarcastically. All I can hope is that he will

come up with a plan, and a good one at that. If not, I've always got at least a few tricks up my sleeves.

"I'll be there!"

"Good, because we've got a rebellion to start," I type, ending the comm connection.

7

Today, I'm the first one in the alleyway waiting for Jax and Leum to arrive. I now understand why Jax never looked around for me that day I first went to meet him. If you look around once, you'll never stop searching, trying to make out a face in the shadows. The more time that passes, the more you want to look. It becomes a sort of game; when one minute ends, you get to scan the rooftops, and then the streets for any sign of a person. Honestly, I don't want to be found searching around, looking like an amateur. So, I stand still, and I don't look at the watch that's strapped around my wrist. All I have to do is be patient. It's hard.

One second bleeds into the next and a minute slides into two. I want to look around, but I can't. *Stay focused. Be patient.* My inner voice doesn't help. Patience was never my strong suit. Five more minutes inch along; it's now an hour and a half before dawn. Seriously, what's taking them so long? I lean against the wall willing my muscles to relax, but it's a futile attempt. I'm about to lose it, so I start to recite poetry, old pre-A.R.T. things.

Although it was my mother who loved stories, it was my father who loved poetry. The two of them were a perfect pair, curving each other's edges and strengthening each other's hopes. If true love ever did exist, it was between them. I guess it was only suiting that they died together, too. I push the memory away before it can take hold of my mind. I don't need that kind of distraction right now.

I start reciting poetry again, though his time I whisper the stanzas of Ella Wheeler Wilcox's "Two Kinds of People, " in the words that my dad always used to say to me. It sort of reminds me of the world we live in today.

"There are two kinds of people in this world to-day;
Just two kinds of people, no more I say
Not the sinner and saint
for it's well understood the good are half bad and the bad are half good
Not the rich and the poor
for to rate a man's wealth
you must first know the state of his conscience and health
Not the humble and proud, for in life's little span,
who puts on vain airs, is not counted a man.
Not the happy and sad,
for the swift flying years bring each man his laughter and each man his tears
No; the two kinds of people in this world I mean are the people who lift—"

"And the people who lean," Jax interrupts, walking into the alleyway, his figure swathed in shadow. His voice is so smooth, like a boat gliding along the surface of a calm sea, and yet his words carry the tiniest bit of an accent. If I were to take a guess, I'd think that his pre-A.R.T ancestors must have been European. To get more specific I'd say that he had a French accent. I don't really know what that means, but I remember once, reading that French people who lived in the pre-A.R.T. eras spoke their words as soft and as sweet as honey, just like Jax.

"I didn't know you liked poetry." His eyes do not hold the arrogance I've become accustomed to as he looks at me. In fact, I think I see a hint of curiosity and an intensity, as if I'm a puzzle he's trying to figure out.

"Well, I didn't think you knew how to read."

"So little faith in the person who's leading you into rebellion," Jax tsks, that famous arrogance of his coming back in full force. "I just was trying to get to know you. After all, we are partners now."

"There's nothing you need to know in order for us to work successfully together."

"How about your birthday, or your favorite color, or even your favorite story-"

"You don't need to know *anything*," I bite back at him starting to get frustrated. It's not like I even know the first thing about him either.

"If you won't tell me anything about yourself, I'll just have to share a few things about myself. My name is Jax. I'm nineteen. My favorite color is burnt orange. My birthday is on June 21. I love the pre-A.R.T story Aladdin, although it's not very popular-"

That makes me stop. Aladdin's *my* favorite story, and Jax is right when he says that it's not popular around here. Most people don't even know who Jasmine or Prince Ali is, and the chances of it being Jax's favorite story... I harden my heart. I don't care if he loves Aladdin. This guy doesn't deserve to know anything about me.

"Fine, you want to know who I am? I'm an orphan whose parents died at eight. A girl who was left with nothing but an empty house and a hungry six-year-old. I'm a girl who learned to hack out of sheer need. I'm the daughter of these filthy alleyways and the child of these dirty buildings. I've learned to live by lying, but I learned to lie by becoming a thief. I try so hard to scrounge up enough food to bring home each night, and finding untainted water is a miracle to me. I've never stopped fighting the inevitable since I was eight, and yet it isn't enough. My sister is dying. So, don't ask me what my favorite color is while people lie on these streets wheezing their last breath. Don't expect me to tell you my birthday when children go to bed starving night after night. Don't even dare to wonder what my favorite story is as our half of this city crumbles to dust, burying the people who are trying so hard to make a living in this horrible place. This is a hard world to live in. I thought you understood. I'm not here to be your friend. I'm here for the rebellion. And that's all you need to know about me."

I walk straight up the alleyway at a brisk pace, passing by a stunned Leum who arrived about half-way into my speech, and not even bothering to glance in Jax's direction. I don't need to see his face to know that I made a point.

I can't believe I was so silly earlier, sending comms to Jax and Leum as if I was a little school girl and they were my friends, letting myself laugh with people I didn't even know. I lied to myself, tricking my own brain into believing that I could have more, that I could have friends. But, I was wrong. See, the thing about friends is that they make you weak. Once you start to care for them, you become selfish, choosing to help a select few instead of all. Because I decided to laugh more, I almost lost sight of the whole point of why I joined the rebellion in the first place. I didn't do it to make friends, I did it because Jax had reminded me that once upon a time I had wanted to change the world.

Stalking up to the nearest building's door, I draw a bobby pin from my hair, slipping it into the lock. I shimmy it around in the barrel, lifting up each of the pins until the lock clicks and the door swings open. One little light flickers on as we walk in, barely providing enough illumination to see our surroundings. To me, it looks like we're in a graveyard on Día de Los Muertos. Leaning chairs draped with plastic coverings look like ghouls dancing at night, and the old broken toys scattered on the floor reminds me of zombies rising from their graves. The room sends a chill racing up my spine. It's the perfect place to hide a secret operation.

Across the room, a staircase is concealed by an ancient shelf that looks as if it's about ready to collapse. I head straight for it. The steps creak and groan like old men breathing their last complaints to the world. But oddly, the noises almost comfort me. Each creak sounds like a cry of pain, a noise I have become accustomed to. It's sad, but it's true. Besides, in a city like this, pain is just a part of life. It comes and it goes like anything else.

In a minute, the winding staircase ends, and I lead Jax and Leum into the room that yawns before us. I smile, proud of my work. Three nights I spent cleaning up this floor of the building, constructing tables from dilapidated chairs, sweeping up the dust that had settled over everything like a blanket, making this floor a place worthy to start a rebellion. By the looks on my partners' faces, I think I did a good job. The walls are a beautiful bright blue that emerged after hours of scrubbing, and I have adorned them with official maps of the city. Light streams through the now transparent windows, illuminating the room in jaunty shades. In the center of the room, a big table stands with neatly arranged stacks of papers and pens sitting atop it. We sink into the three chairs that surround it, gazing around at what I've done.

"Did you do this?" Jax utters in awe, breaking the silence.

"Yes."

"All by yourself?" Leum exclaims.

"Yes."

"But how-"

"We need to get to work." I bite out, cutting off what Leum was going to say. I'm still mad at them.

As if he was not listening to me at all, Jax's declares "I think the code name for this place should be the *Library*: after all, it smells musty and there are lots of books and whatnot around. Besides if someone ever overhears us saying that they wouldn't even think twice about it."

He grins at me annoyingly.

I huff and turn away, ignoring him, neither approving nor disapproving of his stupid but reasonable idea.

"I gathered all these maps so that we could plan the most practical route to the Skyhigh Tower," I say gesturing to the walls. I grab a small map that's on the table, circling two locations in the city. "This is where the skyscraper is, and this is where we are. Now, how do we get from this point," I jab my finger from where we are on the map to where Skyhigh Towers is located, "to that point?"

Jax takes the paper, drawing a zigzagged line across it. I guess he took my hint that this is not a meeting in which he can joke around.

"If we follow this route through the city, it will take us about fifteen minutes to get to the skyscraper; the most efficient way. But," he says making another jagged line on the map, "this is the safest route to Skyhigh Towers. In all, it would take us about thirty minutes."

"I think we should leave twenty minutes earlier and take the safe route. That way we're not really losing time, and we have a better chance of getting out undetected. I don't know about you two, but I don't fancy the idea of being taken to jail," Leum says looking at each of us.

"Sounds good. We'll take the safe path to Skyhigh Towers and back. Now, what's the plan when we get there?" At this point, Leum and I look to Jax.

"The building's going to be the most crowded around one o'clock, the time where families join their relatives for a late lunch or an early dinner. Normally, I would try to avoid a time that supplies more possible witnesses, but in this case, I think the crowds will help. Now, have you two ever been to one of those skyscrapers?"

We both shake our heads no.

"Well then, I'll just have to fill you in. When noon comes around, people start filing into the lobby, and a line forms at the receptionist's desk. Because of the chaos of so many families wanting to get in, any workers or handymen that arrive only have to quickly flash a pass at the receptionist. Honestly, these places don't even know what the word 'security' means."

"So, one of us will receive access by being disguised as a worker. What about the rest of us?"

"Patience, little dragon, I'm getting there. So, I will be the one disguised as a plumber. After I gain access to the building, I will find my way up to room 1009 and pretend that I was called about a plumbing issue in that room. In reality, I'm going to serve as a distraction to Mark Valtin, who should already be eating at that point—I watched him throughout the week and figured out that he starts eating at 12:45 on the dot, and every time he eats, he opens up the window to let in a fresh breeze—you, Kayda," he points at me, "will have entered the building as a maid, and you'll be cleaning the apartment next door. When the time is exactly 1:25, jump from your apartment's terrace to the open window—the two are about four and a half feet apart."

Leum gasps and pales as if he's the one that has to make the jump. Then he looks at me as if expecting me to object. Instead, I just nod at Jax. That four-and-a-half-foot jump won't exactly be easy, but neither will it kill me, especially because the window ledge and terrace won't threaten to crumble like the buildings around here tend to.

"After you're in the apartment, break into his computer, which should rest on the desk located right next to the window. Hack into his banking accounts, and transfer one thousand kimas to the account under *Fredrick Longton,* a person I made up to hide our rebellion's money. When you're done, jump back to the terrace next door. I'll come get you when it's 1:40."

Finally recovering from the news that I'm going to make a four-and-a-half-foot jump from about two-hundred stories above the ground, Leum finds his voice to ask "What am I doing?"

"You'll be positioned at the east side of the lake, with a clear view of the skyscraper. With the earpieces you said you would get-" Jax looks at Leum for confirmation.

"Yep, I got them, they're right here," Leum replies, pulling out three little ebony-colored spheres, each the perfect size to fit in an ear.

"Good, with those earpieces you'll communicate with us. You'll have to tell us when to make moves, and if police ever arrive, you'll have to notify us. Now, when we get safely back here," Jax gestures to the room we're sitting in, "we'll have to advertise what we did—just under a different name."

"Ooh, how about we call ourselves *Honorable Heroes*?" Leum gushes.

"Nah, that's way too cheesy," I say cringing. "We need something cooler, something that actually describes what we are. How about... *The Freedom Thieves*? After all, how else does one manage to come by anything around here? If we want to have our freedom back, we're going to have to steal it."

"*The Freedom Thieves*," Jax says feeling the name out on his tongue and then nodding. "I like it."

"Yeah, I guess it's better than Honorable Heroes," Leum admits sheepishly.

"Then it's settled, we'll spread a rumor that *The Freedom Thieves* stole millions of dollars from right under the rich's noses, and that they did it just because they can. We need every person to know that we plan on doing much more, that we plan on stealing back this city. After all, this mission isn't really for the money. Its purpose is to earn us a name." Jax looks at each of us, his gaze blazing with newfound fire. "If we're going to make ourselves known, why not make us a legend?"

He gives a moment for his words to sink in and then looks around. "Everyone good with the plan?"

"I think we might be able to pull it off," I declare. Turning to face Jax, I add, "Good work." As he talked, my anger slowly melted away. I have to admit, it really is a great plan.

"Yeah, I'm good with it," Leum states, a goofy smile stretching across his face. The kid's joy in the face of possible death manages to find its way to me, and I'm hit with a burst of adrenaline.

"Well then, in two days' time, let's steal us some money. Meet me here tomorrow?" I ask.

"At the *Library*," Jax responds.

I scowl, but Leum just smiles, trying to muffle a giggle.

"Sure, see you guys then!" Leum says, already walking towards the door. It finally hits me that the kid probably has a family waiting at home for him. No wonder he wants to leave. I can't believe he's helping us. Jax and I don't really have much to lose, but a family... that's definitely something. If I had a family, I don't know if I'd ever take a risk again. My thoughts scatter as a hand touches my shoulder.

"Kayda," Jax says once we are alone, his hand reaching out for my arm.

"What do you want, Jax?" I say with a forced sting to my tone, making it clear that I still agree with what I told him earlier. Spinning around, I slip out of his reach.

"I'm sorry about earlier. I just wanted to get to know you better."

"Well, my story isn't so pretty. Besides, my favorite color doesn't matter in a time like this. People need help, and I can't be allowed to goof off just because it makes me happy. This rebellion comes with a cost, and if that cost is my freedom, then for everybody else, I will gladly give it up. If anyone should know that, it should be you."

"You see, that's where you are wrong. First off, it does matter what your favorite color is—at least to me it does. Kayda," he takes a step closer to me, looking me square in the eyes. I don't know how I never noticed them before. Each eye is a deep green, flecked with little hints of caramel and burgundy. The colors fight with each other, creating a sort of chaos, a beautiful whirlwind of commotion. I can't take my eyes away. "you don't have to choose one or the other. Why can't you have both for once?"

"No, that's choosing my pleasure over relieving a burden from so many shoulders. I can't, but I still want to. I'm so selfish." The last few words come out broken, and I force my eyes away from his, taking a step back.

"No, Kayda, you're not selfish. You're trading your happiness for the happiness of others. I bet that ninety-eight percent of the people in this city wouldn't even do that. Compared to most, you're like an angel." I scoff at him. I surely don't feel like one.

"If I'm an angel then this is Hell."

"Maybe it is," he agrees sadly, "But, what if I told you that in this horrible world, I could grant you a wish like the genie in Aladdin. What if I said that you could have friendship and save the world. That sounds pretty good, right? Well, that's what I'm offering." He looks deep into my eyes as if he can see straight into my soul. "I know you've had a tough past, but Leum and I, we'll be here for you, if you let us. So, what do you say? Will you accept the offer? Will you dare to let me grant one wish in this horrible world?"

I pause, soaking in his words like a flower. I know I can't accept, but the fact that he outwardly said he'll be there for me is too tempting of an offer to pass over. My parents are dead, and my sister can barely even move, let alone talk. I've been alone for so long now.

And I'm tired of it. I know I'm becoming as foolish as I once thought Jax was, hoping for a better life, for a brighter future. But, I'm finally starting to believe that maybe there is a chance for that other world.

Is that so bad? Is it horrible to want to laugh more? Is it so terrible to yearn to smile? Is it really dreadful that I hope for a world better than this? If it is, then I don't care anymore.

"I accept, O great and powerful genie," I declare, my voice dripping with dry humor. And yet, not even a hint of regret swirls in my thoughts. "Grant me one wish."

I don't believe in fate, but for some reason, I feel like this was all meant to happen. That in some sense, I'm just like the characters in my mom's favorite fairy tales, making decisions by myself, but secretly being led by a greater being. My story has just started, and if this is my destiny, then it's not so bad.

8

Slipping my feet into two shiny shoes, I recall how they turned up on my doorstep with the rest of my maid uniform. A crumpled unassuming paper lay next to the items. Someone else might have dismissed it as a piece of trash that had been blown onto the house's front steps, but I knew better. When it was unraveled, a message could be seen scribbled across the sheet. It read: "Can't wait to see you wearing that outfit! And don't forget to put your hair in a ponytail, so it doesn't get in the way of the bonnet :) "

I imagine how I must look. Definitely ridiculous with the black dress I wear covered by a creamy colored apron embroidered with tiny blooming flowers. I have little black shoes and a name tag that reads Bethany. To top it all off, is the "famous" bonnet, big and poufy, resting on my head like a miniature ostrich. I just want to tear it apart. Instead, I have to ensure that it won't fall off by bobby pinning it to my hair, which is pulled back in a slick ponytail that hangs down to just above my waist.

I may be pretending to be a maid, but these clothes are still nicely fabricated. Unlike my scratchy garments, the cotton of this dress is soft and light, and the shoes on my feet are so shiny that they mirror the reflection of my face when I peer down at them. My whole ensemble could probably feed a whole family of five for months in these alleys. I can't even dare to imagine what the owner of Skyhigh Towers might wear.

As I walk toward the door, I quickly feel for the four blades hidden beneath my clothes. They rest in their normal positions: one strapped to my back, another snug against my stomach, the other at my forearm, and the last tied tight to my thigh. Each blade is forged from the best quality steal, smoothed by countless fires and with iron handles made just for my grip. They range in sizes from the length of my hand to the length from my fingernail to my elbow.

Even the best assassin in this city would marvel at their beauty. The four knives are the only luxuries I've ever allowed myself to buy, and yet, I use them only for protection.

Yesterday, the meeting I set up proved useful, and by the end of it, any inconsistencies within the plan had been smoothed out. In a perfect world, our plan should run without any troubles.

In other words, if all goes well, it should be as simple as this: we go in, steal the money, and be out without anybody noticing.

"Sakura, are you feeling better?" I ask, creaking open her door. Yesterday, she woke up with an appetite, downing a whole bowl of soup, and ever since then, she's been growing stronger and stronger. In fact, this morning she sat up.

Now, as I walk through the door, I see her fiddling with her hair, trying to weave it into braids. Her weak hands are not as dexterous as they once were, leaving the braids slightly loose and messy. Honestly, they're a lot better than anything I could do.

Despite Sakura's many attempts to try to teach me, to this day I still remain unable to do any type of braid to save my life. It never mattered before because Sakura would always braid my hair for me, and in truth, I'm excited for the mass of tangles on my shoulders to be pulled back again. Seriously, some days I just want to chop it all off. The only thing that stops me is the memory of my mother gently brushing my hair.

She combs through the frizzes on my head before bending down and whispering in my ear. "Hair as shiny as the gleam of afternoon sun on a window; waves like the unrushed movement of wind. My darling, you must be a princess to have such beauty."

I frown at her words. The princesses in fairytales are always delicate and weak. I want to be strong and fierce; the unstoppable knight who saves the blushing young maiden by thrusting a sword through the neck of a ghastly beast.

As if she can read my thoughts, she takes my tiny hands in her own slender ones, whispering "A princess, only because you deserve the respect. But at heart, my darling, you are a warrior. Fierce of heart and strong of will. Promise me, that no matter what this world throws in your way, that you will always be the brave little soldier you are." Her tone hardens and she glances away for a second, her eyes glazing over as if she is imagining the future. "Whatever you must do to survive, whether it be good or bad, never lose the song of your heart."

Carefully, she moves my hand to my chest, right over my heart. "Listen, always listen to that beat. Logic may fool you, but love will never guide you wrong."

Tentatively, I lower my head, resting my chin on my chest, trying to listen to my heart's quick pitter-patter. It kind of sounds like the soft hand of a spring breeze tickling a field of grass—almost like a song of peace.

"Always listen to what it says, do you understand?"

I don't really get what she means. How could I possibly know what each thump is trying to tell me? It's like trying to understand another language. Finally, I decide that I'll just have to keep listening and trying to decode the song the beats make.

I nod at Mom, "I will always listen."

Pausing for a second to study my expression, she gets up looking satisfied with what she must have seen on my chubby five-year-old face. "Go get some sleep then, my little warrior. Many adventures await us tomorrow!" As she speaks, she picks me up and twirls me around. The joy is instantaneous, and I forget the seriousness of the moment before, giggling my infamous high-pitched laugh, and opening my arms to welcome the flurry of motion.

"Kayda, are you going anywhere today?

Sakura's voice breaks through the memory, piercing the fog that has settled into my brain, like a knife. Absently, I find myself playing with the end of my ponytail. I look at it quickly, the corners of my mouth pulling up the slightest bit. For my mom, I will never cut my hair.

"What did you say?" I ask, dropping the black lock and letting it fall back with the rest of my ponytail.

"I just wanted to know if you would be out today."

"Oh, yeah. I won't be home until late tonight. Actually, I was coming to tell you that I was going to head out now. Do you need anything before I go—maybe something to eat?" The question is hopeful, and I know the answer before it comes.

"I had a whole bowl of soup yesterday and an apple today. I think I'm fine Kayda."

"Well then, I'll probably see you in the morning, okay?" I walk to the side of the bed, bending down to kiss Sakura's still damp forehead. She may appear to be better, but the sickness still clings to her like a tattered cloak.

Frowning, I ask again, "Are you sure you don't need anything? How about water, do you want—"

"Honestly, Kayda, I'm good. Go do whatever you need to do, and stop worrying about me. You don't deserve to have to wait over me as if I'm some wrinkly, old, senile person."

She says the words with a light tone and even flashes a teasing grin at me. Forcing a tight-lipped smile in return, I walk to the door, hoping she doesn't notice my lack of joy. I don't find any humor in her words that sound so close to the bitter truth. Quietly shutting the door behind me, I mumble, "None of us deserve this life."

Like a veil, the night covers me. It hides my figure in its shadows as if it recognizes me as one of its children. And like any good parent, it tries its best to protect me, keeping me cached in its many shades of black. In return, I send a quick prayer of thanks up to the heavens.

Numerous people over the ages have claimed to be afraid of the dark. I, myself, would say that such a fear is preposterous. When compared to the possibility of starvation and death, darkness looks like the welcoming arms of a long-lost friend.

Mainly, I think humans fear the dark because it's incomprehensible. What one cannot see, often, one cannot start to understand.

So, when darkness comes around, shadowing the streets and engulfing the city in night, people are reminded of all they cannot control, of how small they really are in the experiment of life. Each and every one of us is really but a puppet played with by our master Time. But who would wish to think of themselves like that? Nobody.

So, we humans live and die, trying to find purpose in the small time period in which we are lucky enough to walk in this world, always ignoring the possibility of death.

Perhaps that's why I embrace the shadows. I understand that one day I will leave this world, and I will not hide from what is inevitable. Before the time comes though, I will make as many marks on this world as I can. So, if I'm just a puppet, then I'll play my role as if there's no tomorrow. And if I'm in only one show, then I'm going to make that performance unforgettable.

Shadows melt away, burned by the shimmering ray of light that puddles onto the street as I creak open the door, arriving at the building I cleaned up. Shutting it behind me noiselessly, I weave through the cemetery of old and forgotten furniture, finding the almost non-existing path that leads to the spiraling staircase. The first step moans like it normally does, and I take a deep breath. *I can do this.* The second step screams out like a banshee. *There's nothing to be afraid of.* Each creak and groan I make into a declaration of my ability to complete today's mission. And when I reach the door at the top of the staircase, I am a perfect example of calm, like the ocean on a mild spring day. My hand grasps the rusty metal handle, and the door swings open.

"Hiya gorgeous!" Jax greets me, a smirk on his face suggesting mischief. He looks over my outfit, his eyes twinkling with laughter.

"Hiya ugly!" I snicker back in return, watching his grin disappear as he registers the meaning of my words. Laughing, I close the door behind me. This new friendship thing is the best. I always have someone to make fun of.

"Isn't she just the sweetest girl ever?" Leum playfully asks Jax who has already regained his composure.

"Oh, my lady," he announces doing an outlandish bow towards me and then holding his arm out as if inviting me to dance, "you are as sweet as the dregs of the finest black coffee."

The blow is expected, but the corners of my mouth still pull up the slightest bit.

"Why, thank you. It seems I will just have to continue with this attitude then if you like it *so* very much." Pushing past him, I ignore his outstretched hand, making my way to the table.

I trace my hand along the map that is taped to the table, outlining the path we will take to the towers.

"Let's go over the plan one last time, all right?" I ask, turning to the other two.

"We've already gone over it so many times," Leum whines.

"Not in the last five minutes." I settle down into a wooden chair, crossing one leg over another and leaning far into the cushioned back. "So, first we will all make our way to our starting positions. I will follow Jax to the skyscraper, while you, Leum, will find your way to the lake. Then, Jax and I will enter the building disguised and head our separate ways."

"I will then distract Mark Valtin, allowing Kayda a chance to break into his computer," Jax adds.

"After Kayda gets the money, I'll tell you guys to get out, and we'll run away, free, and victorious!" Leum raises his arms in a dramatic gesture with a goofy smile on his face.

"That's if it all goes well." I deadpan.

Jax strides toward the door "Oh relax for once, little dragon. Nobody's attacking you at the moment. Trust yourself."

My calm is starting to piece back together when Jax casually pulls off his shirt. I freeze. His skin is a sun-warmed tan, like how I imagine the sands of a desert might look. My eyes rove over his strong figure before I can think to look away. He's lean but toned, the muscles on his stomach and arms gracefully outlined and even more prominent when he bends down to pick something up. It's as if he was carved by the pre-A.R.T sculptor, Leonardo Da Vinci: his figure perfectly chiseled, each plane smooth and shining, a few scars, the only flaws. There's no way that I can deny his beauty anymore. It's obvious.

I'm still staring at him, my mouth slightly open when he glances over his shoulder at me, winking. Dirt! My cheeks start to pinken and I look away before they have the chance to fully turn red. My control is completely and utterly gone, shattered into unimaginably small pieces; a Humpty Dumpty masterpiece of an impossible recovery. Quickly, I glance in Leum's direction, planning on gauging his reaction to the whole fiasco, but he's studying the map across the room. In fact, I don't think he even realized anything happened. Letting out a sigh, I straighten up.

So, I didn't just make a total fool of myself.

"Wow, you managed to pull a shirt over your head!" I say sarcastically as I walk by Jax, who now wears a beige worker's shirt with a little name tag reading William.

"I was going slow just for your benefit." He replies, his eyes dancing with amusement. Dirt, why does he always have to be so arrogant!

"Thank you very much, but I don't really have the time to determine whether your physique is up to my standards or not. I have a mission to complete, and I would appreciate if you helped me out—Leum," I call hoping my voice isn't shaking too much, motioning for him to get up as I try to regain control, "let's go." Turning back to Jax I say "but, if you're not going to come, I can still do this without you."

"Hey, hold on there darling. I'm coming," he declares, crossing his arms in resolution, "and you couldn't do this without me."

"Wanna bet?" The two words are thrown at him, just as I thrust open the door.

"I don't want to possibly compromise the mission so I'm going to say no, but you're going to regret underestimating me in the future. I *am* quite skillful," he proclaims, wiggling his eyebrows and blowing me a teasing kiss, "in *all* areas."

"You know that I don't find you charming, right?" I shoot back over my shoulder praying he doesn't see the color creeping onto my cheeks.

His answer echoes behind me, "Ahh, but a statement that must be declared is a statement that is unsure."

I have no response to that because he is partly true. *Sometimes*, I find him a little bit charming—but only a *little* bit.

"Okay, wise guy, I like the new riddle-thing you've got going on, but it's time to focus on the task at hand. Are we all ready to complete this mission?" I look both Leum—who has just lumbered over—and Jax in the eyes.

"And to become heroes!" Leum chirps out like some student ready to go on a field trip.

"And to steal some money!" Jax says a smirk pulling at his lips.

"And to make history," I declare, walking through the door.

9

Jax and I wind through the streets sticking to the shadows, like spirits raised from the dead, leaving no tracks behind except for the slight whoosh of air that marks our passing. At last, the street widens and, finally, the skyscraper is visible. I gasp.

Each level is molded from polished steel so shiny and bright, I swear it looks like the building is made from little fragments of stars sewn together. And there are not just a few hundred floors—no—there are thousands. They stack up like the wooden logs in that old game, *Jenga*, and I crane my head up, searching for the top.

I can't find it.

Yet, the thing that truly amazes me is that the *whole* city is filled with these towers. They all reach up toward the sky like needy vines, trying to hold onto the sun. Some are stout and made of foggy glass, whereas others twist in spirals and reach up higher than Skyhigh Towers. I don't even understand how some of the more abstractly shaped buildings—a tower made up of various shapes stacked on top of each other or a triangular building rising off the ground from just one point—stay standing. The city itself is an amazing feat of architecture, but for some reason, I have a feeling that technology had a big hand in its creation—technology that would make a Lynk look like a baby's binky.

Jax glances at me and lets out a bark. "You look like you've just learned how to see!"

I close my mouth in a tight, pinched line, erasing the "o" of surprise it had been in and angle my head slightly away, just as an army of red, once again, starts to march its way across my cheeks.

"I bet you were just as taken aback as I was the first time you saw it." I quietly reply, gazing once again at the city; I can't help it, the shimmering buildings just seem to draw my eyes.

"Oh, trust me, I am."

Right as I'm about to take a step forward, something prickles at the back of my mind, a little roughed up boat disturbing the waters of my thought. It starts to draw ever nearer to the surface until I realize just what is bugging me.

The last sentence Jax said—he used the words "I am," not "I was"... which makes it seem as if this is his first time seeing the skyscrapers. But, when he told us the plan, he sounded as if he knew what he was talking about—no—it sounded as if he had *experienced* what he was talking about. If he never visited one before, how did he know all the ins and outs of a skyscraper? If he really doesn't have an inside info provider—which I don't think he does—then where is he getting all this knowledge?

A cold spider of unease scuttles down my spine, and I call out to Jax, planning on getting some answers. But, when I look up, I realize that while I stopped moving, Jax did not. In fact, he's far enough ahead that he couldn't have possibly heard me.

As quietly and quickly as I can, I dart down the street, hoping to catch up before Jax notices I'm behind. By the time I'm about one foot away from Jax once again, all thoughts about where he gets his knowledge have been promptly forgotten, swept away like cobwebs in a cellar.

"Ready? I'll enter first. You can follow in a minute or two." Jax sprints off without even waiting for a response. As he nears the front doors, his gate grows heavy, his speed slows down, and he starts to whistle a common work tune; In a moment he has transformed from an arrogant teenager to a normal everyday plumber.

Dirt... he's good. Now, the question is, can I do that?

Not stopping to find out, I plunge into the crowd outside of Skyhigh Towers. Slipping through the maze of perfumed bodies and hair-sprayed ladies, I manage to arrive at the two front doors, which remind me of two golden giants and have handles carved to look like diamonds. Above these massive doors hangs a cream-colored sign with the name, **Skyhigh Towers**, printed on it in a stiff, bold font. Inhaling a deep breath, I tuck one last stray strand of hair behind my ear and pull open the door.

Everything is glimmering: the couches, the tables, the people waiting in line, and even the air, which smells like delicate vanilla and fragrant rose petals.

If I thought the outside was beautiful, it is nothing compared to what I see now. Couches are draped with blankets of the finest silk, chandeliers are outlined in glimmering crystals, and the front desk is coated in pure gold.

But what really draws my eyes are the paintings that hang all over the walls. Some are as large as my kitchen table, whereas others are as small as the length of my hand. And yet, all of them are absolute masterpieces: paintings that would have each taken at least a year to make—paintings that are worth enough to feed a whole family for decades.

The scenes they depict range from gruesome battles to serene wheat fields, but the one that takes my breath away, is a small forgotten painting in a dark corner of the room—a painting of a desert. The sands are a bloody red, and the sky is a dark violet glittering with stars. A small tear escapes my eye; the desert looks just like how I imagined it would.

I'm not leaving it behind. The painting comes off the wall silently, with no blaring alarms to mark what I've done. I'm already walking away, the painting in a pocket of my apron, before anyone could possibly think to look in my direction. My steps become quick and quiet, my shoulders slightly hunched, and my gaze on the floor. I blend into the background, an unnoticed shadow amongst the rich—the perfect modest maid.

When I reach the front desk, I flash an ID card that Leum managed to paste a picture of me onto. If the receptionist decides to stop me, it'll be obvious that I'm not really a maid. A bead of sweat forms on my forehead, but I maintain the meek smile on my face, continually playing the part of a diligent worker just checking in. One second passes like an eternity, and then another, and another...finally, the receptionist looks up and glances at my ID. She stares at it for what seems like an infinite amount of time, not saying anything, and my legs threaten to quaver. After a long look, she straightens up and gives me a... smile?

"Oh, I'm so sorry, there's just a lot of people at this hour, and I'm so tired that I sometimes daze off." She looks up at me once again and gives me another smile. "Anyway, go ahead, have a nice day." The receptionist waves me forward turning back to the next person in line.

I scuttle into the white hallway in front of me, making sure I turn a corner—finally away from the haughty stares of all those rich people—before slumping against the wall. My breath comes in little puffs, and the thoughts in my mind are swirling like the winds of a tornado, frantic and wild. I bite my lip, trying to calm myself down, but the emotions rise up unbidden.

I can't help but think how flawlessly Jax pulled off his act, waltzing past the line of guests as if he had no care in the world, as if he truly was just a plumber. A hint of admiration seems to creep into and penetrate my thoughts, like a virus I can't be cured of. I shake my head, dislodging the thought, hoping it'll clear away some of my growing nerves.

I need to get up. I need to keep moving. And I try, but the chaos in my mind just escalates, and my thoughts start to veer in a completely new direction, towards the day my parents died. My breath becomes labored like the pants of a dog and my eyes close just when something pointy pokes me in the stomach. Immediately, my eyelids flutter open, and I see what disturbed me—the corner of the painting

I stole; the red of the never-ending sands sticking out of my apron pocket.

The painting combined with my thoughts bring back my mother's voice, and it fills my head once again; "*Promise me, that no matter what this world throws in your way, you will always be the brave little soldier you are.*"

The words rush into me and suddenly strength floods through my limbs. Clarity settles upon me like a cloud. I can't give up. I promised her I wouldn't give up. I need to soldier on, to be a warrior. Grunting, I push the chaos of thoughts away. I'm not doing this for myself, I'm doing this for Mom, for Dad, for Sakura, for the city. I grit my teeth and rise from the floor, shaking off the remnants of fear and squaring my shoulders, preparing for the rest of this mission.

"I'm on my way," I whisper to Leum tapping on the earpiece so he can hear me.

"Good. Jax is going to enter room 1009 in three minutes. You have five to get into your own apartment."

I stalk down the white hallway, moving at a fast pace to make up for the time I lost. Soon, the workers' elevator comes up on my right, and I push the up button on the wall like Jax told me to do. In a matter of seconds, the elevator doors open with a whoosh and a little "ping." Stepping inside the metal vault, I stare in awe at all the buttons on the wall that glow like animals' eyes in the dark.

An angry beep sounds, and I remember how Jax told me that in order to go anywhere, I have to press one of the buttons. I choose the shiny one that reads 300; each floor only contains a few large apartments, making this Tower have a whole lot of floors. Immediately the elevator issues a contented whoosh—which to me sounds oddly like a sigh—and the two heavy doors clink shut and don't reopen. I wait a few seconds, but they remain closed.

Dirt, I'm trapped! My breathing quickens once again. How do I get out? I've never been in an elevator before, but I can't almost ruin this mission again. I sort through all the info Jax told me about elevators, but I don't remember any instructions about what to do if I get stuck in one. All I can think of is to bang on the doors, so I do. But, just as I pound my first fist into the metal, the elevator rockets up so fast that I'm sent tumbling on to the carpeted floor. Struggling to a standing position, I hold on to the little bar that lines the elevator as firmly as I can. For all I know, it could mean the difference between life and death.

As the machine rockets me upwards, my stomach flies into my throat and my brain feels like it's being hammered to mush. I try to make it back to the door, but my legs have become as flimsy as blades of grass. I feel like I'm traveling through time, not up an apartment building.

Just as I'm about to shout out for help, the elevator lets out three high pitched peeps—definitely a cackle in elevator language—and releases its doors. I hobble out like some ancient lady and sprawl on the floor, trying not to retch. If anybody saw me, I'm sure they'd think I was crazy—no, let me rephrase that—they'd think I was insane.

After a minute of deep breaths, I manage to rise up, and the first thing I notice is a small black sign that reads "floor 300" in little white letters. Well... I guess I hadn't been trapped after all. Stepping forward into the hallway, I push my foolishness to the back of my mind and look around.

Leum's voice issues in my ear, "Jax has entered apartment 1009. Two minutes, Kayda."

A quick sweep of my surroundings leaves me with quite the impression: a black and white rose patterned carpet along the hallway, long mahogany doors, flower boxes every few feet, and the same rose and vanilla scent to the air. Wow, this place really went all out when it came to the small details.

"One minute. Get moving."

"Okay, I'm almost there," I reply.

No time to enjoy the surroundings anymore, I hurry along the hallway and spot room number 1007. I continue on, now sprinting. One more... there! Room number 1008 comes into view, the tall mahogany door screaming at me to move faster.

"I'm outside the apartment door," I whisper to Leum.

"Good because you have thirty seconds to use your pass before it becomes useless. Move it!"

Oh, no! I fumble in my apron, searching for the pass—

"20 seconds."

The painting brushes up against my hand, but where's the pass?

"10 seconds."

I reach deeper, searching and... there! The edge of the pass slides over my palm and I grasp it with my fingers, pulling it out.

"5 seconds. Kayda!"

Quickly, I slide the pass into the lock—hoping against all odds that maybe, just maybe this will work out—and a green light flashes. The air in me rushes out, and I send a quick prayer of thanks to the heavens, as the door clicks open.

"I'm in."

"You got me scared for a moment there," Leum replies.

"An excellent performance always has a lot of drama," I say with as much gusto as I can muster, hoping that he can't hear the quaver in my voice. Honestly, I cut that way too close. In fact, I feel like this whole mission has been composed of way too many close calls. I've got to get my head in the game.

I walk into the luxurious apartment, making sure not to pause and gawk at all the furnishings. I head straight to the window, testing out the lock on it. The thing is small and white, located on the bottom of the glass pane. It allows tenants to open the window a few inches, but if someone tries to open it more, it locks up the whole window. I give the building owner credit for safety in his apartments; the normal person could never hope to unlock it. Yet, I'm most definitely not normal.

Glancing at the window, I pull out a nice shiny lockpick that Leum gifted to me—it's a lot better than a bobby pin—and stick it into the little white contraption. I wiggle it around a bit, getting past all the lock's defenses. In a second, the window slides open with a satisfying click.

The view, however, is not as satisfying. I knew it would be high, but this is basically in the clouds! I remove the painting from my apron, placing it on a small table near the window. I don't need that falling 300 hundred stories while I'm jumping!

Inhaling a deep breath, I lower myself out of the window and carefully place my feet one in front of the other on the three-inch-wide ledge. Standing up straight, I spread my arms wide, seeking balance as the wind whips my skirt about. I study the distance between myself and the next ledge. Jax was right it's almost exactly four feet; the length of the blanket my mom wove for me.

I close my eyes. Imagining the soft fabric, the miniature stitches that form vibrant scenes. I think of holding it close, of running my hand down the length of it, of smelling the last vestiges of my mom's jasmine perfume that cling to it, and time stills. The harsh cry of the wind is gone, replaced with the crackling of logs in a fireplace and the soft snores of my father. I open my eyes and see the kind face of my mother, the strands of her silky hair illuminated by the firelight. Jasmine surrounds me mixed with the smoky scent of ashes, and I watch my mother's head turn to look at me. Her skin is young and unmarred, her fingers gracefully stitching the start of my blanket. But, it is her eyes that I stare at; two laughing doe shaped eyes, the same shade of brown as mine. The one part of her that was truly passed down to me.

My heart aches something fierce and I long to reach out and grasp her hand, but as I'm about to move closer to her, the vision starts to fade, my mother's body turning to wisps of color. When all that's left is her smiling face, she whispers, "I love you, now go."

And so, I do.

I jump.

10

Time speeds up, and sound rushes back into my ears, hitting me with the force of a freight train. My heartbeat grows faster and faster, galloping away in my chest like some racehorse on its way to the finish line. I'm being tossed around like a rag doll as the wind fights against my momentum, lifting me through the air 300 floors above the ground. And in the midst of all the chaos, I wonder for a fleeting second if the people milling around on the streets below even see me—I must look like a small speck in the sky.

An odd little chuckle falls from my mouth, encouraging a crazy thought to spread throughout my mind and distract me from my tempestuous descent; I bet they would notice me if my guts splattered all over their fancy shoes. What a scene that would—

The thought is interrupted by the sensation of my feet colliding with the next window ledge, the impact sending a flare of pain like lightning up through my legs. My eyes shoot open, as wide as full moons, and I scramble for purchase on the narrow strip, flapping my arms like an overgrown seagull. One foot slips, and I start to tumble into the open air, falling into wisps of fog. As half my body drops below the ledge, I manage to grasp the metal siding of the window, but my fingers slide down the smooth surface, and I continue to plummet. No! No, no, no!

I shift my grip, straining at the metal and my fingers catch on a small hook, half the width of a copper coin. Immediately, I stop falling, but I shout out in agony, the sound chafing my throat from its force, as all my weight shifts to my right arm, almost wrenching it out of its socket. In a few seconds, my arm is going to become useless, and the last thing I'm going to remember is hanging from this window ledge like some insane bat.

My life doesn't flash before my eyes like everyone seems to say it should, instead I just see the face of my sister, smiling with joy, her eyes glittering. I imagine Jax's face when he told me I was an angel that night, a foreign emotion written into the corners of his smile. I think of the hard-working people of this city, dying so their families live, and I know I could never leave this world now.

I desperately grasp at all my sanity and will, pulling it together to forge a hard ball in my stomach. I want to live out the days with Sakura, playing outside together on spring nights, baking on winter mornings. I want to see her grow, see her survive and lead the life she nearly left.

I calm my nerves, embracing the energy of my fear, turning it into something sharper, something stronger. I want to have the chance to figure out that emotion on Jax's face, to get to know the mischief his smile suggests.

Finally, my thoughts stop swirling, stilled by my determination. I want to—no— I *will* help the people of this crazy land, and there is no way in this forsaken city that I will end my life hanging from one arm like this, scared and weak.

I. Am. Not. Going. To. Die. Like. This.

Gritting my teeth, I sway back and forth, ignoring the shooting pain that licks up my arm like tongues of fire. Swinging up hard one last time, my arm gives out with a sickening crunch, like the sound of snapping twigs, and for a moment I'm airborne, swirling through the air untethered, like a drop of rain flying through the atmosphere.

But as the momentum from my swing sends me upward, a large

gust of wind comes out of nowhere and lifts me higher, allowing me to twist around and manage to grasp the ledge with my toes and my left arm.

Straightening up, I carefully rearrange my feet, shifting my weight as light as a dove, moving my limp arm a fraction of an inch each agonizing second. Scratches run up and down my body, a cut on my forehead has drawn a worrying amount of blood, my shoes have been torn to shreds, leaving my toes a little raw, and my arm feels like it's being gnawed on by hundreds of tiny serrated teeth. Well, at least I'm alive.

Just like Jax promised, the window is open a tiny crack, and I have no problem slipping my hand through and picking the lock on the other side. *Of course,* in a fancy place like this, windows can be locked at any interval, allowing inhabitants to open the window a crack while still feeling safe. Who's going to appear from thin air...well, other than me. My feet hit the floor just as my vision starts to blacken.

Dirt! My shoulder! I feel around the bone and sigh in relief. Although the injury sounded bad, my shoulder is only dislocated. But... if I want to get out of this conscious, I'm going to need to pop my shoulder back in, *now*.

Quickly, I spot the desk with the computer that Jax was talking about and race under it, forcing my shoulder in between the gilded overhang and one of its legs. The overhang is a good five inches long; it should provide enough room for me to be able to pull my arm up, and it should be long enough to hold my shoulder down.

Darkness crowds the corners of my eyes and starts to creep in further, almost fully covering my vision. I'm losing consciousness quickly, and there's no time to think about the consequences; I yank up at my arm with all of the strength I have left, my shoulder bucking against the gilding, and "Pop!" it shifts back into place.

The excruciating burn only lasts for a second, giving way to a dull throb, and then the dark spots slowly disappear and my breathing calms down. Slowly the world comes into focus, re-aligning itself like a spool of film being untangled.

I touch the wound above my brow and feel the hardened, dried blood. Good, at least the cut is closed for now, keeping any more blood from leaking through.

A muffled sound vibrates through my inner ear and slowly sharpens into focus. From multiple rooms away, I hear Jax's voice and the tenor of another man—an angry man. That doesn't sound good. I better get moving.

Slipping into the desk's cushioned chair, I insert a little gadget into the computer—on it is a combination of a few of my hacks that together should find, trap, and send the money in a matter of seconds. 1… 2… 3… 4… 5… 6… 7… 8

A little green light flares from the gadget.

A little gasp bursts from my lips. It's been done. The transaction has been made. I just managed to sneak into one of the most highly-secured skyscrapers, impersonate a maid, steal 1,000 kimas and get away free. At the thought, I grin mischievously, and for a second, I have a wild urge to let out a loud whoop. I quickly restrain it. This isn't some party, I remind myself, this is a mission. Even so, I can't totally wipe the grin from my face.

"Money is transferred. Leaving now." I tell Leum.

"Good. Jax says he can only hold the guy for a minute longer."

An angry huff echoes into the room I'm in, confirming Leum's words. I've got to get out of here.

I grab the gadget, rearranging the desk so that the computer screen is at a twenty-five-degree angle like how it was when I came in. Standing up, I push the chair a few inches to the left and then clamber through the window, careful to leave it only as open as it was before. A good thief is a ghost. We come in unnoticed and leave unnoticed, except for the slight feeling that something may have passed by.

From my view on the window ledge, the city looks majestic, like an oil rendering of the pre-A.R.T. impressionist, Renoir. Each building is brushed with a light that paints their eccentricities, and yet the illumination softens the sharp angles and draws attention away from the slight imperfections. In this moment, the lively night, stroked with such bright lights, and the sophisticated ebony steel buildings, blend together so softly, like an old couple dancing to a slow song, remembering their youthful days.

I nod in appreciation of the beauty and turn my head away, letting the couple sway together in solitude.

The moment tucked away into a pocket deep inside of me, I snap back into focus, scanning the distance between the two window ledges once again. Shifting my feet ever so slightly, I jump. Air whistles below my feet, the world rushing by under me.

I land lightly on the ledge this time and have no trouble climbing through the window and collecting the desert painting.

"Take the elevator to the basement and exit through the back door. Jax will catch up with you." The instructions are easy and precise, but I'm not taking an elevator again. I don't care if I really wasn't trapped. It felt like it.

"Where are the stairs? I'll take the stairs."

Leum replies immediately, asking no questions whatsoever. "Take a right turn at the elevator and the door for the stairs will be on your left."

"Thanks." I need to leave before I do something that will get us caught.

I dash out the door and down the rose-carpeted hallway. My feet fall soft and quiet on the floor, but my breath starts to become frantic, the scented air intoxicating me with its sweetness. And where before the flower boxes seemed like pretty decorations, now I feel as if they are monsters trying to block my way, the flowers in their berths like the ghastly hands of the dead reaching up from the shadows. I need to get out of here.

I'm almost at the elevator when I hear a door open and a terse young man sticks his head out, shoving a handsome plumber into the hallway. I lean back into a shadowed corner to hide my disheveled appearance.

The man starts to scream and splutter, a large vein pulsing in the middle of his forehead. "Tell WHATEVER company you work for to NEVER EVER send someone here AGAIN!" By the end of the sentence, the man's face has turned into, actually, a quite nice shade of deep red. In fact, I would think an artist would use that exact color to paint a perfectly ripe Arkansas black apple.

"Yes, sir!" Jax replies as the door slams shut creating a sound like thunder, and I emerge from the corner. He lopes down the hallway, not bothering to be quiet; I can't believe he can be so calm and laid back, but after all, I guess to anybody else, we *are* just a plumber and a maid.

"Are you okay?" He squints his eyes in worry and reaches out to wipe the smeared blood off my forehead.

I duck at the last moment and spin around with a shaky laugh. "Yeah, I'm fine. Just a little tumble." I change the subject quickly, "And how about you with that guy? Is it really that hard for you to not annoy someone for an hour?" I add hardness to my tone and pick up the pace, so the concern in his eyes will turn to irritation.

"Anger is the weakness of the human race; it's a fog that leaves no room for thought. See, in his wrath, Mark Valtin never thought to wonder why a plumber showed up at his room, despite the fact that according to his contract with Sky High Towers, all his appliances should be automatically fixed by a *technological system*."

"Maybe he just didn't read the fine print," I say, although I file away his words for future reference.

"Even so, it was smart. Admit it." He gives me a goofy smile, and it makes it that much more fun to stay quiet as I turn right when we reach the elevator.

"Wait," he exclaims stopping, "We're not using the elevator? You do realize we're on the three hundredth floor?"

Dirt, he's right! I totally forgot we were that high up. It would take forever to run down that many stairs. I let out a groan and backtrack to the elevator, pushing the button to call it to our floor.

"Not much of a fan of elevators then?" He jokes.

"No."

"Okay... want to tell me what happened?"

"No." I am definitely not telling him about that whole fiasco—nor about my *slight* problems during the mission. I think it's safer to leave it up to his imagination.

"BING!" The elevator issues a loud obnoxious beep, the chuckle of a commander laughing at the return of a defeated enemy. I step inside the metal box. This is going to be one long ride.

Cold, fresh air kisses my cheeks like a prayer as the back door of the skyscraper bangs shut behind us, and finally, I let out the breath I was holding in. It's over... and there are no flashing lights, no black uniforms, no sirens wailing, just silence, cold, blissful silence—well except for the random screams, shouts, and crashes that always seem to come with a city night.

I take off my apron with the painting inside it and lay it on the ground just as the giddiness starts to build in my stomach, filling me up as if I'm a tightly stoppered bottle. It pushes at my restraints, the pressure building, until I can't hold it in any longer. Laughter bursts from my lips, unruly and wild, tumbling into the air like a flame. And once I start I can't stop. The flame turns into an inferno, my laughter becoming bolder, more unbridled.

"You sound like a crazy hyena," Jax says, steering me into the nearest alleyway.

"Well, at least I don't sound like a wild boar." I retort, reaching over and poking him in the stomach, careful to use my left arm.

He lets out a surprised snort that sounds just like a hog, and another bout of laughter rushes through me.

"See, just like a pig," I manage to say in between giggles. I wiggle my eyebrows mischievously, swirling my finger in the air, before I feint to the right, lunging towards him in a mock fencing bout. He lumbers to the left, just in time for me to poke him in the stomach again. His laugh is full and rich this time, and I find myself leaning closer, wishing to hear it again.

"Oh, *I* see how it is," he replies, his eyes twinkling with mirth, "

But be prepared to surrender, little dragon, because you picked the wrong opponent."

"Oh, really? I thought I already beat you once before."

The words have barely left my mouth when he lunges at me, and before I can even think to move, he has already jabbed me in the stomach.

My eyes widen in surprise, and he laughs again, the sound catching me off guard. The rich tones sound like a story about a brave and cunning hero who partakes on wild conquests and yet, appreciates a beautiful sunset. It draws me in, and I can't help but sway ever closer to him, listening with my whole being. And at that moment, I realize his laugh is a story I could spend my whole life reading without ever getting bored.

I tear my focus away from the sound of his laughter, frightened by my realization, and throw myself into the light feeling I felt before. Before I truly make the decision, I'm dashing straight towards Jax, my laugh drawing his attention. He dodges at the last second, but I'm ready for the change. I lean into my momentum instead of trying to break it, spinning to the right and then pivoting a little bit to the left. I poke him firmly in the chest with my left hand, widening my stance so that I slow to a stop, but my momentum is too great and I continue to barrel into him. His arms come around me as the collision sends us stumbling back. And just like that, any traces of unease or pain in my shoulder that still lingered with me, gently are brushed away to the back of my thoughts.

I laugh lightly. "See, I won once again." I tilt my head up so that I can see Jax's reaction, and suddenly, I'm all too aware of how his arms wrap around me, pressing my body flush against his chest. I lightly brush the silver chain at his neck as a distraction, but my eyes are automatically drawn back to his face. His gaze is fixed on my face, his dark eyelashes almost brushing my cheeks. I'm so close I can count the flecks of gold in each of his eyes: four in his right and five in his left. They glimmer in the street light, making me feel reckless, and I can't help but notice that if I leaned forward ever so slightly, his lips would brush mine.

The sound of shoes slapping asphalt draws my attention away, and the moment is lost to the past. Acting on instinct, I push Jax into the shadows and blend into the darkness next to him.

The footsteps grow louder, but I now hear that there is only one set. I let out a silent sigh. One person, Jax and I can definitely handle if we need to, a troop of police officers would have been another story.

Finally, the person turns into the alley, and as he walks forward, a sliver of light from the street lamp illuminates his face.

"Leum!" I slide from the shadows, forcing a quick smile, hoping that he won't see through the veneer that hides the bitter scowl of disappointment. Why did he have to come at this exact moment...interrupting so many possibilities? "I thought we were going to meet you at our building?"

"Well, I decided I might as well head back this way in case there was a chance I would bump into you guys." Oblivious to my sour mood, he mumbles through the whole sentence with a wide grin, as if he's too excited to explain. "Can you believe it? We stole 1,000 kimas! Think about how many cool gadgets I can now get you guys."

"Shhh...!" I hiss, not willing to share in his excitement. "If someone hears, we won't be so successful anymore."

"Kayda's right, we shouldn't talk about it here—you never know who's listening. But, good job, kid!"

Leum beams at Jax's compliment, too joyful to even get mad at the nickname *kid*.

I look up at the sky, trying to lose my foul mood in the endless oblivion of night, and, surprised, I realize that the stars have already come out. In the adrenaline of the mission, I totally lost track of time.

"I'm going to head home now, guys. I'll meet you two at our building in three days, okay?"

Leum yaps, the excitement still with him, "All right see you then."

"Sure," Jax replies much more laid back. The lazy smile on his face making my cheeks flush with pink.

I turn quickly and walk away, stepping into the shadows as if they are tangible things. And as my feet take me along the familiar path home, I try to think about the mission and its flaws and successes. But each time I focus my mind, it just seems to wander to that *one* moment, replaying the scene over and over again: making Leum come a minute later each time, making me fall into Jax's arms a few seconds faster, making my hesitation non-existent. Finally, after I arrive at my house and lay down on my bed, I dream of leaning in, uninterrupted, my lips brushing Jax's lightly.

But it's only a dream, and dreams don't come true in this city.

11

Three days. Why did I have to choose three? Now, I have to wait another day, and I'm bound to go crazy before the night gives way to sunrise. I could have said, "see you guys tomorrow," or "see you in two days." But no, I *had* to choose three, because I had thought that everything that comes in threes always works out: three wishes from the genie, three fairy godmothers in *Sleeping Beauty*, three musketeers—wait there's actually four...dirt! Still, why did I have to choose three?

"Stop fidgeting!" Sakura yells, letting out a long-winded sigh. "Honestly Kayda, you're wiggling as if there are a dozen spiders crawling up your back. How do you think I can braid your hair while you're moving around so much?"

"Sorry," I apologize, the word coming out mumbled and not very convincing. I stare at the desert painting I hung up on the wall yesterday and focus on stilling my tapping fingers, but my feet just pick up the relentless rhythm when my hands become stationary. It's useless, I feel the energy building up inside me, and it makes me restless.

"Well, I'm almost done, okay? Just give me a minute." She bites the bottom of her lip in concentration, weaving the strands of my unruly hair into a neat braid, smoothing away the imperfections with an expert tug of her fingers.

Watching her work so deftly and with such ease calms my body for a moment, soothing the anxious beast inside of me and the realization hits me hard: Sakura's forehead is no longer speckled with sweat, her eyes are bright, and her cheeks once again have a natural rosy glow. Could it be possible? Could Sakura have fought off her sickness for good? For a moment my mind fails to wrap itself around the idea, approaching the thought as if it is some alien creature. But with the thought comes a wave of guilt; I've been so absent recently that I failed to notice the one thing I have prayed for over the past three years has come true: my sister has been healed--and in an unexplainably short time, like the work of a miracle. And although I want to punish myself for my selfishness, my excitement quickly wins over. I want to shout it from the rooftops, I want to whisper it into the smallest alleys, I want to show Fumihiko just how wrong he was, and I may sound like some eager hawker on the side of the street advertising goods, but I want the whole city to know: my sister is healed!

The glee bubbles up, a wild creature pulling me into a reckless mood. It's an all-consuming feeling—the type that only comes from the discovery of a truckload of intense joy.

"Sakura, let's go!" I'm already rising, the decision made without a doubt.

While frantically trying to tie a rubber band around the end of my French-braided hair, which sways wildly due to my sudden movement, Sakura asks, "Go where and why, Kayda?"

"We'll go to the market, the bakery, the park. I don't care where, let's just go! You're no longer sick and I want to go have fun again."

"Umm... I've been healed and moving for a few days, and you're just having this revelation now."

"Well..." I almost shrink under her words but I decide instead to plow on, "you want to go or not?"

My sister hesitates for a second, her lips scrunching up into a tight square, wondering what could possibly make her older, normally very cautious, sister so reckless. And although she ponders for a moment or two, it's just for show. For Sakura, there's not even a decision whether she wants to go out or not, the answer will always be yes.

Sure enough, her carefree nature wins out, her pinched eyes softening into big brown orbs of excitement, shedding seriousness like it was a costume just a few sizes too tight.

"Alright, let's go!" exclaims Sakura, flinging her arms up, not quite able to contain a little shriek of delight. It's a small sound, even more minute than the patter of a single raindrop, but the ease it portrays, the simple gladness to be uttered, warms my heart as if it hears an old tune it once knew.

Maybe some god up there in the sky makes moments like these, forming the joy into shimmering balls, rounded to perfection. And just maybe when he sees a person in despair, he throws one glimmering orb down to the dirt, like a falling star, gifting the weary with one moment of pure, unmarred elation.

In truth, perfect moments probably just happen by chance. And that might be true, but still, I grab at the pleasure, holding onto it as if it is a tangible thing, as if it is truly that glittering orb thrown down from the land of angels. I hold on to it and I will not let go.

Rising to my feet, I grab my sister's small smooth hand, rushing to the door and leaping outside into the fresh summer breeze. Sheaves of light turn her hair into a dazzling amber as the wind casually tosses the strands about, and quietly Sakura tilts her head, doe-eyes slowly waning into half-moons and then crescents and soon her eyes are completely closed, mimicking the cycle of the moon. She breathes not deeply, but carefully as if bottling up the fragrance of her home, tucking it away on a shelf that only she can reach in dreams. And then out of the blue, she starts to run, sprinting past the heaps of trash and darting around the corner, skimming close to *Li Jin's.*

"You'll never catch me," she shouts back with a laugh that immediately slows her down, "I'm as fast as a hare." The words are part of a joke Sakura and I made up awhile back based on an old folk tale. In a sense the childish line is true because Sakura is—even with only being healed for two and a half weeks—faster than me when it comes to a short distance, but we both know that in a long race, I would beat her by several minutes.

"Well, I am the tortoise, the tortoise who beat the hare." I complete the saying, and push my toes into the ground, leaping from the asphalt into a steady fast-paced jog. As I chase after Sakura, who is no longer in sight, I start to speed up, my jog turned into a run. Buildings and lights blur in my peripheral sight, smears of butter on the burnt-toast gray of a smoggy city afternoon.

My breaths become short staccato puffs that create a battle march tune as I run forward, my velocity increasing by the second. A cramp seizes my left side, right below my ribs, but I just grit my teeth and run faster, focusing on the outline of my sister that has just come into view. I hear the slap of her shoes against the road, and I finally allow my short strides to lengthen like a shadow in the afternoon. A wild drum beats in my chest as the distance between us closes from eight-hundred meters to six hundred. I start to sprint, my feet barely touching the ground just when I recognize the old building in front of Sakura; it's a grand gray-brick building with a tiled red roof and ornate green wooden doors—an odd mixture that makes it appear almost quaint—but what makes my heart jump, is the fact that this could only be where Sakura is heading... and she's almost there.

Quickly, I calculate the distance between Sakura and the building, about two-hundred meters, and then how far I am from the building, about three-hundred meters. I note the way Sakura's legs are starting to drag, how without her realizing it, her body has started to cool down, too tired to pick up any more speed. A sharp grin pulls at my lips. I can make it.

Putting on one last burst of speed, I rocket forward, practically flying, my body weightless, only held to Earth by the strength of gravity.

Two-hundred meters... one hundred meters... fifty meters, I pass Sakura and slam to a stop, slapping my hand against the red brick with a loud thwap.

"I won! Who won? *Me*. I won!" I turn around with a little victory dance, laughing at the defeated look on my sister's face as she recoveries from the six-minute run. She rests her hands on her thighs, bending over and heaving in and out, sucking in air like the goldfish that swim in the stuffed marketplace tanks.

"You—" she breathes in, "only won—" she lets out the air and gulps in a new mouthful, "because I let you." The air whooshes out of her lungs with a big huff.

I laugh. "No, *I* won because you," I wiggle my finger at her hunched-over figure, "are out of shape."

Sakura grins, and then her eyes scrunch up a bit in curiosity. "Actually, you're right." An incredulous laugh hits the air as I realize she just told me I was right. "I am out of shape, but how are you so fit, yourself, hmm?"

My smile flutters and I spin around, heading for the large doors of the brick building. "Maybe I just lift you up and down while you're asleep to build up my arm muscles," I joke, the words missing the natural levity that should come with them. My fit state and the scratches on my arms, legs, and forehead that Sakura "tutted" at this morning, have not been forgotten about. In fact, I'm surprised Sakura didn't outright ask me what I'm involved in yet.

Reaching the two humongous eight by five feet green doors, I wrap my hand around one of the handles. It's a golden dragon carved from metal, flying with one of its clawed hands extended forward, as if calling to the other handle on the left door, which is molded in the shape of a little girl. What always interests me is the apparent anguish in the dragon's stature as he reaches for the small girl, as if he's trying to save her but was just a little too late, rather than hunting her and being disappointed about losing a possibly delicious meal.

I tug at the dragon, feeling the resistance that comes with disuse, and after a bit of pulling and pushing, the door yields and slowly begins to creak open, the wood grinding against the cement floor. It comes to a stop, and an enormous dust cloud envelopes me. Coughing and spluttering, I swat uselessly at the millions of tiny particles that settle themselves in my hair and clothes. I imagine the dust particles as old people awoken from slumber, chatty little things recounting to each other all the stories of the past thousands of years but settling down to a hush as they notice me, the one who has woken them up.

Sakura slides past me and through the doors with a laugh, "You look like you've aged ten years!"

I frown, trying to brush off the white particles, but they just won't come off. Sighing, I give up. I might as well let the oldies have some fun and give them something new to gossip about.

As I enter the building, memories start to crash into me, one after the other, piling all the way up to reach the high gilded ceiling. I'm just about to say something, but Sakura gets to it first.

"You remember when we first found this place? We were so excited to have discovered an old theatre. I remember it being like waking up on Christmas morning." She smiles slowly, imagining that day years ago.

"No, it was better than Christmas morning! And when we found the old costumes behind the stage—that changed the whole course of our childhood! We put on so many plays here, you and I." I laugh softly, reminiscing.

"Kayda, what about that time we wore princess costumes into the marketplace," Sakura giggles, "do you remember all the looks we got that day?"

"Yeah!" I giggle too, the old joy bubbling up once again. "People looked at us as if we were mentally insane, but I guess we kind of were." Still smiling, I step further into the theatre, inhaling the musty air and looking out over rows and rows of cushioned seats.

If I close my eyes, I can almost imagine the thunder produced by thousands of hands clapping, the bright lights shining on a stage full of actors dressed in wild costumes, the smell of roasted nuts as vendors offer goods to audience members. It's all so believable, so real with my eyes closed, but if I open them once again, it's just a large dark room falling into disrepair.

And maybe that's all it ever was, but for today, I bring back the audience, the lights, and the vendors.

In my best announcer voice, as I walk down the center aisle, I bellow, "Ladies and gentlemen, prepare to laugh with joy, to cry tears of anguish, to be forever changed! The play is about to begin." With a great flourish of my arm, I summon Sakura to the stage.

She walks down the aisle with a straight spine, waving to invisible fans, every bit the famous actor she's pretending to be. When she reaches the stairs by the stage, I take her hand and we ascend to the platform in unison. Once at the top, I let go of her hand and stride confidently to the center of the wooden floor. I glance at Sakura and she nods. Trying to hide a smile as to not break character, I take a deep breath in and exclaim "Tonight we will be performing a version of the beloved tale, Beauty and the Beast." The crowd roars in pleasure, and I exit the stage as the play begins.

Sakura starts off the play with a scene of Belle proclaiming her want to see the world. Then Sakura, as Belle, flees the stage in search of her father, whom she saves by imprisoning herself in his place at the Beast's castle. Playing the father, I pretend to rush back to the village and cry for Gaston's help. In the next scene, Sakura, in a magnificent red ball gown we found backstage, dances with me, and this time I'm the Beast. We exclaim in agony, as imaginary Gaston invades the palace, and sends a bullet towards my chest, but Sakura quickly moves in front of me, and it hits her instead. She artfully shudders and cries out in anguish falling to the floor, clutching her chest.

"My Beast," she whispers, "live for me." Sakura presses a kiss on my cheek, and pretends to die, collapsing into a still red ball of satin. Faking tears, I huddle over her, hiding my head behind her dress, and taking off my beast mask. I raise my face to the empty theatre seats, and the crowd goes wild.

Laughing, I bow sloppily and help Sakura to her feet. She does a brilliant curtsy, smiling, and then finally she breaks character and lets out a great big snort, followed by loud laughter. The sound fills the whole empty room, bouncing off the walls in echoes.

I turn to face Sakura, and exclaim, "That was a great spin on the ending!"

"Why thank you, Mr. Beast. You were a great actor too!" The

words come out a little garbled, the sentence interspersed with high giggles.

At that moment, I realize that I have missed this—this frivolity, this childishness, this kinship. I've missed my sister.

And I know I will not be able to truly find this feeling again if I keep my secrets.

Mustering whatever scrap of seriousness I have left, and all the courage I bear, I start, "Sakura, I have something to tell you." I slowly sit down, pulling off my costume, and patting the spot next to me. Sakura quietly settles down next to me, calm all of the sudden, her eyes calculating and filled with curiosity. She gives me an *it's-about-time* look, that makes the corners of my mouth lift.

"While you've been sick, I've been doing things," I say carefully.

"Yeah, duh!" Sakura interrupts, "Of course you've been doing things! Just get to the point. The suspense is *killing* me." She rolls her eyes and pokes me in the side.

My stomach tightens, and I let out a nervous laugh. Silence descends around us for a minute.

"Oh, come on, Kayda. It's not like I'll be mad at you. Besides, sisters don't keep secrets," Sakura makes a pouty face, and something inside of me breaks.

"I'm the hacker, *Dragon*, I kind of started a rebellion—well a three-person one, and I stole 1,000 kimas from a random rich guy, and we're going to save the city," I hurriedly confess, the words tumbling out of my mouth. Realizing what I had just uttered, I glance around nervously noticing the way my every word bounces of the walls and echoes, but the big green doors are closed and no sound will get through the walls. I sigh in relief and finally allow myself to look at Sakura, expecting a frown or anger, anything but the wide goofy smile that's on her face.

"No way!" She exclaims. "Not fair! While I was sick, my sister became cool without me." She laughs and then looks me in the eye. "I'm in."

She hops up and scurries across the stage and down the steps, while my mind rushes to give my mouth something to say so that I'll stop spluttering random sounds like a lunatic. Finally, my brain comes up with, “No, it’s not safe.”

Sakura stops in the center aisle of red chairs, blinking her eyes up at me innocently. “I know you want to protect me and all, but I’m not that young anymore, and besides, you know I have great people skills.”

“You could get hurt,” I plead.

“*You* could get hurt,” she just replies. And then wiggling her eyebrows at me, she adds “You know you need me, Kayda. I could persuade a person to give me a thousand kimas in just a few minutes, no other plans required.” She turns her head and continues to skip towards the green doors.

Descending the stage, I try to think of a good argument, but there really are none, and truthfully, she’s right. Jax, Leum, and I *could* really use her help. But, if she gets hurt, that’s all on me, and I don’t think I could live knowing I caused her harm. I weigh the risks versus the benefits and reluctantly give in, only because looking at Sakura’s stubborn face now, I know there’s really no chance that I could stop her from getting involved.

“Fine,” I huff, “you can help us.”

Sakura lets out a “whoop” and stops at the last row of chairs, waiting for me to catch up, and as I approach her side, she says, “Well, if I am to be a member, I need to know what we’re called.”

I finally allow myself to let out a breath. “The Freedom Thieves.”

She laughs. “Of course, that’s your name. Is your slogan like ‘we’re thieves, so why not steal our freedom back’?”

“We didn’t make a slogan yet,” I say defensively, crossing my arms.

“Oh, even better!” She cries, laughing once again.

“What?” I say a little annoyed.

“Nothing, it’s just that you are *so* lucky that I’m your sister.” When she sees my face, she pats me on the shoulder, saying “Oh, relax. I just meant that I’ll fix all your problems because I’m your amazing sister,” her voice becomes more serious, “I’ll always be here for you,” and then the levity comes back, “because you can’t get rid of me.” Sakura goofily grins at me, and I can’t help but smile, too.

"I've missed you, Sakura." I lay my head on her shoulder, and she embraces me softly.

After a minute, she lets go. "Come on, we've got a lot of work to do if you really want this rebellion to work."

"Yeah, but first let's get some food."

"Definitely," Sakura agrees. "How about we get a few *pao douce* buns?"

"No, let's get a meat pie!" I argue.

"We'll get both, and then we'll get blueberry pie, and dumplings, and soup. We'll buy the whole market." She laughs and then widens her eyes at me mischievously, "After all we do have a thousand kimas to spend."

I gasp, but can't seem to hold in a laugh, too. "That's not for us!"

"I know, I know," She says rolling her eyes, "But think of all you could eat with 1,000 kimas."

We both laugh, the notes filling the theatre like music of the most beautiful kind. I push on the big green doors, and as they creak open inch by inch, I realize that little by little the broken strings of my heart are being glued back together.

12

"Is it that building with the pretty windows over there?" Sakura says pointing.

"No."

"How about that one with the bright red door?"

I snort. "Like I'd choose one with a bright red door. That practically says '*we're over here!*'"

"Fine, how about that one?"

"Shhh, be quiet. You're drawing more attention to us when we want the opposite. You know I'm starting to regret allowing you to come with me."

Jokingly, Sakura whispers, "That's just because you're realizing how great of a conversationalist I am."

"That's definitely why," I say my words dripping with sarcasm.

Finally, in silence, we continue to make our way down the street, keeping to the shadows. After a few minutes, the building comes into view, and I quietly open the door. Turning to Sakura, I put my finger to my lips. She nods. We slip in without a sound, and once again, I wend my way through the sleeping, dusty furniture, Sakura precisely following each of my footsteps.

As I start to ascend the creaky stairs, Sakura says "So, abandoned building hideout, huh? Kinda cool and probably super smart, too, but it honestly smells like a pack of wolves lives in here. I mean, could you have taken the time to place some air fresheners here and there?"

"When you have a city to save, you don't really think about that," I reply leveling an annoyed expression at her as she put her hands up in defense.

"I'm just saying that it would be a nice addition."

"That would attract unwanted visitors," I huff at her.

At the top of the stairs, I open the door to see that Jax and Leum are already there.

We walk in casually, but my heart pounds fast nervously, "Hey guys. This is my sister, Sakura. Sakura that's Jax and that's Leum," I say pointing to each of them in turn. Jax looks at me questioningly, but I just smile reassuringly back.

"Hi, Sakura!" Leum waves at us. Jax just nods in our general direction.

"Okay guys, we need to make a plan on how to get our name out there." I walk over to the big wooden table, grabbing a piece of paper and a pen. "I think the best way to do this is by word of mouth. We'll tell twenty or so people and they'll want to tell others and those people will tell others, so on and so forth. News spreads fast around here. Soon the whole city will know our name and what we did."

"That makes sense and its simple," Jax agrees looking at me in the eye. I quickly glance away, focusing my eyes on anything but him

"What exactly should we say though?" Leum asks, "It's got to be consistent each time."

"Skinny guy's right. We need to say the same thing each time." Sakura ponders for a moment, oblivious to the exasperated arms Leum throws up into the air. "It has got to be short, and straight to the point. After all, if we're leaving it up to the people to pass around what we did, it's going to change every time it's said. If we don't want our name to be associated with crazy deeds, we've got to make the starting message simple, so that even when it's modified it will still resemble what you guys did."

I hesitate, thinking, "How about... The Freedom Thieves have come to steal back the city bit by bit and have started by stealing 1,000 kimas from the corrupt rich?"

"That's not bad," Sakura considers approvingly, "It's simple, it's short, and it will do its job, but we should add a sort of slogan to the end... like the reign of the rich will end, or all will be saved. I don't know, something that people will say consistently, something that would unite all the stories. Anybody got a suggestion?"

Jax speaks up. "What about something as simple as 'Get ready, the oppressed will soon rise'?"

"Well, everyone will remember it, and it does get the point across. I think with what I suggested before, it should be good," I say looking to Sakura and Leum for approval.

"That's fine," grumbles Leum, still upset about his new nickname.

Sakura smiles, "I approve."

"Well then, we'll go into the city for a week, a different place each day, like the market or farming fields, and tell someone," I quickly jot the message onto a piece of paper, 'The Freedom Thieves have come to steal back the city bit by bit and have started by stealing 1,000 kimas from the rich. Get ready, the oppressed will soon rise,' I pass the paper with the message on it around, ¨Okay, memorize it quickly, and then someone can drop it in a city street for the people who can read."

"I can do that," Leum says folding the paper into his jacket pocket after everybody reads the words one last time.

"Okay, good. Everybody in accord with the plan?" I ask.

Leum, Sakura, and Jax nod.

"We're done for the day then," I say surprised, finding myself unsatisfied, wanting something else to do.

Jax gets up from one of the chairs and arches his back. "Anybody want to go get some food? I'll pay."

"Sorry, but I've got a special dinner tonight, beef stew. Don't want to miss that," Leum says excitedly, waving goodbye.

I turn to see if Sakura wants to go, but her eyes are narrowed a little bit, looking between me and Jax. She sees me staring at her, and a slow mischievous smile lights up her face. Dirt, I forgot how observant she could be. A bright color of red begins to seep into my cheeks.

"You know what, I think I'm going to skip out on that dashing offer, but thanks anyway cutie." She turns and starts to walk toward the door. I'm about to follow her out when she says, "Oh, but Kayda you should go anyway, you'll have fun." With a wink and a smile, she turns and saunters out the door.

I swallow nervously and turn to Jax.

"Well," I say not daring to meet his eyes, "I guess it's just us."

"Yeah," he says slowly, drawing the word out in that deep, smooth voice of his. "Just you and me, Kayda." I can't help but look up as he says my name, and when I do, his eyes catch mine. They twinkle mischievously, and a chill runs down my spine. Thankfully, before I start to shake with nerves, he breaks eye contact and lopes over to the door, gesturing for me to follow. "I know the best place."

We dash through alleyways and streets until we take a turn onto a small, dark road I've only been on a few times. Boisterous laughter, although muted, makes the air come alive. Oh, and the heavenly scents—fresh-baked bread, cardamom, grilling fish, and something else sweet that I can't recognize—waft from the light-ringed door at the end of the road. My pace starts to pick up and I can't help it when I start to salivate.

Even if that door led to Hell, I don't think I could walk away.

Jax glances at me, and when he sees the look on my face, he bursts into laughter. "Who knew you could win a girl by just bringing her to a good old bar."

"Oh, you could win me over with just a single well-made meat pie," I say without hesitation. After all, it's true. I do enjoy—well, *really* enjoy—eating good food. You really learn to appreciate the food you get when you only get a little.

I can't hold myself back any longer, and I start sprinting towards the door, excited to get a bite of the merriment and food that seems to be inside. "Come on you slowpoke," I yell back at him, "by the time you arrive, I'll have already cleaned five dishes—food that you're still paying for!" I laugh at my own words.

With a roll of his eyes, Jax runs to catch up with me. "You're way too excited about this."

"Oh, a poor girl should *never,*" I stare him straight in the eyes with a mocking smile, "be denied the thralldom of eating fine food."

"Well then, in you go, little gastronome." Jax sweeps his arm out dramatically and opens the door. Immediately, the chatter of common workers and thugs rains down on me, the volume amplified tenfold. I uncertainly take a step forward, expecting to be knocked over by the sheer force of life that is packed inside such a small place.

Jax presses up against my back making my heart start to thunder as the door slides shut behind us. People jostle me from every side; tattooed men, tired workers, and women dressed in punk-like clothes filling every inch of the place.

"Careful there are people in here who will steal anything that's not five-times nailed down." Jax presses a large hand against my back urging me through the crowd, standing tall over me, watching the movements of every single person with hawkish intensity.

"Who knows, maybe I'm one of those dangerous thieves who would steal the chain necklace from around your neck without you even noticing." A slow smile spreads across my face, as Jax's hand automatically searches for the little silver chain he never seems to take off—the necklace which is now gone. At finding its absence, a sliver of panic traces its way across Jax's features, but it disappears almost immediately as I show him the little necklace hanging from my right hand.

"Never underestimate me," I say handing it to him with a smile. He snatches it quickly, his hand moving so fast it almost appears as if it did not move. Only after the chain is securely hidden inside his shirt, does Jax let out a soft, but still tense laugh. His shoulders don't relax, but the intensity in his eyes mellows.

Confused by his sudden rigidity, I fall quiet.

But a moment later, all signs of fear or unease have fled Jax's manner, and he breaks the silence. "Can thee not smelleth that lovely aroma of scrumptious food that embraces thee from ev'ry angle?" As he impersonates the language of an author who wrote many books a long, long time ago, Jax swings out his arms dramatically whacking a few people on the back in the process.

Giggling, I straighten my back, carefully folding my hands at my waist, and with the most ladylike voice I can pull off, I say " T'was these v'ry scents that brought me hither."

With a mock look of surprise, Jax says, "My lady, I am disgrac'd to has't bethought t'was I who hath drawn thee hither, but I shalt desire to proveth m're enjoyable to thee than the food tonight." The foreignness of his words is finally starting to pierce through the crowd and some heads turn our way. I just smile at them like a real lady, and to those who really stare, I give a little cupped wave of my hand with a muffled giggle.

Continuing the conversation, I reply, "Valorous sir, thee'd has't to be a downright god to beat food."

"Ah, but my lady, the gentleman who pays for the food to cometh shouldst be praised just liketh a god, is that not true?"

"And with this, I must be in concord, good sir," I say matter of factly.

"Then alloweth us not to wait a moment longer—To the food!" Jax exclaims proffering me his arm.

Linking my arm with his, I shout, "To the food!"

With a laugh, we both—very un-politely—shove our way through the crowd, leaving a whole wake of grunts and curses behind us. Upon pushing one last group of people away, Jax and I finally discover the shabby little bar counter, and as if we are in a fairytale, there happens to be—in this extremely crowded place—two open bar seats right next to each other. We don't dare to question the absence of people on the two worn bat-wing-like leather seats, instead, we just quickly take the luck, not giving it a chance to look over our grubby clothes and dirty hands and decide to leave.

Jax waves over the thick-armed bartender with a small flick of his hand, and when the dark-haired man comes over, he orders a small cup of whiskey, and I order a green tea.

"Can't hold down a drink, huh?" Jax says with a smirk.

Smiling, I respond, "I can, I just like to always be sharp."

"You can relax with me here." He says seriously, looking at me with those green eyes.

"I'm never relaxed when you're around," I mumble quietly. Jax doesn't acknowledge the words, other than the slight smile that touches his lips, and for once I don't even care that he knows how I feel.

Playfully shoving him and rolling my eyes to try to hide my growing smile, I grumble, "Just go get me some of that delicious smelling food."

With another flick of his hand, the waiter comes back, and Jax murmurs something unintelligible to the man. The waiter leaves with a nod, and Jax simply smiles mysteriously at me, purposefully not giving me any clues whatsoever.

To pass the time, I try to think of a normal question... something that doesn't mention the rebellion, but all I can think of is, "So your favorite color is burnt orange, huh?"

"Don't worry, I won't ask about yours." He winks at me playfully, but I just continue on with the list of things I know about him—which I'm realizing is super short.

"And you laugh like a boar."

With a light chuckle, he agrees, "Ahh yes, that has been confirmed."

"And I knocked you out in five minutes."

"You can't seem to forget that can you?" Jax throws his arms up in mock exasperation. "Am I always going to be the guy who was beat up by a little dragon?"

"For the rest of your life," I say, keeping my face as serious as I can manage.

"For the rest of my life." He repeats resignedly. "Well, at least I was beat up by a *beautiful* dragon."

I ignore his comment with a slight blush, and get back to my list, until I realize that I have nothing else that I can add to it. Frustrated I exclaim, "what else?"

"What do you mean 'what else,'" he says, amused by my sudden irritation.

"I mean, tell me something else about you that I can add to this incredibly bare list of facts I know about you."

He looks like he's about to refuse, but then something inside of him urges him to continue. "Fine, I'm an orphan, never knew my parents. I like the sourest green apples that can grow, and I am unbelievably handsome." He slightly tilts his head to the side, runs a hand slowly through his dark, unruly, hair, and gives me a stunning grin—the exact position that models take on magazine covers, and I don't even try to stop the snort and high-pitched laughter that follows. It actually ends up making Jax's grin broaden into his true—slightly goofy, but mostly charming—smile.

Jax stops laughing and focuses the full heat of his gaze on me. "Now it's your turn."

"No," I say quickly.

"Fine, be like that," He says, his eyes sparkling with amusement. "I'll just have to start making my own list—"

Jax is thankfully interrupted by the clatter our waiter makes as he shoves his way past other bartenders with ten large, food-filled, delicious smelling, platters in his hands.

First, the man sets down two large mugs, one filled halfway with whiskey, the other filled to the brim with hot green tea. But that's only the start. Our waiter then places one platter of steaming hot and oiled naan bread and golden *pao douce* buns in front of us. Paté de campagne formed in a perfect circular cake with a small dill pickle like a crown resting on top of it is wedged between the pieces of bread. Two golden bowls are presented, one with a delicious smelling red curry and one with some sort of beef stew. After that, a long silver platter with a whole grilled flounder finds a place on the small bar counter. A wooden bowl of spinach, a ceramic ramekin of rice, and a container filled with little metal cups of different spices and seeds are also placed in front of me. Finally, one miniature piece of goat cheese and one powder-sugared chocolate cake are set down; the poor waiter has nothing left to juggle and promptly leaves.

"This is a real feast; how did you get a normal bar to serve this type of food?" I whisper breathlessly, trying to comprehend the sheer amount of food in front of me, while also trying not to visibly drool. The fragrant scents almost overwhelm me, and I want nothing more than to gorge myself upon the food, but I just can't.

¨I know the owners, and besides, they owed me.¨

"Jax, how can you pay for all this?" I drag my gaze away from the dishes, and stare intently into those green eyes.

All he says in response is, "I save money to spend on the occasional special treat."

"Yeah, but this would take all the extra money that you've saved for the past year. Jax, you can't do this. Come on, at least let me chip in a little." I try pleading with him, suddenly reluctant to eat all this food, knowing every forkful is a kima that Jax has to pay for.

"No, Kayda, you have a sister who depends on you to provide food and shelter," he says softly but with a firm edge that tells me, he won't change his mind. "Besides, a whole year of savings is worth that wild smile of yours." At his words, he gives me a tentative grin, this one lacking all his normal cockiness and audacity, and I just can't find it in myself to argue any longer.

"Alright then," I say, sweeping our previous conversation away, "What exactly is in that gold dish?" I peer at the red sauce curiously.

Jax makes room for the bowl in the mass of dishes and places it right next to me. "That is red curry with tofu and bamboo stalks."

Before he even finishes his sentence, I take a large scoop of the curry and lay it carefully on a blanket of rice. A second later, I'm wiping my first spoon clean. A low groan of pleasure escapes my mouth, and Jax laughs at me, but it's not long before he, too, joins me in picking apart this feast forkful by forkful.

Dish after dish I taste, each one a blessing to every single taste bud on my tongue. And even once every single bowl has felt the smooth metal of my spoon, I can't seem to stop myself from taking some more, from filling my belly with the warmth of spices and good food. The taste of a creamy meat spread that Jax declares was invented by French people hundreds of years ago, makes me sing with joy. Oh, but a spoonful of some sort of stew, leaves me yearning for ten more bowls. And the bite of flounder I have, makes me believe that I've discovered love.

In short, what I've eaten today, has totally altered my definition of food.

However, once I've had my fill of savory dishes, I finally allow my eyes to gaze upon the chocolate cake. It sits confidently on its white throne, lording over all the other wrecked dishes; chocolate drizzle perfectly zig-zagging across its body, powdered sugar gracing its top like a glowing halo snatched right off an angel's head.

I always believed that nothing was perfect, but looking at this cake has just about changed my mind.

Slowly, I push away the other dishes and with great care, I lift the plate that holds the cake and settle it in between Jax and I.

We stare at it—I, as if it is a wish come true, and Jax as if it is an old friend he once knew and loved.

Without taking my eyes off of the cake, I hand Jax a new clean spoon, and as if we rehearsed it, we dig into the moist delicacy at the same exact moment. I bring the spoon to my lips and gently place the moist cake on my tongue, and...

It tastes like heaven, like bliss, like a warm spring afternoon on a perfect day.

My teeth sink into the airy cake as if it is a cloud of moon dust crumbling under the touch. And yet, as light as the cake may be, the first bite introduces such a distinct taste—a smooth and velvety chocolate that makes my mouth tingle with an overflow of flavor. I savor each bite, running my tongue over my teeth, making sure not to lose one morsel of the delicacy. But even with small bites, Jax and I finish the cake all too soon. We place our shining spoons on the table, and our waiter comes and clears away the wreckage of our feast.

I gaze at the empty bar counter, relishing the spices and sugar that still linger on my tongue, but after a minute, Jax breaks me out of my reminiscing.

He smiles mischievously all the sudden, and says "So, now that the feast has been devoured, it looks like it's time for me to make up my list of things I know about you."

"Oh, no," I groan, playfully ducking my head into my arms.

"One: you laugh like a hyena-"

I interrupt, cocking my eyebrows at him, "Starting with a classic, I see."

"Don't worry I'll get more specific." He smirks at me and edges his chair a bit closer before continuing on. "Two: your smile when you're really happy is cutely lopsided—tilted ever so slightly to the left."

"Is it?" I respond, looking straight into his eyes. My cheeks automatically blush, but I don't look away, too entranced by the way the little flecks of gold in his eyes seem to dance and shimmer in the lights of the bar.

"Yes, it is," he whispers, his voice husky. Slowly, he brings his hand up to my face, cupping my cheek, and gently, he brushes his thumb across the dimple on my left cheek. I shiver at his touch, but he doesn't draw his hand away, instead his thumb continues its steady caress drifting down over the long scar that stops right above my lips. My heartbeat speeds up, and a million thoughts fill my head, but I shove them away, leaning into the warmth of his touch.

"And three," Jax whispers, leaning in closer, his nose almost grazing mine, "is that since the moment I saw you, I've wanted to kiss you." His warm breath smells of spices and a woodsy scent that always seems to cling to him, and my heart skips a beat, my own breaths becoming heavy. He leans in slowly, giving me time to turn my head away, but for some reason I don't.

I glance away from his gaze for a second, wanting just a moment away from those intense green eyes, and one white paper that is tacked up on the bulletin board of the bar draws my attention. I look back at Jax, trying to forget about it, but inevitably my eyes go back to it, and finally I can read the words that are printed on it in large black, boxy letters. At the last moment, I jerk away from Jax. His look of utter confusion and betrayal pierces my heart, but I'm too shocked, bewildered—even a bit angry, to dwell on it.

"Jax," I try to keep my voice quiet, but it's starting to shake, "What is that paper over there." I discreetly point at the paper I'm talking about.

"Which one?" He asks quietly, his tone not at all light.

"Tha-that one," I try to point again, but my finger starts shaking. "The one with the black letters-"

I stop speaking when I notice Jax's face pale to a shade fitting of a ghost. He swallows and closes his eyes, saying nothing. He's seen it.

"Jax, why would it say that?" He doesn't answer, but instead rummages into his pockets.

"Jax?" he pulls out a wad of cash leaves it on the bar counter and gently takes my arm.

All he says is "come." We head into the crowd and as we pass by the bulletin board, I discreetly snatch the white piece of paper, my hand trembling into a fist around it. Jax doesn't stop until we're out the door and a few alleys away. When he finally stops walking, I face him.

"Why did it say that?" I ask calmly. Hoping against all odds that he'll answer me with some reasonable justification. Instead, Jax just swallows and averts his gaze.

"Jax," my voice breaks, "look at me." Finally, he glances up, his eyes dark and unreadable. In that moment, he actually looks dangerous, like some muscled thug who could make someone disappear in one dark night.

I take a step back, and a flash of pain registers in his eyes, turning him back into the person I know, but just seeing that other side of him has made me weary, and I don't move forward.

"Tell me why." My eyes grow watery as silence stretches out.

But finally, Jax very slowly walks forward and says, "I'm sorry." His throat bobs and his voice almost breaks. "I'm so, so sorry." He steps closer, but I stiffen and walk back again.

"Why, Jax, why!?"

"Because," he whispers, his voice cracking. He swallows again, and then so quietly that no one else could possibly hear, he says "Because I'm a seer."

I'm quiet for a moment, thinking, hoping... I shake my head, pinch my arm, anything to make sure that this is reality, that this is really happening.

"No, no, no!" I shriek, and Jax looks around nervously. I lower my voice. "Why didn't you tell me before?" I say almost about to sob.

"I didn't know you before." He responds.

"So, you didn't think I deserved to know that you are a-"

"I know and I'm sorry, I really am. Please, Kayda. You have to understand. I didn't know what type of a person you were."

"You're right, you don't. But it seems like you're more foreign to me than I am to you. How many days did we have to spend together until I would earn your trust? How many lies did you speak to me before you would tell me the truth? Were you ever going to tell me?" I ask him, the volume of my voice dangerously close to a shout.

"I was going to, Kayda. You have to trust me, please." He looks at me, his eyes pleading.

"But I don't trust you, Jax. Not anymore." I wipe a tear from under my eye, and harden my gaze. "I have to go."

I walk away from Jax, from the water glistening in his eyes, from the pleading look he wears. I walk fast into the shadows, and then break into a run. I stop after a few minutes and finally let myself look back, but of course Jax is gone, probably still in the alleyway I left him in.

I unclench my fist and smooth out the paper. The white sheaf stares up at me innocently and I glare at it, my tears falling on it and wrecking the ink, smudging it so that it becomes illegible. But it doesn't matter, the words are already imprinted in my memory.

"Kayda Kobayashi is wanted alive for conspiring with Jax Moreau, a dangerous criminal who is also wanted for committing various crimes against the government. She is also accused of leading a rebellious movement. 1,500 kimas will be rewarded to the person who brings her in."

The words flash in my mind again and again along with what Jax told me. I had wanted to know what he did to get the government chasing him. I had wanted to know why he hadn't told me what trouble I was really getting into when I first associated with him. I had wanted to know why he didn't tell me. And now that I know—that Jax is a seer, a magical fantasy, someone who gets flashes of the future, a type of people that are thought to be extinct—I wish I didn't.

My whole world starts to crack around me, chunks falling to the floor, raining from the sky. The cracks spread, and I feel a scream building up inside of me. It grows and grows in my chest, and I don't have enough energy to stop it, so I let it out.

The deafening noise pierces the air and drowns out my worries for one moment. But all too soon, it just blends into the odd night sounds of the city, leaving my throat sore and raw.

All my questions return at full force, almost knocking me over.

What will happen if they catch me?

What will happen to Sakura?

Why did I do this?

And the worst one by far:

Why didn't Jax tell me?

I hate that I care more about the fact that Jax lied to me about who he was than about the fact that he got me in trouble, that I could die any day now. I hate it, and yet I can't get rid of the thought. It haunts my mind like a ghost in a mansion, coming back when I least expect it.

I focus my eyes on the paper, trying to think of something else, but it just makes me angrier, more confused. I tear the white sheaf to shreds and throw them in the air, but I feel no better. Tears start falling hot and fast, and standing alone in the middle of a dark alley at midnight feeds my growing terror. With nothing else to do, I run home, cautious not to be seen, my tears still staining the asphalt as they fall, one by one, faster and faster, writing out the pain and confusion of my heart.

13

"Kayda, you have to get up now." Sakura says, her voice annoyingly chipper. She jabs my back with her long and slender fingers. "Just because some rain sprinkled last night, doesn't mean you can deny the sun is shining today!"

Groaning, I roll away from her merciless poking. Last night, I told her everything, well *almost* everything. Sobbing, I recounted the feast, and the 'conversation' that had happened afterwards, but for some reason, I had not divulged the fact that I had almost been kissed; even though my anger for Jax sits heavy, writhing in my stomach, I still can't deny the fact that I have feelings for him, whether I want them or not.

"Seriously, Sakura! '*Just because it rained yesterday, doesn't mean the sun isn't out today!*'" I respond, raising the pitch of my own voice, mimicking Sakura's higher and more cheerful one. "That's such a cliché saying. Nobody wants to hear that as a wakeup call. When you think of something better, come wake me up." I put my hand back under my pillow and tuck my head into the crook of my arm, closing my eyes again.

"Fine," Sakura huffs, rolling her eyes at me, "How about: get up because the early bird catches the worm?" She smiles at me, her eyes twinkling with amusement when I peak one of my eyes open and frown at her.

"That's honestly so much worse. I am *definitely* not waking up to catch a worm."

"Oh, did I say worm?" Sakura says with a smirk, "I meant bacon. But since you don't want it, I'll eat it all, anyway." She dashes out of my room with a light laugh, while I'm left struggling to pull off my covers.

I arrive in the kitchen to the lovely smell of sizzling bacon, a special treat that I haven't had in a few years.

"Oh, look who decided to get out of bed," Sakura says spotting me walk into the kitchen.

"So, where'd you get the bacon?" I ask ignoring her comment and sitting down at the kitchen table.

"Went to the market this morning," She replies casually.

"What?" I exclaim dramatically, swiveling in my chair to look at Sakura, "Did you just say that you--someone who regularly sleeps till eleven--got up early, went to the market, and had to deal with all those crazy, loud people, just to get me bacon?"

"Yes, I did," she responds not looking at me.

"Awww..." I gush sarcastically and Sakura blushes, rolling her eyes, but with a smirk I change my tone and holler, "bring it over!"

"Ahh, for a second there, I thought an alien took my sister and dressed up in her place." Sakura comes to the table and sets down a plate of steaming hot bacon in front of me. "Luckily, your impoliteness reassured me of your identity. It would have been a real shame," she whispers her eyes widening, and she puts her hand to her mouth with a mock gasp, "for you to miss out on bacon because I thought you were an alien."

"A real shame," I repeat, focused only on the delicacy glistening before me. I dig into the bacon and take a forkful of eggs that sit on the plate next to the delicious meat. Chewing the food in my mouth, I savor the flavor, which then makes me think of the feast I had last night, which makes me think of... suddenly the eggs don't taste as great as they did.

"Why are you frowning? I know it's not because the eggs are bad--they're amazing. I made sure of it. So, what is it?" Sakura pulls her chair over next to mine and tilts her head to the side in a concerned, sisterly fashion. "Spill."

Reading my silence and the way I pick at my eggs, Sakura says "Ah, I see. Thinking about what happened, huh?"

I shrug, making a face at my plate that reflects just how vulnerable and pathetic I feel.

"Well, guess what," she says and I look up, "You're going to have to get over it."

I scowl at her.

"You know what I think?" she asks and I can't help but take the bait.

"What?" I shoot at her, my tone flat and annoyed.

"You overreacted a bit because you felt offended that Jax had kept such a secret even though *you*," she wiggles her finger at me, "thought he had feelings for you."

The statement manages to worm its way to my very core, making me feel off balance.

"No, I'm mad because Jax has basically given me a death sentence, himself." Although I say the words with conviction, I turn my head away from Sakura just in case she can pick up the flicker of doubt that swims in them. My words still don't affect her though, and her face remains unconvinced, one eyebrow cocked up, her lips pursed.

"Mmmhmm... whatever you say, Kayda."

"Well, you don't have to believe me for me to be right. I'm going back to bed!" I declare indignantly standing up from the table, feeling a lot like a whiny child. "And I'm taking these with me!" I grab the plate of eggs and bacon and march off to my room.

As I storm away, Sakura yells after me. "You can mope around now, but sooner or later, you'll have to confront him. And if you take too long, I'll drag you to him, myself."

A WEEK PASSES by and I don't contact or meet up with Jax. But even though I don't go to the *Library*, I've still been spreading word about The Freedom Thieves.

Murmurs have rippled through the city people, rumors claiming that there is a group of the most powerful and cunning rebels preparing to take back the city.

Every person tells it differently; some say we are orphans of the city who seek revenge against the rich. Others say we are a group filled with the most daring and audacious criminals, ganging up to steal some money from those who won't notice. And, as always when rumors manifest, there are always those few wild tales. Ours shape us into angels fallen from the clouds, or saviors to all those who cower in the dirt of inequality and poverty.

The first theory impresses me by how close it is to the truth, yet I find myself taking more of a liking to the second theory, which makes me puff my chest out with pride... to be called one of the most audacious and daring criminals in this city is one of the highest compliments I can imagine. But the third one... well, I snorted when I first heard it.

There is no way that someone--if he or she actually knew what Jax and I have done in our lives--could consider calling either of us an angel. It's simply improbable, practically impossible, considering the things I've had to commit to survive. Just imagining it makes me feel ridiculous.

So, although the speculation is, in most cases, quite far from the truth, I still listen into the conversations, and I've realized that, already, a general story is starting to develop in the way that merchants whisper and children play more boldly in the streets; the Freedom Thieves little by little are becoming legends, and I don't want to be left out of the story I've created.

"Sakura," I call out suddenly invigorated and filled with a purpose: I'm going to make myself part of that legend again, even if I'll have to apologize on my hands and knees.

"What?" she cries out immediately, popping her head out of her room's door, "Have you finally realized how wise I am, and that you should take my advice?"

"No," I say slowly, giving her a look, "but I have realized that I've been a bit over-dramatic and that I'd rather have one friend than none."

Sakura pouts and says, "Hey, I'm your friend,"

"No, you're my sister," I respond matter of factly, trying to hide my smile as I turn around and head for the door .

"Whatever, same thing," she cries out behind me, "And you better come home with a smile on your face, or I will... I will," looking behind me, I see Sakura thinking with her face all scrunched up, grasping for something good, threatening. After a moment, she gives up and goes with a feeble warning, "I will never wake up early and deal with all those annoying marketplace people just to get bacon for you."

With a laugh, I open the door and holler over my shoulder, "Don't worry, I never expected you to ever do that again anyways."

I stare at the building, the *Library*, for a count of eight seconds. Millions of concerns run through my head, all contemplating my decision to be here. But quickly shaking them away before they can mold into something real, I take one deep breath in and push the door open. The familiar dusty furniture stands right where I saw it last, no signs that anyone has been here, just like it should be. My shoulders relax a bit, and the wild thoughts flying around my mind become sluggish and one by one float carefully to the edges of my mind. After all, this place has become a second home to me over the past month, and just the sight of the old furniture and stairway and the familiar lines of code hanging around them, makes my heart's pounding soothe to a calm and steady rhythm.

Slowly, I walk the last length of the floor, arriving at the stairwell, and with a smile I lift my leg and shift my weight onto that first wooden step, hearing it groan and howl all it can, as has become tradition, before ascending to the next one. I take each step slowly, listening to the complaints and pain of the wooden boards as one by one, they bear the burden of my weight. By the time I'm about exactly halfway between the first and the second floor, I'm so soothed by the familiar sounds that all my worries completely disappear. Suddenly, a joy long trapped inside of me bubbles up as I imagine bursting through the door and into the grand room upstairs, and I can't hold back any longer. Sprinting up the rest of the stairwell, I slam into the door, practically falling into the room.

Jax, who is sitting at the large wooden table scribbling on a piece of paper, whips his head up from his work, alarmed. Upon seeing me, a dozen emotions flash across his eyes: surprise, joy, shame, and something else I don't quite recognize.

Before I lose the courage fueling my will, I say everything that has been on my mind for the past week, letting the words spill out of me like stepping stones leading to a new life, "I'm sorry Jax," I begin, laying out all the passion and regret I feel into one, simple sentence, "I know I might have overreacted a bit and that I shouldn't have stayed away for a week, but it hurt that you held such a big secret from me and for so long, too." A tear rolls down my cheek and my voice hitches. "You told me I could trust you Jax--"

"You can-"

"Please let me finish," I ask quietly closing my eyes and collecting my chaotic thoughts, and Jax's lips slowly close as he nods.

"You said you would grant me a wish, and I-," my hands fling up trying futilely to carry some of my pain as my voice starts to break, "I believed you."

"And I don't know why; maybe it was because Sakura was getting better and it gave me hope, or maybe it was because I was tired of living like a rat thrown to the cats, or maybe it was both, who knows. But for some downright foolish reason, for a second, I believed that you could do something that I can't even do: grant a wish."

"But I didn't care that it was foolish," I say my voice starting to harden, "No, because for just once, I was taking a risk. And for dirt's sake, Jax, I wanted it." I look up at him, my eyes blazing with a sorrowful fire, "That mischievous smile on your lips, the easy flirting, the thoughtless laughter; I wanted it all, I craved it... that thing you called friendship."

"The possibility to finally be happy haunted me for days, and I tried, trust me, I tried to forget about it, but when my heart stopped craving it, my mind would just remind me of your name, and just like that I was hooked again."

My voice thins, the flames in my heart slowing, burning to ashes, "Jax, you offered me so much when we met for the third time. You said you could give me the possibility to help the city and my sister. But what you don't know, is that I didn't agree to help because of any of that. I agreed to help because of the friendship that you showed me, the casual way in which you talked to me--something I thought was impossible for someone like me. You offered me normality" I pause sucking in a breath, "and all I ever wanted to be was normal."

A silent moment stretches between us, as I compose myself, sniffling and carefully wiping my eyes. I fold my hands together, tightly, pulling my emotions back together, and after a moment, I stand up straighter.

"But, I've realized that it wasn't fair of me. I put it all on you... my dreams, my hopes," I sweep my arm through the air, gesturing as I talk in my nervousness, "and after all, no matter how much you may want to grant my wishes, you're just one person in this dirt forsaken city, after all." I purse my lips sadly, my eyebrows wrinkling with grief. Looking up, I see a single tear roll down Jax's cheek, his eyes sad and tired. I almost break apart, but instead I gather my courage and continue on.

"And uh," I laugh quietly, "I've realized that one person can't really do much by themselves around here, and I want to change things, I really do," I walk towards Jax, carefully laying my hands on his chest, a small smile hesitantly spreading across my lips. "After all, I'm a true thief, and I know someone who said that thugs and thieves would be the ones to save this city--he's a crazy person, but I still think I believe him."

Jax chuckles softly, rubbing his eyes dry, before lifting his head to meet mine.

"So, what do ya say, ugly. Partners again?" I whisper, holding out my hand, my eyes soft, but questioning.

Grinning, he pauses for a moment pretending to contemplate his choices, "Sure, partners," he takes my hand in his grasp, but a few seconds later, drops it and moves back a few steps, before continuing, "First though, I have to apologize, too. Kayda, I'm sorry for... everything. I really am, and I'm glad that you're back," he studies my expression and in seeing something in it he smiles deciding to continue on, "but--"

"Oh, no," I groan, relishing how light I feel after saying all my thoughts, and how easy it is to slide back into this friendship.

"But," he repeats, mischievously arching his eyebrow at me, and I can't help but laugh. "I don't agree with one thing you said."

"You don't?" I say, once again cautious.

"Nope."

"What don't you agree with?" I ask a little nervous.

"Well you said that we are, basically, friends."

"Yes, I did," I respond, now a bit confused on where he's heading with this.

"I don't agree with that." He states plainly, a tiny little smirk hiding in the corners of his lips.

Completely bewildered and most definitely shocked, I just stand there with my mouth slightly open. Jax walks closer to me.

"I don't agree," he continues, "because we aren't *just* friends, are we Kayda?" He emphasizes the 'just,' adding an extra weight to it that makes my heart skip a beat.

"No, we aren't." I whisper, and then I turn around and head for the door, smiling all the way there.

He laughs, "Bye, my little dragon."

14

The door softly closes, leaving me in silence, standing at the top of the stairwell with just the loud and rapid beating of my heart to fill my ears. I listen as it pounds out a persistent rhythm, never missing a beat, always on time. The world could be blown up to bits and reduced to ashes, but as long as that steady beat continues, life will still go on.

I'm so focused on the rhythm of my heart that I almost miss the bleating of sirens. At first it only sounds like a distant scream, but as it grows louder, I recognize the loud alarm that belongs to none other than the city's police cars. Automatically, the nice, steady beating of my heart increases, and all I can think, frozen on the top stair is, *have they found us?*

The shock wears off in a moment, and I start moving towards the second-floor door, ready to get Jax, who I hear shuffling around, too, and prepare to jump out the window to the next building if I need to. But just as my hand starts to turn the doorknob, the police are already at the building… yet, they don't stop. Four swift cars race past the *Library*, heading deeper into the city.

I watch them rush past me, their flashing red and blue lights illuminate the windows and walls creating an eerie sort of picture, something akin to an abstract painting. The colors look as if they are locked in battle: the blue charging at the red and the red slashing back, spilling on the blue light like rivulets of blood. I stare at all the walls, a shudder slowly running up from my feet to the top of my head. But no sooner do the cars fully pass the building, and the walls and windows instantly fade back to their normal dull shades of gray, leaving me with only the memory of the war between the colors.

And maybe it's because I'm reckless or because the police cars have shaken up a long-buried fear, or perhaps, it's because the cars were headed in the general direction of my house--I don't know--but I start running down the stairs and out the door, following the now-distant screech of sirens.

Swift and silent, careful now more than ever, to not be seen, I dash through the streets, the soles of my beat-up sneakers hitting the ground in pace with my heart. My breath puffs in and out, my lungs burning, but despite my frantic efforts, the sirens start to fade away. I grit my teeth, urging my legs to go faster and faster, but it's no use and the sound disappears. With nothing left to follow, I slow down to a jog. And although disappointment fills my head at losing the police cars, it is coupled with relief that I won't get to see who they will take away this time.

With nowhere to go, I jog home, passing by the familiar shops and landmarks that are ingrained in my mind. Before long, I sight the stooping outline of Li Jin's, humbly wedged in between all the towering buildings at the corner that leads to my street.

My sore muscles protest the fluency I demand of them at a jog, so I relax and walk, enjoying the warm day. A slight breeze tickles the hairs on my arm, balancing the sticky heat of the air, and I find a light smile gracing my lips.

After everything that's happened, I can't believe joy can still find me so easily.

Strolling down the street, I approach the faded, and dusty stone wall that makes up the side of Li Jin's, and as I glance at the dark windows, wondering if I should stop in and see if I can help Chen Tao, the restaurant's head cook, the door swings open and out comes a short old woman with strikingly severe eyes and choppy black hair cut to her shoulders.

Her eyes widen in surprise when she sees me, but a second later a desperate relief and urgency replaces it. I'm about to laugh at what a coincidence it is that I would be thinking of Chen Tao, someone who I haven't talked to in years, right when she manages to bump into me, but I'm not given the time.

Staring just beyond my shoulder, she starts speaking incredibly fast, her hands cutting the air wildly, and I only manage to pick up a few words, some of which are in Chinese. "Jǐngchá...taking nǐ de sister."

At first curious and a bit amused, I kindly listen to her, but at the word sister, my whole body freezes, and my brain changes into survival mode, intensely processing every word it understands, which is about two words for every fifty Chen Tao spurts out.

"Chen Tao, slow down. I don't understand you." She doesn't hear a word, continuing on with her hysterical babbling.

I grab ahold of her shoulders, gently turning her face towards me, so that her eyes finally meet mine. And all of the sudden, her body shudders, and a tear begins to tumble down her cheek. She starts repeating only one word, "Bào qiàn," again and again. The sound of the word awakens a memory in my mind, and I try to grasp at it, desperately wanting to understand what she's trying to tell me, but as soon as I reach for the memory, it slips away from my grasp, like a slippery fish. I try once more to remember, but I reclaim nothing.

Now disturbed, my pulse unusually fast and my hands starting to sweat, I ask again, trying to sound calm, "Chen Tao, I don't know what's wrong, but if it concerns my sister, you need to tell me."

Swallowing her tears, Chen Tao says quietly, her voice wavering a bit, "The police ta-take your sister."

Immediately my hands fall from her shoulders to lie limp at my sides, useless, and before my mind has time to process the words fully, I'm running in the direction Chen Tao's shaking finger points towards. As I round the corner, sticking to the shadows, I'm met with a scene from my nightmares.

At the end of the dusty and cracked road sits six menacing police cars. They squat in front of my house, lights flashing, like lazy beetles, too curious to fly away, too tired to truly care. And yet, I feel as if a ring of hungry panthers surrounds my house, black pelts reflecting the now threatening clouds in the sky, lips pulled back in growls that reveal pearly white fangs.

In my nightmares, I always see the cars coming, always try to escape, but inevitably, every single time, no matter how hard I fight, I always get caught. The sirens blare in my dreams. The lights obnoxiously flash. The police curse and hit me while Sakura has to look on helpless; but that's nothing like the scene unfolding before my eyes now.

The sirens are quiet now with the police following suit, and the air is heavy, saturated with my fear. But the greatest difference is the fact that the uniformed man is walking down my front porch steps not with a screaming and thrashing criminal in his grasp, but instead a beautiful, dignified, innocent girl, her chin held high--Sakura.

My mouth flaps up and down like some odd fish, changing from horror to shock and back again. I stare at the round sliver of metal circling her wrist, cruelly appearing as a simple bracelet, but its looks betray its true complexity. I know how there are five locks to keep it in place, and I know how it's made of steel and not of silver. I know how it may look just to be skimming the surface of her wrist, but that it's actually strangling her blood flow. I know that it has a tracker in it, and that it can send bolts of electricity into its wearer. I know because I remember when that same silver bracelet was strapped onto the wrists of my parents.

My heart hardens at the thought, and automatically, I'm a soldier again. I slip my hand under my left sleeve and grasp the knife that is strapped to my biceps, making sure to not fall out of the shadows. Stealthily, I creep forward behind a trash pile to gain a better view. I count seven police officers, each with at least two obvious weapons. If I can get past the first two cars and slip towards the side of my house, I might be able to disarm the police officer that's holding Sakura, using the element of surprise to my advantage. I watch as he firmly holds my sister, while keeping his right hand hovering over his gun. If I hit his right hand, he'll most likely release his left hand, and with it the hold he has on my sister. If I do it right, I also won't have to worry about him shooting us because his gun hand will be nonfunctional. Honestly, it's a tough shot, and the officers will be alerted immediately, but at least we can make a run for it. Besides, I always have three more knives that I can use if I need to.

As I run through the last details of the plan in my head, Sakura glances at my hiding spot behind a heap of trash, as if she can feel my presence. Her eyes meet mine, and my breath tightens, fear for her well-being threatening to overwhelm me.

I take a few breaths, steadying the beat of my heart. "I'm going to save you, don't worry," I mouth, my resolve once again firm.

She stares at me for a moment, and then shakes her head firmly.

"They came here for me, not you" I mouth slowly, "I won't let them take you."

Reading my lips immediately—we used to do it all the time as kids so we could silently communicate when playing games against others—she mouths back words that I can just make out, "But, I could never let them take you, either."

As Sakura's lips form the last of her sentence, the policeman holding her roughly jerks Sakura to the right, and her gaze immediately snaps away from mine. She's dragged up the path, and as my eyes follow her staggered walk, I realize that during the whole talk with Sakura, she has been slowly pulled, bit by bit closer to the cars, and now, she's only about ten feet away from the nearest vehicle.

Frantically, I scrap my last plan and quietly start advancing towards the cars. I leap over a pile of trash, but slip on a tin can as I land. A large crunch slices through the air as aluminum bends and folds under my heel.

I still, my legs chiseled from stone, my fingers stiff as a statue, my breath trapped inside my chest. If I'm caught now... The heads of the police start to swivel in my direction, their damning eyes a second away from landing on my figure... a half-second away from realizing that I look at lot more like the blurry picture of a girl on the wanted poster than Sakura does... a quarter second away from obliterating every single one of my dreams. I prepare my knife in my right hand, lifting the weight off of my toes so that I'll be able to dodge at least the first bullet. But, at the last moment Sakura shrieks convincingly and points her finger to an abandoned house that's in the opposite direction of me, "He's over there, and there's something shiny in his hand."

Immediately, like picturesque soldiers, the police—even the one holding my sister's arm—whip their heads around and simultaneously walk forward as a troop. Guns flash out of belts as the uniformed men scan the broken windows and shadowed doorways of the old house.

I don't spare a second for thought, dashing towards the car Sakura is standing next to as quietly as possible. Trash blurs in my side vision, and my feet hit the black asphalt of the road in rapid succession. Two hundred meters separates me from my sister, and I've only got a few seconds before the police discover that there's no one in that abandoned house: but a few seconds is a lot better than none.

As I run, I swiftly grab the knife strapped to my leg, so that I have one dagger in each hand, the silver blades flashing in the sun. And maybe that's what draws her attention or maybe she's just used to the feeling of my presence, but for some reason Sakura looks back at me once again. Her locked eyes soften as she sees me, many emotions flickering across them: hope, sadness, resolve.

I stare at her unflinchingly, my jaw set, my legs pumping up and down, and for a moment, the world slows down, all sounds muffled, but the loud thumping of my heart. Right now, the whole world only consists of Sakura and I. We stare at each other, a whole life of laughter and tears, of stories told on winter evenings and nights gone to bed hungry, flashing between us. Images of playing with Sakura and Doc in the summer from years ago float through my mind, and more memories start to surface. I think of all the days I spent wiping the sweat off her brow, and all the times I fed her spoonfuls of hot soup. I remember the way she put her hands on her hips in the old theatre just a few weeks ago and mischievously giggled, telling me that there was no way she would be left out of the rebellion. But, I most clearly imagine the roundness of her laugh when she declared four years ago, that sisters are like a pair of chopsticks, you can't have one without the other, and they're not useful unless they're together.

All the moments in my life with Sakura surround me. I see it all: the joyful moments, the sorrowful ones, and I'm instantly struck with the realization of just how much I have to lose.

A single tear runs silently down my cheek, a proclamation of my enlightenment found just a second too late.

At that moment as I near a police car, five vehicles away from Sakura's, I see the sadness, the love in Sakura's eyes morph into a determined blank hardness. But just before her eyes become devoid of emotion, she turns to me and whispers "I love you, but I'd rather they have me than you" a small tear, matching mine, slowly rolling down her cheek.

I run faster, exhaling the air from my lungs and heaving in another mouthful as fast as I can, trying to reach her before she does something stupid, something heroic: because I know that look in her eyes, that glazed stare of hers. I know it, because I, too, wear it. It's the *all-or-nothing-face.* A reckless expression that basically translates to "I've made up my mind and I'm going through with this, even if it means I die."

Of course, Sakura knows that the only way to stop me is to play the same game as me, and so that's exactly what she does.

Four cars away from her, I'm not even surprised when Sakura shouts out "The guy, whoever he is, obviously is gone. It's best to just leave before he can make his move."

Automatically, the shoulders of the police stiffen, annoyed at being ordered around by a prisoner. They stand and stare at the building a moment or two longer, so to appear unaffected by Sakura's sensible words. I keep running the whole time, realizing just what Sakura's trying to do. She wants the officers to look my way, knowing that I'll hide before they see me. If I'm spotted, Sakura will be taken hostage as leverage against me, and any leniency she might be given will automatically be withdrawn. But, if I hide, Sakura will get in the police car, and I'll lose my chance of saving her. It's a lose-lose situation, *unless* I can make it to Sakura before the police turn around. That way, I could protect her from being shot and give her a chance for escape even if I died.

Yet, when I reach the car behind Sakura she yells out again, "Come on, I could escape any minute now, you fat old men!"

I pick up my speed, but it's too late. At her words, the officers immediately snap around, and as they turn, I feel the terrible moment of my defeat. I almost keep running forward, but at the last moment I roll to the ground and under the nearest police car. Even though I want to stand up and do as much damage as I can before going down, for Sakura, I have to face the fact that if I survive, I'll have the ability to plan for her liberation later.

So, I lay quiet under the belly of the car, hard road biting into my cheek, gravity forcing blood from several cuts on my face to carve a crimson path down my skin and spill into my mouth. I taste the hard metallic fluid with a numb feeling, frustration crawling up my throat, daring to burst out in a scream. I want to weep at my loss, laugh at my feebleness, and yell at my sister whose heart proves bigger than her head. But instead, I remain motionless, watching the one person I love be shoved into the back of a police car. I don't budge as the door slams closed. I don't even flinch as the motor snarls and the car speeds away. I just wait, silent, like a predator stalking its prey, until the motor of the car above me starts to growl. Four cars pull away before the wheels beside me start to spin, grinding against the earth. I flatten myself into the road as much as I can, while at the same time tightening my muscles, preparing for motion. Thunder crackles in the distance, and the car moves forward, exposing my back to the bleak sky, and as soon as my hair feels the tickle of fresh, humid air, I jump up and run after the car while its speed is still at a leisurely pace, bending my knees and leaping onto the vehicle's roof with my newfound adrenaline powered by the absence of my sister.

My ascension makes not a noise, and the car speeds on, oblivious of its new passenger.

Clutching the light bar on the roof and squatting, so that my thighs are almost resting on the back of my calves, I watch the path the car follows with squinted eyes, the relentless wind drying out any moisture they hold within seconds. At first, the car tails behind the five others in front of it, and for a moment I dare to think that luck is on my side, and that I'll be taken directly to where Sakura is to be held, but after five minutes of driving, the cars ahead of us start to turn onto different streets, splitting up, so that someone like me won't be able to track a prisoner back to the correct holding unit. It's a tactic that's only used when transporting class one criminals, and police officers are supposed to be incredibly circumspect of possible following accomplices.

I think luck's on my side, though. The car I'm on is going about twenty-five miles an hour, driving in a swerving line that if traced out would look like the sound waves of a low yawn, as if the police officer inside is drunk on too much coffee and doughnuts. No one is sitting in the passenger seat watching for any pursuing criminals, and the red and blue lights aren't on and flashing my shadow on the buildings that slowly drag by. In all honesty, I couldn't imagine a more leisurely ride.

Streets lights illuminate dark puddles of water on the streets, but I remain in utter darkness, fully concealed, stretched out like a spider slowly wrapping its oblivious prey in a silky and fatal web.

After about ten minutes have passed, the car slows down at a shoddy intersection between two side streets, taking a left turn and pulling up next to a tall unassuming building. Confused as to what's happening, I quiet my breathing so that I can hear the soft mumbling of the police officer in the front seat.

"These stupid, overly cautious people! Making me stop at ten million checkpoints every day, and for what! Oh wait, it's in case a random criminal was following me," he laughs gruffly, detaching his seatbelt, "like that would ever happen..."

His words trail off as he fumbles for something in his car, and I immediately slide down from the roof of the car, landing next to the front passenger door and hoping against all hope that any lookouts didn't manage to spot me.

Just as my boots hit the ground, the driver's door slams open, two shiny black work shoes visible as I peer under the car. With an obnoxious huff, the heavyset policeman starts to shuffle towards the building's side door, walking towards it, completely conspicuous, breathing loud as a pig.

I decide to follow him, the temptation to shadow this incredibly loud man, too inviting to resist. I wait until he walks through the door before rising. Silently I creep to the door, scanning all the surrounding rooftops and windows to make sure that no snipers are lying in wait, fixing the mouths of their guns on my chest.

Once I verify that I, indeed, am not going to die from a sniper's bullet, I slip through the door.

"Two flights up... humpf... door on the left... humpf... password is, um... oh, yeah '*We work for the good of all people!*'" the officer mutters, saying the last few words in a mockingly chipper voice, as he struggles up the stairs, panting and wheezing between each word, "Who do those new office people think they are! Besides, no matter how cheery they make the passwords, everybody knows that police officers sign up because of the free lunches and snacks that are paid for with everyone's taxes!" He laughs, pleased at his own joke, and has to stop to catch his breath halfway up the second flight of stairs.

I wait, slightly annoyed that my supposed "enemy" is only an overweight, bald man in his thirties, who's only a policeman because he gets free doughnuts. I know I should be happy because it will make my job easier, but still, what superhero ever had a lame villain? Imagine what the title of my comic would be! Next to posters that say "Superman fights off Lex Luthor" and "Batman destroys the Joker," (old pre-A.R.T. superheroes) will be a small sheet of paper that says "The Dragon fends off the psycho Doughnut Devourer!" I wonder who would ever buy that comic!

Shaking away my trivial thoughts, I ascend the stairs, nearing in on the policeman who now stands next to the door to the left of the stairway.

He says loudly, "We work for the good of all people," and the door immediately swings open, allowing him entry. I only manage to see a dimly lit room and another man in a police uniform who's probably in his late thirties, too, before the door closes once again. Stealthily, I creep up to the door, leaning my head against the wall to the right of it, so that if someone opens the door, I'll be behind it and have a better chance of remaining unnoticed.

After a second of silence, a loud surprised laugh echoes behind the door, joined by a second lower one.

"I didn't know you were assigned here today, James! I thought I was in for a long night with that annoying new supervisor!" exclaims the police officer I've been following.

"Oh, do you mean Harold? He really is quite the perfectionist. Anyway, the boss sent all the other officers in this building home for a holiday break, but I took mine last week, so I'm the only one here now."

"Oh, *really*...?" says the officer in response to James' news, "Want to party tonight in the city? We can go to a nice bar, have a few beers, make this working night fun. What do you say?"

James hesitates, looking from side to side nervously as if his boss is overhearing the conversation.

"Oh, come on, James, it's not like anyone's really going to break out that girl we caught! I'll tell you what, if that small girl escapes before her sentencing tomorrow, next night out, all drinks are on me, alright?" his chuckle is low, but his confidence that everything will be fine, must rub off on James, who answers,

"Well then, to the bar, it is!"

Hearing those words and the shuffle of feet brings my heart back into motion, pounding again and again like a mill grinding grain.

In an instant, I whisk myself onto the staircase railing, and taking a deep breath, I leap into an open window on the wall lining the stairs. Lowering the sound of my breaths, I blend into the shadows, and crouching down, I grab the bottom of the old window frame and swing myself once to the side, letting go to grab an old metal pipe running along the building's side. Before the policemen even make it down the staircase, I shimmy down the pipe and disappear into a dark street, five buildings away.

Once my feet rest on the ground motionless, the reality of what the men said starts to sink in, and my heart begins to gallop away in my chest, a horse untamed, loose from its bridle. Before despair fully overrides my thoughts, I try to weigh my options in my head: If I keep following the policemen, I'll end up at some crazy bar, waiting all night for the policemen to drive back to their stations; even if they exit the bar at midnight, there's no knowing if they will go back to the station Sakura is being held at or just one of the many others. I think about the chance of me finding Sakura by following these officers. It's low. But... if I leave now, I could run back to the *Library*, find Jax, and plan how to break Sakura out.

My jaw clenches, but after thinking for a minute or two, I realize that if this car never goes to the right police department, then I'll barely have time to plan the jailbreak before morning comes and her sentence is announced. Once Sakura's punishment is released to the public, her cell will become heavily guarded, and there will be no chance of a breakout.

Carefully releasing my fingers from their strenuous grip on the lightbar, I stretch up a couple of inches, and as an alleyway opening comes into my vision, I leap off the roof, fly through the air and immediately, as the ground comes to greet me, roll.

Rising up, I stretch my aching back and tired legs. But suddenly, once I'm standing still, without the adrenaline of riding a police car or hiding from officers, I start to crumble, all my panicked thoughts crashing into me.

What if I can't figure out where she's being held? What if I don't save her? What if I'm already too late?

The thoughts slam into me again and again, chipping away at my confidence bit by bit, attacking me without any true purpose but to cause pain.

The assault is unending, and the memories I thought of earlier are starting to penetrate into the flood. With everything swirling in my brain, I can't think logically, and the emotions manage to sweep me further and further away from where I'm standing. My strong exterior disintegrates as my memories take hold of me, and I'm left battling all the emotions with my weak and confused heart.

Every new question that my mind proposes makes my heart shudder with uncertainty. Once I push away one question, another more painful one flies at me. Again and again they come, and again and again my heart tries and fails to fight back doubt.

Of all the street scuffles and gunfights I've dodged and taken part in, I have never, ever, felt as out of control, as powerless, as I do now. There is no harder, more strenuous fight, than one against one's self, for a war in which both sides know every single weakness of their opponent, is a war without an end. It's a war I'm fighting now.

Just as my resolve is about to crumble like the flaky crust of a singara from the market, an enormous clap of thunder draws my body back to attention. Looking up, I see a whole sky of angry clouds like fiery eyes tightly knit over the city. The slight breeze from earlier has picked up its speed, and the moisture in the air no longer as pleasant, but plainly threatening. A true summer storm has whipped itself into existence.

I could easily find an old building to shelter from the rain, but for some reason I don't. When the first drop hits me on the forehead like an angel's very first tear, I close my eyes and let my whole body relax, leaning into the sway of the storm. It pulls me in as if I'm its kin, as if it understands the deep sorrow that fills my chest. So, I answer its call; every drop that explodes against my skin, I turn into a worry, a fear, a fault and when the water shatters, flying away from me, so do they.

Minutes and minutes pass by, the rain thoroughly slicking back my hair and turning my shoes into cups of water. Soon, all my thoughts have left me except for one. It emerges so suddenly as if a magician dumped it out of her hat.

After all that has happened, I finally remember what *Bào qiàn* means: sorry.

For some reason, the simplicity of the word, brings up true sorrow, no anger, confusion, or pity attached. For the first time that night, I truly grieve for my sister, for our relationship that, by the events of today, has been forever altered. My grief digs deeper, and I lament how Sakura got sick, how we lost so many years being together. But too soon after, for the first time since I was eight, I really let myself mourn all the years Sakura and I lost of our childhoods because our parents passed away.

My shoulders don't slump, but instead straighten, as my first tear falls, just like that first raindrop I felt upon my forehead, announcing the beginning of a storm. It rolls down my cheek, warm and salty, mingling with the cold of the rain. Tear after tear falls, flowing down my face and dripping to the ground like individual prayers. My heartbeat steadies, my breathing calms, but my tears keep falling. And for my sister, I let go of everything, my tough facade, my hopes, my fears, and I gently lean into the steady rhythm of the storm whirling around me, whispering one word, "sorry," into the tempestuous air before I totally become free. Then the storm takes hold of me, and I know nothing but the rocking of its wind and the caress of its wet tears.

15

Sometime after the rain stopped, I somehow managed to drag myself back to the *Library*. And here I am, walking up the steps, dripping and shivering like a soaked rat.

I push the door open, a part of me hoping that Jax is still in the room, and luckily for me, he is. Upon seeing me he grins curiously, but as I step into the light, his smile immediately curves downward.

"Kayda, why--what happened?" He asks concerned, rushing out of his seat towards me.

At my shudder, he takes my hand and more gently says, "Here, sit down and I'll get you a shirt of mine to change into. It won't do you any good to sit there cold and wet." As he ruffles through a box of his that holds spare clothes, I curl up onto one of the chairs at the table, resting my pounding head on my forearm. A small tap makes me open my eyes to see Jax holding up a large sweatshirt.

"Thank you," I say nodding at him and rising up, "Could you, uhh, turn around?"

"Oh, sorry," he says as he turns around, trying to restrain a smile.

Quickly I remove my soaked sneakers and peel off my wet clothes, stripping down to just my underwear. I snatch the sweatshirt from the ground and slip it on, noticing how the scent of spices and wood clings to it. It falls a little short of my knees, the fabric ensconcing me in its warmth.

I spread out my wet clothes and shoes on the floor to dry, before returning to my chair at the table. Once I'm seated, Jax turns around and sits down next to me.

"Kayda, you need to tell me what happened, or else I won't be able to help you."

I ignore his words for a moment, relishing the simplicity of just resting with my eyes closed, warm, dry, and comfy, but after a moment I can't ignore reality any longer.

With a sniffle I open my eyes, red and raw, still bearing the temporary scars of what just happened, and lift my head, staring off into the distance, "They took her."

"*Her*? *Who,* Kayda?" Jax looks at me confused, fear shadowing his eyes.

Without looking at him I answer quietly, my voice hushed and broken, "Sakura."

Saying her name makes my heart want to crawl up my throat and start digging its own grave, but I just continue to blankly stare past Jax's shoulder, out the window at the dark streets.

For a moment, not a sound acknowledges the horrible truth I've just told: only silence greets my pain. But right when the absence of sound starts to pull at my seams, Jax speaks, and I finally look at him, at his messy hair, hardened face, and sad eyes that are smoldering with anger and determination.

All he says is, "I've got a plan."

"Beep, beep, beep."

"Sakura, get the microwave! Whatever's in it is ready!" I yell flipping through the pages of one of my mother's story books.

"Kay," she replies and I hear her footsteps as she walks to the kitchen.

I refocus on the story laying on my lap. "She was taken by the police on a stormy evening. It was unavoidable, her involvement was destined to be ill-fated," I read out loud, the words tingling up my spine eerily with deja vu.

"Beep, beep, beep." The sound interrupts my thoughts.

"Sakura, why is it still beeping?" I yell out, perturbed. There's no answer.

"Sakura?" I call again, now a bit afraid for a reason I can't quite pinpoint.

"Beep, beep, beep."

At her silence, I decide to go check out the kitchen to see if Sakura is all right, or if she went outside for a moment.

Placing the book on my bed, I leave my room, and choosing to go with caution, I tiptoe to the kitchen. "Beep, beep, beep."

As I turn the corner into the room, I call out quietly once more, "Sakura?"

When I get no answer, I turn into the kitchen.

"Beep, beep, beep."

I gasp with horror, my heart stopping in my chest.

On the kitchen floor lies Sakura, her neck bent at an odd angle where half a shaft of an arrow protrudes from her flesh. A steady stream of blood trickles from the wound creating a crimson puddle that has started to stain the ends of her dark hair.

Heaving air into my lungs, I whimper with disbelief and immediately sink to the floor cradling her in my arms.

"Sakura wake up, wake up!" I say shaking her, but she doesn't stir. Instead, she flops in my arms as limp as a dead fish. Tears start to stream down my face as I keep shaking her without any response.

"Beep, Beep, Beep," the microwave cries out for the sixth time, but I ignore it.

Terrified to try to wake her again without success, I rock Sakura back and forth in my arms, murmuring "I love you," over and over again.

As she sways in my arms, I notice something golden shining on the side of the arrow. Carefully laying Sakura down, I lean closer to investigate what it is. When I'm about eight inches from the arrow, I realize that the shimmering is not a trick of the light, but golden letters crudely inscribed into the wood of the arrow. It reads, "This is your fault."

A silent scream scratches itself out of my throat violently, as grief, anger and pain take over my thoughts.

"Beep, beEP, BEEP!" All of a sudden, I jerk up, my eyes flashing open, the dream immediately disappearing. I sit straight as a rod, trembles coursing down my spine like mini earthquakes. My breathing is a harsh, cutting sound that beats the air with its panic, but after a minute, it regains its normal pattern, and I am able to realize that the beeping tainting my dream was the alarm I set on my Lynk last night. Quickly I stop it with just a simple shaky thought: "Lynk stop alarm." Immediately the awful ringing ceases, and I'm left with the after-effects of my dream. Fear wafts off of me like an odor, but it is coupled with extreme relief that what I saw isn't real.

Wiping my sweaty palms on my thighs, I take in deep breaths to calm down the panicked tattoo of my heart. I push away the nightmare, trying to erase it from my memory, trying to convince myself that it is not some sort of omen.

And before my thoughts can grow into something more, I decide that it'll be easier to shake off the last bits of my dream if I get up, so, reluctantly, I scootch out of the warmth of the blankets that Jax covered me with last night, proceeding to bury deeper into his sweatshirt so that the chill of the morning, which has seeped into the building won't touch me. Stretching, I look around for Jax, but it seems as if he's already gotten up.

Sitting in one of the chairs at the table, I look over the plans with a yawn. Last night I hacked into all the security cameras of every single police department. I couldn't get through their barriers in the little time that I had without setting off an alarm, but after a bit of prodding, I figured out that if I break into one department's security cameras and set off that alarm there is a one-second loophole where I can skip to another department's feed without setting off that new security system. If I hack into Department Five's cameras (a department only used for keeping records), I can check the feed of all the other departments' cameras, as long as I do it in a second, without anyone getting any notifications.

In other words, I ran a simple code, stole the feed I needed like a true thief, and the police still think I'm oblivious to the fact that Sakura is in cell 8b of Department 22. After all, how could someone track a code of invisible numbers that, in a second, breached every single department's camera feed without leaving the slightest trace behind? The answer is simple; they can't... well unless they're the *Dragon.*

However, the whole hacking ordeal took at least three hours to accomplish, and I ended up going to bed at 3:15. Jax insisted that we break Sakura out early while it's still dark, so I'm now up at 4:45 in the morning.

I yawn again.

With nothing else to do, I start putting on my clothes from yesterday, which have thankfully dried overnight. I shove my black shirt, pants and sneakers on, tucking my daggers into their correct sheaves. Once I'm fully dressed, I tug the sweatshirt back over my head, choosing to be comfy for the last thirty minutes before I have to leave.

Just as I'm about to go on the roof to look for Jax, the door swings open, and he waltzes right in.

"Good you're up," he calls over, "Eat fast, we have to leave in five minutes."

Thinking about the mission brings a flutter of fear to my stomach, and it takes a great deal of my will to keep images from my dream from popping into my head. Looking for a distraction, I walk over to the brown bag Jax left on the table.

Opening it, I find three pieces of warm roti bread sprinkled with herbs. Immediately my mouth starts to water and I stuff a tiny piece into my mouth. Sending a small prayer up to the God I hope is watching, I thank him for the magical foods created from a bunch of ethnicities squished into one small city, and more seriously, I pray that Sakura is okay.

Finishing up the piece of bread, I ask, "Is Leum in position already?"

"Yep, he is officially Teddy Dinkum for the day," Jax responds quickly as he packs things into a small black backpack, "Can you toss me the map and a piece of roti before it's all gone?"

I toss the bread and the map, before fingering the last piece of roti, "So... there's an extra piece... " I say smiling, "Is it for anyone in particular?"

"Eat it," Jax calls back with a chuckle, "I bought three because I knew that if I got two, I wouldn't get any."

I laugh and take the warm bread, eating it slowly. But when finally my hands are empty and licked clean, the false lightness I played at, falls away, and my nerves come back tenfold.

"Jax... do you really think we can pull this off?" I whisper, slightly afraid to hear his answer, wondering if he has already foreseen what will happen.

He turns around slowly, purposefully looking me right in the eyes, "When I asked you to join my rebellion, Kayda, I knew just by looking at you, the way you stood so grounded, the way your eyes were filled with such defiance, that in short, if you set your mind to it, you could do anything. If nobody ever gets in your way, I have no doubt that you will spin this world on your pinkie finger. And honestly, I wouldn't be surprised if you still manage to do just that even if every single person lines up in front of you to hinder your success. But, remember, some things we can't control... not even I *saw* this whole situation coming.

If you want your sister back, clench your jaw, summon your fire, and get her back. And if for some reason you can't bring her back, I'll be here for you, but you'll-*we'll*-have to keep on going. This world-," he says and then corrects himself, his voice becoming softer, his gaze cautiously leaving mine, "*I* need you more than you need yourself. Don't forget that."

I blink a few times, pushing back the tears that threaten to spill over onto my cheeks. Gritting my teeth, I pull together my strength, sharpening my thoughts to become as lethal as the tips of my blades, "Let's do this."

16

We stop a few streets away from Department 22, and in the darkness behind one of the buildings, Jax dons the uniform of a police officer over his clothes: a dark jacket, boots, and black pants. I don't exactly know how he obtained the uniform on such short notice, but I don't really care as long as it will help us pull off this mission.

When he's all dressed, I slip my hand into my pocket and pull out a red badge marked with a small dove on it bearing a chain shackled around it's left foot, keeping it from flying away. Below the picture are four words: steal your freedom back.

It's the emblem of our rebellion, which I designed two weeks ago. When I wasn't communicating with Jax, I wasn't helpless, wallowing in my sadness. In fact, I contacted a few other hackers and thieves that owe me and arranged a deal with them to make several hundred of our badges with the symbol on it, throw them from rooftops, leave them in work areas, and spread them to every corner of the city.

"Let the people pick them up," I responded when they asked how I would hide the flags from officials, "If a man whose family has been persecuted again and again for simply living in poverty picks it up, then good. But if an officer picks it up, then even better. I am done hiding. Let our oppressors get angry, it will just rally more men and women to my side when a police officer acts out blindly in rage. Our enemies will be standing in a cage of my own making when finally their rage subsides!" My words were bold, I knew it when I said them, but I meant them then and I mean them now.

Whether those hackers and thieves believed me or not, they did what I asked of them. The badges spread like wildfire. They were exchanged like money, passed from hand to hand, quietly and quickly. To have touched one, was to have pledged support to the rebellion. It was the thing that nobody talked of, but everybody whispered about it. Petty arguments between vendors and customers in the marketplace ceased when the red insignia was carefully slipped from the customer's pocket.

Nobody who had known pain could outwardly declare that the rebellion wasn't the savior this city needed, and so the distrust between everyday people dissipated in the wake of their mutual belief.

Just as I had expected, about two days after the badges had been released, police officers surrounded the market square, but what I had not foretold was the increase of rebellious activity.

Once the people had the attention of their oppressors, they went wild. More red flags were created, stitched together from old t-shirts and rags. They were hung from the highest windows of abandoned buildings and the words "STEAL YOUR FREEDOM BACK" were spray-painted on buildings all over the city.

Some avid supporters would yell the words out in the market square in front of the police and then slip through the masses before a gun could be raised.

I had given the people just a single crest, but they took it as a sign of hope. And in the name of hope, people would do just about anything. In fact, I was quite surprised when one day, while I was roaming the city streets at night, I heard a chorus of murmured voices coming from a building that had been abandoned since I was a kid.

Crouching on the broken first-floor window, I overheard the conversation of a group of people who called themselves the

Freedom Thieves Supporters. I had been surprised enough to find that people had organized a group of adherents, but I was blown away that such a group had created a code to show which houses held other supporters: a small shackled bird, about half an inch wide painted on the left-bottom-corner of a door.

Now, I take the red cloth and remove a small jar of sap from Jax's backpack, which my mom used to make homemade glue for the various art projects she always did. Holding the petite glass container, its label "pine sap" written in curvy and fast letters, my mom's handwriting, brings a surge of emotion to my chest, but I tamp down on it.

There's no time for sentiments.

I place a dot of the substance on the back of the badge and quickly stick it to the shoulder of Jax's black coat.

"Be careful," I whisper to him, but before the words have fully left my mouth, he's already disappeared into the shadows.

I heft his backpack onto my shoulder and grasp a red brick of the building next to me. Leveraging the grip, I rest my weight on it, so that I can swing up and grasp another handhold. Brick by brick I scale three stories until I reach the roof.

Without a moment to spare, I unzip the sac and pull out my computer, setting it down behind an old air conditioner. With a few taps, I connect to the camera installed into Jax's badge, so that I can track his progress. Right now, he is a street away from the back parking lot of the police department. I have a few minutes.

With time to spare, I send Leum a short message from my Lynk in a heavily encrypted conversation platform; it'll expire in an hour, but while it is running, every message in the conversation will be concealed in code bubbles that are almost impossible to break. It's a code I made years ago, and it's never been breached.

Jax is nearing the building. I estimate he'll enter through the back door in 6 minutes. If my estimation is correct, be ready and in position in about ten minutes.

He responds right away: ***Already in position, send the signal when you're ready.***

Satisfied, I switch back to Jax's camera feed. He is turning into the parking lot now, no officers insight. Immediately, I open the coding canvas on my link and decide to use two codes that I've already created: one that works as a sort of blitzkrieg (an ancient military tactic) by breaking through one link in an encryption, and another one that basically does the job of a construction man. I tie the codes together, but add a line in between them which will make the building code activate exactly a minute after the blitzkrieg runs. If the code runs properly, the building code will repair the original encryption, therefore leaving behind no evidence of a breach--not that anyone will be expecting one.

When Jax is about ten feet away from the door, I put my work to the test on the security system that monitors and locks the back parking lot door.

I receive a message from Jax: *Kayda, can you open the door for me, now?*

At that moment, my Lynk notifies me that the Blitzkrieg worked and that the second part of the code will start in a minute. I smile and send back: Already done! The door closes in a minute, though, so you better start moving faster than that slow walk you got going on there.

;) he sends back, before slipping through the door.

I smile but ex out of his feed. I won't need to follow him anymore. In fact, I need to start moving.

I place my computer back into the backpack and kicking open the side of the air conditioner, I store it inside.

Be ready in three: I send to both Leum and Jax. Then I tie my shoes and start to run. The first building's roof is so close, I barely have to leap. The second building is four stories tall and about five and a half feet away. It doesn't prove to be such a challenge when I jump to one of its windows and scramble to the top. Four more roofs and I'm on a building adjacent to Department 22.

As I squat on the roof, a burst of energy licks its way up my spine fanning out into my chest like a rage of fire. It focuses my thoughts, sharpening them to a single, lethal tip, of anger: *I will get my sister back.*

This morning Leum signed up to become a new police recruit.

After hearing the police I was trailing last night talking about all the new recruits, I realized that it wouldn't be weird if another person showed up this morning asking to join the force.

Sure enough, Leum was accepted within five minutes of gushing about how "helping the city's security is his only purpose in life." I can only imagine how hard it must have been to get those words past his lips.

During his introductory tour, Leum snatched the key to Sakura's cell from the pocket of the guard officer; a task that should have been simple and easy.

In reality, it was the work of miracles and the four hours of Jax trying to teach Leum the trick of stealing, which helped him pull it off.

Leum may have been good at procuring high-tech goods out of thin air, but one-on-one thieving didn't suit him.

The kid simply had shaky hands and slow feet.

However, after those long hours, Jax gave in and handed a relieved Leum a packet of sleeping drought. I still wasn't so convinced the kid could steal keys even from a sleeping man. Luckily though, he did.

I glance back at the feed on my computer, only to see a blank screen. With a huff, I remember that I am alone now. All I can hope is that Jax and Leum are on their way to the side door.

"Beep," the alarm on my Lynk flashes in the corner of my eye, and immediately, I send the command to make the cameras loop back to yesterday's feed without even having to hack into them: when I accessed the security cams last night, I placed a little bug in them, which when I type a certain command, gives me temporary control over them for about four minutes.

I send a message to both Jax and Leum, which reads: forever or never.

It's the signal for: It's time.

We first came up with it as some sort of team slogan, resembling the choice we made to always be rebels at heart, always fight for what is right, and the choice we didn't -- to just lay low and wait for another chance that may never come. It's a sort of oath that we say, a promise to always have each other's backs.

Just sending those words washes a wave of confidence over me and I stand a little taller, braving what I have to do next.

Right now, Jax should be two minutes from the exit. Any second, he will purposefully hit one of the intruder alarms on the wall. This will activate Shut Down Mode, which orders all officers to stay in place and await further commands from the head policeman unless they have eyes on the intruder.

At the sound of the alarm, the boss will check the video feed to verify the threat, but he will only find empty corridors with roaming police; yesterday's feed. Confused by the lack of a threat and annoyed by his officers' insubordination, the head policeman will hesitate to set the alarm, and hopefully, by then Jax will be in the corridor that leads to the side exit.

During all the chaos Leum should be outside, taking his break with the elderly officer, Bruno, who, conveniently, is more than halfway to deaf and won't hear the alarms.

Because the side exit is watched by two guards, Jax will have pursuers. We planned for that though.

He will run out the door, the guards thirty seconds behind him, pull off his badge, stick it on Leum's companion, and then disappear, Leum already lost in the shadows.

When Jax's pursuers reach the side exit, they'll find one innocent elderly officer, standing with a red badge on his shoulder, completely bewildered.

It's a perfect getaway with a flare of theatrics and our sign of the rebellion marked on it... if everything goes right.

I cross my fingers and pray that it will go just as planned and then proceed to turn off my Lynk, cutting off any communication I have with Jax and Leum and with the rest of this city.

I'm all by myself now.

In the cells, all Lynk activity is monitored. Even though mine is heavily coded, it still communicates with other electronics, and therefore, it will show up on the scanner for the jail cells. If someone notices that two people are in the jail unit, Sakura will never escape, and I probably won't either.

And so my Lynk is off. Maybe I can really call myself a ghost now.

Before another second passes, I start to run, the air wispy and warm, stroking my skin like a dear old friend. My strides stretch longer and longer, the muscles in my legs bulging as they assume the new strain of my movement. All of a sudden, a strong gust of wind propels me forward, and I lean into it, using its momentum to smoothly glide across the gap between buildings, my legs perpendicular to my body. If I were a bit more graceful, I might have resembled the pre-A.R.T ballerina dancers, but instead, my grand leap is nothing but a precise movement of muscles that gets me across the gap efficiently and does nothing else. I hit the building's roof quietly, unscathed, and unnoticed. Perfect.

Streaking across the roof, hunching low, hiding behind any objects that I can, I am as inconspicuous as one could be. After half a minute, I arrive at a ceiling vent installed on the edge of the first building.

Department 22 is composed of three buildings that are all connected. The first one, is the work office, the second is the holding unit, and the third is the unit open to civilians.

With that in mind, this vent should lead to the second building. To my sister.

I pull out a lock pick, and use its slender shape and strength to my advantage by sliding it under the screws and popping them out. The vent comes loose.

I find myself peering into an empty white, intensely lit hallway. The walls and floors shine unnaturally, and I get a strange feeling that if I were to turn off the lights, they would still be glowing.

Glancing at the old-fashioned watch on my hand--I was lucky my mom kept one in her drawer and that I was able to get it working--tells me that two minutes have passed since the security cameras started looping. That means I have two minutes to get Sakura and get out.

That's not too bad.

I slide through the opening, my hips scratching the metal sides as I wriggle them through. Inwardly, I curse the heavy meals I have been splurging on recently.

I leave the grate slightly open for when I exit and drop to the ground in a crouch.

Immediately, as my feet contact the shiny floors, an uneasy feeling rushes through my stomach, and my vision wavers, bringing tears to my eyes. Ignoring the sudden pain, that I suspiciously believe is coming from my contact with the odd white substance that makes up this hallway, I rush to the steel door at the end of the hall. It's a large door: probably five feet across and eight feet tall. I stick my hand under the small crack below the door, feel along the bottom of the steel. My fingers find a small divot and when I apply pressure to it, the tiny chunk of steel comes away, revealing the door's hollow inside.

I can't help but snort, the police didn't even make the door solid steal! It's just a ruse to make people believe that the jail is heavily guarded. I should have just brought a small bomb and blown my way through.

Well, I guess that would have been a bit dramatic.

Pushing the wild thought away, I wiggle my fingers in the small hole, and feeling a little metal object, I grab it, and sure enough when I pull it out, it's a key.

The thing is also made of steel, no adornments or writing on the top like keys in fairy tales, just a piece of metal roughly cut to have teeth.

I insert the key into a slightly hidden hole in the large door, and with a single satisfying click, the door slides open. Slipping into the unlit, but continually glowing room (made from even more white stone--if that's possible) beyond, I am met with a second, stronger, wave of nausea that rips up through my stomach like a bolt of lightning. I cry out, tasting blood in my mouth, as another bolt slices through me. I clench my stomach trying to fight off the wave of pain, but it only grows stronger. I can barely fend off the pain, let alone ponder the reason why it is plaguing me.

Sinking to the floor, an unimaginable heat bursts in my head, causing my eyes to squeeze shut. My brain starts to shut down, reaching desperately for unconsciousness and the bliss of feeling no pain when a single thought breaks through the agony: *Sakura.*

The small whisper startles my brain awake, and I grasp the small part of me that is still struggling against the pain. I push against the blinding heat in my head, imagining it shrinking and being stuffed into a small box. Then I grab the pain in my stomach and pull it into the box, gasping with the effort. Once it is all stuffed in, I shut the imaginary box, locking it with five chains.

For ten seconds I just sit, heaving cold sterilized air into my lungs, warding away the shakiness that had consumed my limbs just moments before. After I feel the blackness creep away from my vision, I blink, clearing the water that sits, ready to fall, from my eyes. When finally I can see clearly, my eyes are met with the same blank and shining white walls. Except in this new corridor, electric lights are blazing on the ceiling, buzzing like trapped lightning bugs. Dark cells line the walls, the metal bars a stark and ominous contrast against the immaculate walls. A chill runs down my spine along with a wave of nausea that I force away.

Without another thought, I start to walk down the hallway, my shoes clanging against the glassy floor no matter how lightly I walk.

I arrive at the first cell and glance through the dark bars, seeing a dirty floor with multiple dark stains that look suspiciously like blood. A small pile of straw lays abandoned in the corner. Just that one glance makes the hairs on my neck raise, and I speed up my pace wanting to get Sakura out of here as fast as I can.

I almost call out her name, but at the last second, I decide not to in case it draws attention to me. Besides, I know what number cell she is in: 4.

I rush on, passing cell three until I reach the dark bars I've been searching for. My heart lifts and I fumble in my pocket for the lock pick. Pinching it between my fingers, I peek into the cell.

"Sakura," I whisper softly, the name barely lifting off my lips, and yet the hope in my voice is evident.

The click of the lock opening echoes in silence.

I bite down on my lip, trying to steady the frantic beat of my heart.

I swing the door open slowly and whisper a little louder, "Sakura!"

Maybe she's just sleeping?

I enter the cell slowly, my eyes adjusting to the darkness.

As I walk deeper in, trying to make out a figure in the darkness, straw crunches beneath my sneakers, creaking like old bones.

Looking down I realize that it is scattered all over the floor, no longer in a neat pile.

My throat tightens.

It looks like there was a struggle.

Maybe she didn't like sleeping on the straw.

My mind registers that such a thing is unlikely, but my heart wraps the idea around it like a blanket, hiding away from the world.

I walk further into the cell, my eyes still blurry. Nothing moves or rustles.

Where is she...?

I swing my head back and forth, lowering to my knees, so I can feel the ground for Sakura. I grope around in the darkness.

Where is she...!

My eyes finally adjust, and as my vision expands I see a wall in front of me. Turning I realize I'm at the back of the cell, and there is no one in it with me.

"Sa-Sakura??" I say quietly but, in my head, I'm screaming her name.

I crazily throw around the straw, looking everywhere for a little sleeping body.

"No," I whisper as I hold all the straw in my hands, looking out at a totally empty cell, "No, NO!"

I spring up to my feet, rage fueling my footsteps.

The cell door closes with a clang as I rush down the corridor, glancing in every cell.

Every empty cell.

When I reach the end, I throw my hands against the horrible white wall, scraping my fists raw as I beat against the surface again and again.

Why? Why? WHY?

The fight drains out of me, and I sag against the wall, my stomach still roiling and my head once again burning up. I squeeze my eyes shut to keep tears from spilling down my cheeks.

"Sakura," I say, the sound forlorn and broken. The whisper of a fracturing heart.

Where are you! I'm here for you.

I'm here!

"I'm here! Sakura!" I yell, getting up and walking down the white hall, throwing caution to the wind.

Please answer.

"Sakura!" I scream louder, my voice cracking in a sob.

I need you.

I push open the metal door, the wind of its movement fluttering a small scrap of paper. From the corner of my eye I read "no trial ex". The words are nonsense to me and the little shred of paper offers no explanation other than those few letters, so I keep moving, pulling my body through the door and out into the first corridor. I shut the door behind me, not even caring about the loud sound it makes as it scrapes closed, and slide the key onto the other side. They won't be able to get in anytime soon without another one.

As I walk away from the door, the pain in my stomach slowly subsides, the giant talons that are squeezing my organs, relinquishing their grip, confirming my suspicions that the white stone is what is affecting me.

Just as I breathe the first full breath I have since I entered the cells, the sound of pounding shoes reaches my ears. The police. Of course.

I look back at the cells, tears streaming down my face, but anger swiftly rising to take its place.

My thoughts start to sharpen like daggers, my fingers burning up in fury.

The police grow closer.

My hands clench into tight fists and I grit my teeth.

The shoes are right outside the door.

With one seething look in the direction of the police, I run and push off the wall, propelling myself up toward the vent. Wildly grasping with one hand the side of the opening through the small crack, I swing myself up and through the vent, feet first to knock away the covering. I crouch on the roof, dexterously screwing the vent back in place. Just as I am about to leave, I see the police storm into the room. My hand shakes in anger where it sits on the vent, and I imagine an angry fire consuming the building. When I lift my hand, a black hand print smolders on the metal grate.

Impossible...

I close my eyes and run, confusion, pain, and anger swirling in my head like liquor in a drunk man's stomach.

I leap off the building and on to the next, landing rough and rolling to a stop. With a yell, I run and jump to the adjacent roof. Tears spill down my cheeks angrily, and I throw myself across the next gap so I don't have to think about that burning handprint, about the fact that no one is running beside me.

17

I realize it at the last minute.

I didn't jump far enough.

I curse loudly even as a tendril of fear stretches awake in my stomach like a dormant dragon rising from sleep, and the feeling spreads through my mind, muffling any other emotions.

My mind reels, trying to find a solution where there is none.

At the last minute, I straighten my legs while I soar through the air, throwing my arms forward in an attempt to catch the building's ledge.

My heart pounds out a frantic rhythm, hoping for the impossible.

Dear God if you are up there, please save my stupid soul.

Seconds slip by like molasses, slowly but inevitably, and the moment my fingers miss the ledge by several inches is frozen with my shock and denial. I hang in the air for a fraction of a second, my eyes wide, staring at my lost chance of safety.

And then I start to fall.

My stomach twists like a corkscrew as gravity pulls my body down. For what feels like an eternity, I plummet, tumbling down in a confused flurry. I squeeze my eyes shut against my impending fate.

This is it.

A few feet from the ground, a burst of wind swoops in and cradles me, lifting me up. I keep my eyes shut tight, wondering if I am already dead and being taken up to heaven.

I always thought I'd have a more fiery ending.

Wind continues to buffer me from each side, and after a moment, I automatically take a deep breath, my heart beat slowing.

Wait, my heartbeat is still there...

Confused I open my eyes to see my body floating in midair, a few feet above the building's roof as if held in place by invisible strings.

My jaw drops open.

With a quick glance, I find nothing wrapped around me or anything I could possibly be suspended from. The only odd thing is a slight glimmer that outlines my body: something so fine, so minute, that one would only really see it if the sun struck the shimmery particles at the right angle.

It looks like magic.

The thought comes out of the six-year-old child in me still sitting on my mom's lap as she tells a story.

Once the sheer preposterousness of such an idea and the impossibility of my situation finally hits me, my brain wakes up, and without another thought as to what exactly is holding me, I start thrashing against the air, a panic attack right around the corner, my breath quickening, sweat starting to form, and I silently will the air to let me down.

It does. Immediately.

*As if it is listening to me...*whispers my six-year-old voice in my head.

The eerie thought is immediately forgotten as I land roughly in a pile of sore limbs, on the top of the building.

Groaning, I untangle myself, stretching out my legs and flexing my seemingly unaffected muscles satisfyingly. After a moment I rise, focusing on my movements to distract my brain from many unwanted thoughts.

As I walk to the end of the roof, I realize that I am not going to be able to keep jumping across buildings. It's risky, especially if the police have already sent out search groups. Instead, I decide to shimmy down a drainage pipe and make my way back to Jax and Leum on foot.

I let out a sigh as I slip into the shadows and all unseen eyes lose track of me.

My heart jumps as I realize someone must have seen me... *floating.*

If that even happened.

People would probably just chalk it up to a delusion, anyway. Impossible, crazy, things happen every day in this city.

My *incident*—the image of a hand burnt into an iron vent pops up into my mind—*incidents,* I correct, are just more examples of those impossible, crazy things.

I exhale, satisfied with my explanation.

Now, I just have to never mention what happened to anyone. *Ever.*

I keep moving in the shadows, running fast past buildings. I count them. Three. Ten. Twelve.

I turn right.

With only silence around me, my brain begins to think. And since I tucked away the strange events of earlier deep into the dark recesses of my mind, it starts to ponder over the one thing I have been trying not to think about. Sakura.

The fact that she is not beside me.

The fact that I didn't save her.

Tears start slipping down my cheeks, silent and soft.

My immediate anger when I first realized she was gone has faded, replaced by sorrow.

How many times can I fail someone?

My throat tightens, more wobbly tears drifting down my cheeks like sea-wrecked ships trying to find calm in the storm. And yet even with all their struggles, each one inevitably falls to their doom, splattering against the asphalt in salty sorrow.

For some reason, the sound of my tears plummeting to the ground brings a memory to my mind. When I was running out of the corridor of cells, angry tears leaking from my eyes, I remember seeing a scrap of paper on the floor. My mind struggles to remember the words that were written on it.

I stop running, tucking myself in a dark street corner, trying to think.

"No trial ex"

Remembering the words brings a wave of disappointment. I thought they might be a clue, but they mean nothing! It was probably a random scrap of paper that a police officer accidentally dropped.

The sentimental part of me caves in on itself, but the other half of me, the cunning part, keeps mulling over the words, convinced that they have some meaning.

Just as I'm about to start running again, something in my brain clicks. The answer unfurls slowly and I recoil in horror.

The piece of paper wasn't just a random scrap, it was probably a piece of an officer's orders.

My mouth sours, and my stomach churns.

Why does everything have to be so DIRTY complicated!?

I clench my fists and start to run even faster than before.

I need to alert Jax immediately.

We won't have much time.

I look up at the sky to see that the pitch black of the night has started to make way for a lighter blue. Dawn should be here in about an hour and a half.

I curse, running ever faster because if I don't get there soon, if I don't—the meaning of the note repeats in my head:

No trial. Execution at dawn.

I finish my thought, a feeling of finality settling heavily in my belly: if I don't get help now, then I won't ever have a chance to fail Sakura again.

18

"I had a vision--just a blurry dark image of restless black colors seething against each other--that something bad was coming when I was leaving the police station, and when you got here, I was so relieved, but now *this,*" Jax shakes his head, dragging a hand over his face, "this is worse than I could ever have imagined."

I pace the room, my feet hitting the ground so furiously that I'm afraid they will soon leave imprints in the concrete if I keep this up.

"Well, what can we do with the time we have?" I say, "We can't just jump out into the execution and single-handedly fight off a bunch of officers with guns: that would be a massacre!"

I clench my fists into hard stones, my knuckles turning white from the effort.

"We need a diversion. Something so big that the firing squad will be distracted long enough for me to go in and grab Sakura."

"That's suicide for you even if the firing squad is distracted. Someone is bound to notice that you look even more like the picture on that wanted poster than your sister." Jax says, annoyed.

"Well, I'll just dress up!" I throw my arms up wildly, "if I didn't know that we would both be killed, I would turn myself in right now."

"You have so little care for yourself! We can't have you throwing yourself in front of a bullet today, just because you can." Jax says angrily, his lips pulled down in a frown.

"Maybe we can use the public as a distraction," Leum interjects sheepishly, his eyes darting between my furiously pacing figure and Jax's angry scowl. When neither of us responds, he swallows and plows on.

"If we tell people that the head of the rebellion is being killed, naturally there will be a riot. I mean people have just started to begin to hope. They're not going to let their chance at peace slip past them so easily."

I stop pacing, mulling over his words. A plan begins to form, and I give him a slow, thoughtful nod, "Perfect. Nobody will know that Sakura is not the actual leader, and if only twenty people show up angry then that's still enough of a distraction for me to grab Sakura and run."

Jax looks back at me a bit reluctantly but offers no verbal dissent.

Viewing this as agreement, I start to prepare.

I pat my left arm, right thigh, and back, making sure that every knife is in its spot. Satisfied, I stretch each of my arms and then legs in turn, finishing by cracking my neck. Without waiting for Jax to persuade me to stop and think, I stride towards the door, my mouth turning into a grim line.

This might just work.

19

I slither through the streets approaching a large, writhing, and howling mass of people. I smile bitterly: Sakura finally has people who care for her, although I would say it's a bit late, as they have come for the spectacle of her death.

I let my eyes unfocus and slide across the crowd. 124 commoners. Leum did a good job of spreading the word.

I'm about to slip into the crowd when a hand gently touches my arm. Jax gestures me into a shadowed corner a few feet away. His anger has faded now, replaced only by worry.

Before he can speak, I make a decision.

"Jax, I have something to tell you," the burning handprint flashes in my mind along with the memory of floating, held up by a gust of air.

Maybe he already knows. Maybe he can help me learn how to use it...if it is real.

"Is it really important?"

I close my eyes for a second as my confidence wavers.

I guess he didn't have a vision of this moment or of my "powers". Well... I'll just tell him later then.

"No," I say opening my eyes.

"Good, because you should focus on what you'll have to do now. You can always tell me later...." he hesitates before continuing, "I still have the feeling that something bad is coming." He scans my disguise, making sure everything is in place. When he's satisfied, he steps back as if to leave. At the last moment, though, he looks back at me, something flickering across his eyes, "Just be careful, okay."

"I will."

He swallows, his eyes flitting to the ground, but when he looks back up, he continues on, although quietly.

"Promise me you won't get yourself killed today. Please, Kayda..."

His words automatically hit a mental shield that I have carefully forged over many years.

Never promise anything...never leave Sakura behind.

"No." My voice sounds like ice, cold and detached.

Sakura is worth dying for.

"Kayda..." he pleads quietly, a tenderness, a pain, hidden in the way he says my name.

I look back at him, "I can't promise that. Jax you know I would die for her."

But if I died today, I would...

I look into his eyes: two dark green orbs swirling with caramel and burgundy flecks. They stare back at me, soft and pleading. Fear is etched in the minute wrinkles spreading from their corners, but there's something else in them, something tender and unguarded when Jax looks at me.

My breath catches, as a realization hits me, hard and heady.

If I died today, I would lose Jax.

My heart pounds out a frantic pattern, not in fear, but anticipation. There's no more time to waste. I might die today.

I remember that day in the bar, our almost kiss—the one I ruined. I always keep myself so tightly bundled, so afraid to be hurt. Honestly, I should have just trusted Jax, should have realized that he had his reasons for not telling me what he is.

A smile touches my lips, small and mischievous despite the chaotic circumstances.

I guess I'll just have to fix what I ruined.

I step closer to Jax, our bodies mere inches apart.

This close, his scent envelops me, spices and wood overwhelming my senses.

His eyes widen.

My smile grows, and I lean in closer, my lips just below his.

I feel him breathe in shakily, and my heart skips a beat.

"My birthday is on February 18," I whisper, and at first Jax looks confused, but understanding dawns on his face with a grin, "my favorite color is banana yellow—not the outside of the banana but the inside," he laughs, cocking an eyebrow at me as if saying *you're so weird,* "and my favorite story is Aladdin."

He smirks, his arrogance finally returning, his own wall that he built after our fight, breaking down.

"Of course it is." He lets out a breath he's been holding, and laughs a bit incredulously, "so does this mean we're friends again?"

My smile turns into a wicked grin, "No."

"No?" Confusion passes over his face, and sadness quickly flits across his eyes.

"No, I won't agree to that." My smile is barely contained.

"You won't?" He asks, now suspicious of why I am smiling like some crazy hyena.

"No, because we are more than that aren't we, Jax?" I respond, looking up at him through my lashes, a sly smile playing at my lips as excitement and apprehension flash through my stomach in waves.

He looks at me for a moment, his eyes searching for any flaw or hesitation that will tell him I'm joking. When he sees none, he cautiously looks at me. His eyes on mine. Something alters within his face, and all of a sudden, the intensity of his gaze, the strength of the warmth that flows from it, threatens to sweep me off my feet. He stares at me for a few seconds, and then as if waking from a daze, he smirks.

"For dirt's sake, I thought you'd never say that," he declares, before he leans down, tipping the hood of my cloak back. Gently, he cups my cheek, his touch blazing against my skin like fire and closes the last inch between us.

His lips touch mine, soft and questioning, a barely contained hunger hiding behind the tender kiss.

At first, I don't respond, my body tensing up in surprise—after all, I have never really been kissed before—and Jax starts to pull away. Panicked I lean in, pressing my mouth against his in a desperate move. Nervous that it was too much, I almost step back, but Jax responds immediately, his lips moving against mine hungrily, deepening the kiss. He nibbles my bottom lip with his teeth, and I sigh in pleasure, melting into his body.

Finally!

Wrapping his arms around me, Jax gently pushes my back against the building's wall.

I gasp and experimentally, I kiss his cheek, short stubble grazing against the softness of my lips. Immediately, he pulls me closer to him, dipping his head to press feather-light kisses to my neck, mumbling breathlessly in between them "You're so beautiful."

I shiver, the softness of his mouth on my neck awakening a recklessness inside me.

He groans when I slip one hand into his hair, my fingers pulling at the dark strands when the kiss deepens, my other hand sliding under his shirt, hard muscles lined with scars flexing under the whisper of my fingers.

After all the struggles and pain, the fights and the losses, I became worn and haggard, my old joy and laughter forgotten, blending in with the darkness so often that I had become but a hard shadow of what I once was.

But here in this moment of absolute bliss, all my insecurities, worries, and griefs fall away, and my mind flies far away from these dirty streets back to a time where I was happy, reading about beautiful princesses and dashing princes.

And in this moment, I am inclined to believe that fairytale endings may actually exist.

And that wishes are not forgotten...

Because this is surely a wish come true.

"Kayda..." the gravelly whisper is barely loud enough for me to hear, but he says my name like a prayer, as if it is the only thing holding him together.

Gently, he nudges my head up, our eyes meeting for a second, both wild and burning before Jax leans in again.

His lips are an inch from mine, and I'm an inch away from losing myself, from melting into his arms and never coming back out, but suddenly, a stray thought manages to cross my mind.

Sakura.

The name awakens a silent panic in me, and I start to pull away.

What am I doing? She's going to die in ten minutes and I'm in an alleyway kissing a guy.

My heart flutters when I think those last words, and I curse my teenage hormones.

"Kayda...? Did I do something wrong?" Jax asks worried, letting me go.

"No, no... I just, I'm sorry, I've got to go... Sakura..."

He nods with understanding, his face already hardening, preparing for what's ahead of us.

"Don't die today little dragon," he says, a somber smile on his lips.

"Don't call me that, little...," I search for a good comeback, but my mind draws a blank, still feeling the remnants of our kiss, "little... seer," I shoot back at him, about to turn away, my heart still pounding, but something in me whispers "*no.*" And so at the last moment, I turn around, whispering "forever or never" as I press a quick kiss to Jax's lips, pouring into it all my emotion and fear.

Before he even has a chance to respond, I slip into the crowd, my mind still focused on those few moments we shared together, still feeling his lips on my skin as I head to the spot where my sister is to be killed in less than ten minutes.

Some old part of me whispers: *you're a traitor.*

The new part of me screams: *No, I'm alive.*

20

I slip my way through the crowd easily, ducking under meaty men's raised arms and past hardened mothers' dirty skirts. I even pass some children with surprise.

It seems that everybody has come to save Sakura or well—I gasp in realization—all these people are here for the so-called head of the rebellion, which is *me* and Jax...but mostly *me*.

A new respect settles inside me for these people who are risking their lives for the rebellion, but at the same time, a heavy burden settles on my shoulders.

I am responsible for all their lives: for that boney man, that beautiful, worn lady, that cute little fidgety boy. I am the reason they are standing here, and if I'm not careful, I'll be the cause of their death.

One thing at a time. Get Sakura first and then save all their lives.

I almost laugh at the arrogance of my thoughts.

But it is better to hope for a lot than to never dream for anything else. I know that now.

Hurrying along, I notice with confusion that everybody is so far from the execution square. I can't even see Sakura yet, or the firing squad for that matter.

A small wave of doubt rushes across my body.

I move faster.

"Steal your freedom back," yells out a voice I immediately recognize.

The signal.

Glancing back, I spot Jax crouching in the shadow of a building lining the execution square.

I give a small smile of recognition.

He grins back before disappearing. His job is done. The signal sent.

Automatically, the crowd starts to move, shouts ringing out into the air.

I wiggle through to the front of the roiling crowd, and a wave of horror washes over me.

Ten squads of police, five officers in each, guard the whole square. If they were unarmed it could almost be a fair fight, a little more than two commoners—more showing up every minute—per one trained officer, but each police officer carries two guns and a hard plastic shield.

If we fight, we will be slaughtered like lambs.

For dirt's sake, is life never easy!

From my vantage point, a group of highly decorated soldiers walks into the square, red coats lined in gold thread cover black shirts, each one with a different symbol stitched into it according to the soldier. Golden tassels fall from the jacket's shoulders, shaking clumsily as the soldiers march. To finish the costume off, each wears the finest black pants and pristinely polished ebony black shoes.

The Bullets: the city's finest execution shooters, rich pets that do the dirty work for old graying billionaires.

Cries of outrage slash against the air, when a small beautiful girl dressed in rags is pushed to her knees in front of the pompous shooters.

Her hair falls down in a shiny black wave, and a large red cut runs down her beautiful face, but instead of it making her look weak, it gives her a fierce appearance. She keeps her shoulders back even in the uncomfortable position, her head held regally, her eyes two twin fires of anger.

The perfect picture of the head of a rebellion.

It looks as if she was born for this.

She holds up her hands in the symbol of a flying dove, and the people immediately quiet, hands up in the air mirroring the flying dove back at her.

I raise my hands up, too.

A righteousness, a peace, pervades the air at the connection between so many people.

This is how it should always be.

A Bullet strides forward and kicks Sakura in the back of the head. She slumps forward, her hands falling to the ground.

Chaos erupts.

Commoners charge forward into the lines of police guarding the square, hitting hard plastic shields again and again, but the Bullets don't even blink an eye. They drag Sakura towards the white wall.

I scan the line of police, frantically looking for a hole between their shields.

One Bullet drags a ladder up to the wall.

I spot a space I can dive through, but it is on the far side of the square. If I make it through, I will still have to run across the whole square to get to Sakura.

The Bullets force Sakura onto the ladder, hitting her when she refuses to move as fast as they wish.

The people of the city, hit harder against the police, crudely sharpened pieces of wood and scraps of metal now held in their hands. Men run and jump at the officers, trying desperately to break a link in the chain.

I glance at the writhing mass of people. There's no way I could get them organized in time.

Instead, they keep pounding wildly against shields, aggravating police officers that are already trigger happy.

I glance quickly to my left and see a man charge at an officer with a lead pipe. He makes it six feet away from his target before a shot rings out.

I cringe in horror as the man, whose clothes are tattered and worn, falls to the ground, blood spurting from a bullet hole in his forehead.

I close my eyes and whisper, "I'm so, so sorry," but the man doesn't move. A tear leaks out of my shut eyes.

One life on my shoulders.

I open my eyes and focus on the spot between shields.

I start to run.

Another shot rings out. A scream follows.

My heart clenches but I don't turn to look.

Two lives.

Two more shots ring out. Two more screams. Two more tears fall.

Three, four lives.

I keep running.

Five...

I dive through the opening just as a group of men clashes with the police, distracting them.

My knees burn as they scrape against the white rock that marks the execution square, but I ignore the pain, leaping to my feet.

I turn to see that Sakura is already on top of the white wall, the ladder being removed as I watch.

I scream in frustration, momentarily turning to look for Jax in the crowd, hoping he has a plan, wishing for his calming presence. I meet his gaze as he's running through the crowd. He shakes his head, his eyes filled with pain. My face falls.

I look up at Sakura and start to sprint. Her eyes meet mine and she smiles—while her executioners line up in front of her—gesturing that she saw my exchange with Jax.

"I knew you would love him," she mouths at me.

My jaw drops open.

What nerve she still has even when facing death!

"I don't...I love you." I respond, my lips moving slowly so she can read them.

She makes an exaggerated face of disbelief. I almost laugh.

After a moment, she lips, "I love you, too, but it's okay to love more than one person, Kayda."

I snort.

She's approving my love life while guns are being pointed at her!

"Just hog all my love while you can," I want to scream at her, but I bite my tongue.

I need to focus on saving her now. I scan the line of Bullets. There is one row of them, with their leader on the right side, 200 meters away from me, ready to give the signal to shoot. If I can just knock him over, the rest will be disorganized and therefore the execution will be delayed. Then I will figure out how to get Sakura. I nibble my lip in hesitation.

Well... at least it's a plan.

I try to pick up my pace.

150 meters away.

Sakura stares at me, a sad smile on her lips.

She thinks I won't be able to save her, I realize.

I run faster.

I will.

90 meters.

I'm so close, I can see the pin on the head Bullet's shirt.

I look up and grin at Sakura. Her mouth opens in horror. She waves her arms at me, gesturing for me to get down. Confused I turn around, ready to duck if I need to, but before I can do anything, a searing pain envelops my right shoulder.

21

Crying out, I fall to my knees, darkness threatening to swamp my vision. I hear people screaming all around me, but I clench my teeth, already pushing myself off the ground with my left arm, making sure my hood stays in place.

Pain races up my arm swift as fire, and although I may have control of it for the moment, I understand that it is an enemy I can fight for only so long. The truth is, I'll probably pass out from blood loss or pain in a few minutes.

I sway, unbalanced, my knees on the verge of buckling, but I lock them, refusing to fall again.

Angry tears race down my cheeks.

I glance at my arm, a small opening ripped in my cloak allowing me to see a dark bloody hole close to the top of my shoulder. Rivers of blood gush out of it, dripping thickly down my cloak sleeve and splattering against the ground like drops of red paint.

My eyes widen in morbid fascination.

So this is what it's like to be shot.

I should probably apply pressure to it and tie a piece of clothing around the wound to staunch the bleeding, but I don't have time, and besides, I can always take the pain.

I grit my teeth with determination even as waves of anguish crash against me, each time stealing a bit of breath from my chest.

I start to run, my gait slow and awkward with my right arm swaying limply by my side, adrenaline pumping through my blood too fast for me to feel any real pain anymore.

Well then, all considered, getting hit by a bullet is not too bad.

Sakura's eyes stare at me, pleading for me to back down, but I can't, not now. Not when the lead executioner is raising his hand, ready to drop it and condemn a girl to death.

I shake my head.

Not now. Not ever.

I am ten seconds from tackling the captain, and I decide to swerve to the right so my left side will take the brunt of the impact when I knock him down.

A bullet whizzes by where I was a moment ago. It hits one of the executioners in the leg. He crumples to the ground and stays lying there awkwardly, groaning.

Got a taste of your own medicine, I think with grim satisfaction.

The other Bullets don't even react when their comrade slumps to the ground.

A shiver travels down my spine.

They're practically human robots.

I chase the thought away, focusing on my target. My strides lengthen and my muscles scream in protest. The pain from my arm sits like an elephant on my chest, making my breaths labored. But I keep going.

Once I am close enough, I lean on my back leg, using momentum to push off the ground—

The head Bullet whistles in preparation for the execution.

All the shooters pick up their guns.

Sakura's mouth hardens into a grimly determined line. Her thumbs lock above her head in the shape of a flying dove, and she shouts out, her voice strong and unflagging: "Steal your freedom bac—"

My feet leave the ground and I hurtle towards the head executioner, my heart being held together by hope, my stomach being chewed apart by doubt.

This is it.

The seconds drip by like honey from a spoon, giving my frantic brain plenty of time to calculate if the head Bullet will be able to raise his arm before I hit him. His hand twitches and my stomach clenches, but it's too late for him, I realize with a winning smile—right before my ribs knock into the back of a beautifully made red coat.

I did it.

The head Bullet sways before the force of my attack causes him to fully fall, and as I hit the ground, I smirk, imagining how his red coat will look covered in dust and dirt.

I relish his descent with satisfaction, watching as my enemy is pulled to the ground by gravity, utterly incapable of doing anything but watch himself fall into his line of soldiers, ruining their focus and concentration. My smile starts to grow—*maybe I can* really *save her now*—but immediately my lips draw back, my mouth opening in an anguished but silent cry, "*NO*".

As his body crashes into the dirt, his chest, his legs, his head, all parallel to the earth, one single arm is raised, the bloody knife that murders my hope.

22

I scream, a raw sound ripping out of my throat in agony.

This can't be happening. Not now. Not when I was so close...

Something inside me snaps, a barrier that has been slowly crumbling crashes to the ground. In its absence, some existence that recently opened its eyes from a long, long nap, finally stretches up, uncurling like mist in my chest. As it spreads out, yawning and shaking off the last vestiges of sleep, I swear I hear it whisper something, as clearly as if someone were talking directly to me.

Hello, Dear One.

My mind freezes in panic, but another part of me, a part I didn't know existed, cries out in joy, welcoming the *thing* that has awoken inside of me like a lost friend.

My brain fights itself, trying to figure out what part of me to trust, going back and forth between "*Yes, come out*" and "*There's an alien in my head!*"

I decide not to listen to any of it: I can figure out the *why* and *how* later. Now it's time to trust my heart.

And it's telling me to embrace whatever this thing is inside of me.

So I do.

Immediately warmth rushes through me, and I feel *whatever it is* seeping into my veins, into my heart, into me.

I clench my fists, dirt crackling beneath them, and focus my newfound power on my sister, on my determination to save her, on my love for her.

It all builds up like a tsunami wave, looking for land to crash against, and so I give it what it wants, an outlet.

I unclench my pale, bloodstained, and trembling fingers, spreading them wide against the ground. Taking a deep breath--*here goes nothing*-- I let go of the last hold I had on whatever is inside of me.

My back arches violently, my spine threatening to break through my skin, and I scream as raw energy bursts forth from my hands, golden and sizzling, dancing on my fingers like mini lightning bolts. It almost appears to be happy--if that's something that energy can be--like a genie released from its lamp after thousands of years.

I concentrate on Sakura, all other thoughts long dead and buried deep into my mind.

Save her, I scream in my head, and in the blink of an eye, the energy rushes away from my hands, pouring into the earth. As it leaves my body I feel a slight pull, and then a small twinge of pain, as if I had just pulled out a loose tooth.

As I'm pondering the odd feeling, a slight tremor vibrates out from under my hand, pulling my attention away. Immediately another shake courses through the earth but this time my whole body vibrates and I'm thrown roughly on my side.

A small smile manages to grace my lips, a little bit of hope growing inside my belly.

Shouts cry into the air, but I ignore them, focusing on the executioners, expecting them to be on the ground. All, but the one who was shot, are still standing.

I curse. My eyes starting to water. It wasn't enough. I WASN'T ENOUGH! My fists clench as anger and despair prickle hotly through my skin. I realize this is it. I have no more plans, no more tricks up my sleeves. I can't save her. I *can't*.

But I HAVE to. This isn't fair!

I slam my hands against the ground. Not even a small tremor responds. I try again. Nothing.

The Bullets move their fingers toward their triggers, organized once again.

My heart shatters and I crumple to the ground, my eyes flickering closed. My hope, if any remains, disappears.

My breathing becomes so shallow that I feel my lungs start to burn, gasping for air. I ignore the pain. What does it matter if I die now? Then I wouldn't have to watch this. My lip quivers, tears falling freely down my face.

If I don't die now from my gunshot wound, I will when I watch Sakura di... my mind won't let me finish the thought.

I curl in on myself. Maybe the world will just disappear, the gunshots fade away, the blood vanish if I close my eyes for long enough. Maybe Sakura won't be facing death, maybe my parents will be alive, if I just stay curled up here long enough.

You know that's not true, some part of me whispers.

I don't care, ANYTHING's better than this, I scream back, wrapping my arms around my legs tighter.

Are you sure?

Yes, I CAN'T WATCH THIS HAPPEN.

Have you really given up all hope?

That question causes me to hesitate, but after a moment I answer myself.

Yes.

Then you have failed her--

I KNOW THAT--

But not because you can't save her, but because you have given up while she is still alive...

I'm about to respond to myself when another voice starts talking; it's my dad's, reciting his favorite life lesson, his voice quiet but stern, the sound of the last page of a book being flipped: *Death is not something to be feared, but a moment that everyone must live through.*

I always thought it was foolish of him to say that one must live through death when they obviously were to die, but I finally understand what he meant. If you die afraid and a coward, many will remember you like that, but if you die with hope and joy, your spirit will live on; something that is much easier to do when someone you love is at your side.

23

My eyes immediately open, and I stand up, glad I'm not too late.

I glance towards the Bullets, watching nauseously as they start to press their fingers against their triggers, knowing that I won't stop them.

I turn away and don't look back, my eyes locking with Sakura's. Her hands are still raised in the air in the symbol of a dove, but they tremble ever so slightly and her face is trying and failing to hide her growing terror. Her proud shoulders curve inward, and although she is taller than I, her body looks impossibly small as she stands alone on that wall.

Tears well up in my eyes at the sight, but I push them away, and as best I can, I smile. Although I wish to say goodbye, I don't, knowing that it's a luxury I can't afford to take, one that would break Sakura's strength. And I won't do that to her. Instead, I mouth, "It's no fair, you look prettier in prison garbs than I'll ever look in any princess gown."

Her mouth opens in surprise, her full lips forming a small circle before turning into a smile, but I continue, "but, dirt, I can get a hot boyfriend and you can't!"

At that, she throws her head back and laughs, the sound coming out pure and beautiful. It's bubbly and wild and I love it, and I wish I made her laugh out of accident, but I didn't.

The first bullet hits her in the heart before the sound of her last laugh even reaches my ears. Tears stream down my face now, but I don't look away, I just keep my eyes on hers, a loving smile on my face, even as the bloody hole in her chest tears my own heart apart. The rest of the bullets penetrate her flesh, and she starts to fall off the wall, her main organs failing her one after the other until her heart finally shuts down, and her brain slowly stops sending out signals, once it realizes her body is no longer alive. But even though she's dead, for a second, when the sound waves yet to stop traveling through the air, I still hear her laugh.

THE COUNTDOWN…24 HOURS LEFT

The Countdown

Time: 9:00

My eyes at first refuse to open, a certain weight resting on them as if the invisible fingers of the universe are trying to hide some horror from me.

I thank whatever God that was trying to watch out for me, but I open my eyes anyway. It's best I know what's coming.

My eyelashes are damp and stuck together, the fragile skin around my eyes puffy. I've been crying.

Why?

My head bounces against a thick pole—no an arm, Jax's arm. He's cradling me against himself, my head tucked under his chin as he runs through dark streets, his feet hitting the ground quietly, his breath huffing gently.

For a moment I just gaze up at him admiring the chiseled line of his jaw, his mussed-up hair and his beautiful eyes—that are filled with agony and rimmed in pain. A chill crawls up my neck slowly, the feeling of wrongness settling in my gut at the sight.

I now notice the paths of fallen tears lining his cheek, the slight tightness of his jaw as if he's holding back a growing amount of anger.

My gut clenches and my mind resists one last time, but then it all comes back. No wonder God wanted me to keep my eyes closed and sleep away.

I wish I had.

I wish I never remembered.

But I do.

I remember the exact moment that the first bullet hit Sakura, splitting through the layers of her skin, delving into the core part of her body until it lodged itself into her heart, snuggling close like Doc to lead her back with him to Death's doorway.

I remember her body falling off the wall, dark hair spreading around her shocked face like a halo, her hand still in the shape of a dove as it fell into the sky, giving the symbol the appearance of flying away, free. If only that was true for Sakura.

But she was not ready.

She was too young, had too many things to still check off.

And yet life is not fair; she died anyway.

The thought is too horrible that I just want to somehow forget it for a moment.

I need to move, clear my mind.

I need to go for a run.

Immediately, I start struggling against Jax's arms, my legs kicking furiously in despair, yearning to hit the ground and carry me far away. But as soon as I start to raise my arm, a sharp pain rushes through me, blurring my vision to pinpricks. I yelp in agony.

"Kayda, your bullet wound caused you to faint from blood loss. I was only able to wrap it with part of my shirt I tore off. It won't hold for long, and the more you struggle, the more blood you will lose. So please just wait until we get back to the base where I can properly fix you up," Jax says, his words stiff and tightly reined in as if he has too much emotion and little control over it.

Watery tears start to form in my eyes as my helplessness becomes evident.

"What..." my voice wavers, "are we going to do now?" I ask, staring numbly at the faded-out buildings around me, my urge to flee subdued by a great sadness that feels like the small hand of my sister resting on my shoulder. But when I glance behind me, no one's there.

At the emptiness behind me, even though it was expected, my throat becomes sore, and I swallow dryly, my nose pinching up against the water puddling into my eyes.

I turn my head into Jax's chest, curling into his warmth, but not even his distinct scent of spices and wood manages to dissolve the lump in my throat.

His arms tighten around me as if he's trying to protect me from the pain of my own thoughts, but it's useless, my mind won't stop remarking on what I've lost.

"I've let them all down...not just Sakura," a tear slips down my cheek, "but everyone, everyone who dared to believe that we could change the city. I've let them all down."

More and more tears fall coldly onto my skin, and I close my eyes, hope finally leaving me. I sniffle, my nose starts to run, my breath becoming short and erratic as I dissolve deeper into grief.

Jax's steps slow and he comes to a gentle halt.

A warm hand cautiously brushes my cheek, gently wiping away my tears. He runs his fingers ever so kindly through my hair, untangling the dark heap, tucking it behind my ears and smoothing it back behind my head as I continue to sniffle and shudder. He softly presses a kiss to my forehead, causing my stomach to flutter even in my despair, and I find myself snuggling deeper into his arms.

He doesn't speak for a minute, just runs his fingers through my hair calmly, but then he clears his throat, straightens and slips his hand from my head to wrap around me.

I open my eyes slowly and he's staring into them. A feverish passion like a blazing fire burns in his eyes, lightning up the golden flecks in them like pieces of heaven. And for some reason, his expression reminds me of that day in the alleyway a long time ago when he first asked me to join the rebellion.

He starts speaking, his voice soft at first, but slowly gaining strength, "Don't give up on me yet, little dragon. I need you, more than you know. When I asked you to join my rebellion, I was the only member, but once you agreed to join, the tide suddenly turned: you found us a headquarters, supporters, and gave the rebellion a symbol. You made my dream come true," he pauses for a moment before continuing on, as if lost in a memory, "And a while ago, I, too, took a chance at dreams. I promised you that I would make one of your wishes come true: that you would always have a friend. And I swear Kayda, I will *never* leave you. I am here for you, and I know you lost your sister today, I know how hard that must be, but you still have me. You are not alone, Kayda."

His words swirl around me, soaring straight to my heart, and the ice that had slowly started to form over the muscle starts to melt. I am so consumed in his prior words that I almost don't hear him whisper, "I love you."

Immediately I tense up in surprise, but I don't even have time to truly process his words because he has already started speaking again.

"We can't give up, little dragon. No. We will finish this together. We haven't lost yet and I don't plan to. Look how far we have gotten, how many people we have inspired. We can't stop now--not when we are so close to the end! So come on, pick yourself up, find that inner strength I saw in you that first day you knocked me out," he smiles in remembrance, "and let's make this rebellion happen."

His hope grabs on to the last vestiges of mine, cradling the little bits back to life. But what really gets my heart beating again, is the sound of the whispered words, "I love you" that repeats itself over and over in my ears.

Against all odds, Jax somehow makes me want to believe again.

"We have followers, believers, supporters! We have equipment and money, a team, and a base! For Dirt's sake, the police think that the leader of the rebellion is dead, and for the next day, from nine a.m. now until nine a.m. tomorrow, they'll surely be hosting their customary celebratory party--those stupid cops who are so unused to trouble--partying after every small success! Well, their ignorance will keep them from seeing us coming until it's too late. After all, what could be a better time to finish what we started than now? So what do you say: are you ready to overthrow the entire lifestyle of this city in twenty-four hours?"

After everything I lost, Jax's words manage to take my mind off grief, stirring the same wild excitement in my gut for an adventure that I first felt when he asked me to join the rebellion. I suddenly crave the journey, the trials and tribulations, the shifting sands, the victory. If this is my life story, then this rebellion is the quest I was written to be the hero of. How could I possibly deny the chance at my own fairytale ending?

And so, there's no other choice for me than to say, "Yes."

THE COUNTDOWN...23 HOURS LEFT

Time: 10:00

"That speech of yours was all fine and dandy, but--ahhh," I growl in pain when Jax pulls a needle through my skin as he stitches up my bullet wound, "we still need a plan--and some better medical tools. You're lucky they shot me with a dissolving bullet. If you had to take a metal one out of my arm, I would be dead by now."

Jax just laughs, "At least *I'm* stitching you up, not Mr. Nervous hands over there," he says gesturing towards Leum who's pacing the room like a nervous wreck.

He pauses his frantic walk to shout back, "Well at least I was able to find you a needle and some thread!"

I sigh in annoyance, "Stop it you two. We actually have things to do and only a day to do it, so does anybody have any idea how we are going to turn things around in twenty-four hours?"

"Well," Jax says, tying a knot at the end of my stitches, "What do the rich people value the most?"

"Money!" Leum replies excitedly.

"Exactly," Jax concludes leaning back in his chair with a satisfied smile as if he single-handedly proposed a marvelous plan when in reality he literally just stated the obvious.

"So-what," I say, " we already knew that."

"So," Jax drawls, "all we have to do is," he puts his hands out to his sides and gives me a mischievous grin, "steal it."

THE COUNTDOWN...22 HOURS LEFT

Time 11:00

I scowl, "we already stole a thousand kimas a month ago!"

Leum helpfully chimes in with, "We did use more than half of that between creating more badges, procuring high-tech gadgets, and maintaining friendly relationships with those that supply me with those gadgets," and I shoot him a sharp look.

He raises his arms in mock surrender and theatrically replies, "What I meant was that it's a horrible idea to steal more money."

Jax chuckles. "The money's not for us. We have enough from that last job. I was thinking that we could hack into all the bank accounts--"

"Wow, wow, wow... that would be almost impossible!" Leum interjects.

Jax continues, "Just hear me out. If we hack into all the bank accounts, we can take money from the really rich and distribute it among the accounts of those who are either bankrupt or pretty poor--after all, every accounted citizen of the city that is of age is designated their own bank account for free. It's how the government keeps track of people around here. Of course, those who are really rich will still have more money than those who are poor: some of that money they, after all, earned and therefore, deserve it. Anyway, it would be unfair of us to force anyone to automatically go from a lavish lifestyle to a plain one in a day."

"But then there's more than enough money even if we give a good amount to each city person. What are we going to do with the rest of it?" I question.

"We'll make a new representative government and the rest of the money will go into rebuilding the city and its economy." After finishing his sentence, Jax leans back in his chair, his arms casually behind his head, his feet crossed and resting on the table: the exact picture of smug.

It bothers me, but I have to admit it's a pretty good plan, and we have no other options.

"Well, that *would* work, but... it's quite ambitious. I don't know if we could really pull it off," I ponder.

Leum adds, "I don't know how we would hack into all the bank accounts. There are thousands of people who live on the other side of the lake. Sure, not all of them are rich enough to spare that much money, but even so, that's a lot of people. Not even Kayda could hack into all those accounts."

Leum's words ring true, but I feel like there's another solution. Silence fills the air as we all think for a while, but then I realize that I might just have a solution.

"By myself, I could probably hack into the bank's mainstream, which then opens up the possibility to hack into any bank account, but I would never be able to get into all the bank accounts at one time...but if I assembled a group of about fifty hackers, we could probably do it in less than an hour!"

"There's the spirit, Kayda!" Jax exclaims, "Where are we going to find fifty hackers that are willing to work for free?"

"I know some people," I reply, this time the one to lean back in a chair, "who still owe me. However, we'll have to pay them a bit. After all, I already made some of them make us the badges for free."

"Alright, sounds good, lil' dragon. I guess we'll need to talk to them early today. Now, what else do we need to get figured out?" Jax asks.

"There's one more critical thing that must be done to transfer money from such a large number of accounts," Leum explains. "In the building, there is a hand scanner that must be activated when money on more than 5,000 accounts is being transferred. It was created so that no single hacker could just steal all the bank's money easily. Instead, we will have to hack *and* do a physical mission. The problem is, the handprint can only be that of the owner of the bank, and we have no time to find Mr. Grenell. The only other possibility is to heat the sensor up to at least 1,600 degrees Fahrenheit to deactivate its reading abilities, which is basically impossible to do on such a small surface and in little time."

I pause at the news, my heart starting to thump faster in my chest, my mind toying with a dangerous possibility.

Jax sighs, resting his head in his hands, "This is too complicated. You were right Kayda, we'll have to make another plan."

My body tenses, my mind spinning in frantic circles, weighing the disadvantages against the benefits, and yet, I can't help how my stomach clenches with a crazy sense of excitement.

We may never find a better plan after all. And...what have I got to lose? Besides, I owe this to the people of the city.

I finally make my decision, folding my hands in my lap, trying to contain my adrenaline and anxiety.

"No," I say.

Jax chuckles and smiles questioningly, "Are you saying you weren't right?"

I ignore him and continue, "No, I meant we don't need to make a new plan. I can do it. Leum will have to lead the hackers, but I can heat the hand scanner to 1,600 degrees... I *think*," my confidence wavers as I realize what I have committed to. What if I can't do it?

"How are you going to heat it up?" Leum asks curiously.

"I...uh...I have powers."

THE COUNTDOWN…21 HOURS LEFT

Time 12:00

"You have what?!?" Leum says incredulously as if he is sure he heard me wrong. Meanwhile, Jax just sits perfectly still, an astonished yet unsurprised look on his face as if my confession made something suddenly clear to him.

"I have… powers," I repeat, a bit nervously this time, the adrenaline of first sharing my secret seeping away from me.

A gasp breaks the silence, and Leum stands bewildered, his jaw opens as wide as a dog's at mealtime, staring at me, his eyes blinking slowly.

After a moment, the shock wears off, and he asks slowly, " I heard you right, didn't I? You said you have powers?"

I nod.

"But… I thought that only people in stories had powers. How is this possible?" he asks.

"Well, Jax is a se-," I stop mid-word at the look Jax shoots me, and I realize that he must guard his secret closely. After all, it took him a few months and a fight between us to tell me.

Not to make Leum suspicious, I rephrase the sentence, "Jax seems to believe me."

Jax nods at me in thanks, his eyes conveying "I'll tell you later," before he verifies my words, "It is extremely unheard of to have powers...but if Kayda thought it was important enough to tell us, it must be true."

Leum takes a step back, still in awe, his eyes squinting and then widening, his forehead scrunching, visibly showing the millions of thoughts that are running through his mind.

Finally, after a few minutes, trying to sound casual, he manages to ask, "so... what types of things can you do?"

His voice heightens on the last few words of the sentence, giving away his true excitement and curiosity.

Just to fool around with him, I reply, "Nothing, I was just joking about having powers!" Nimbly, I slide off the chair to sit on the floor, spreading my fingers wide in preparation. I steady my thoughts, focusing...

Instantaneously, his face falls in disappointment, but he tries to cover it up by chuckling, "Of course, you were! If you had powers that would have been insan-" his sentence is interrupted as the building gives a little tremble sending Leum clumsily crashing to the ground.

"What was that?!?" He exclaims looking from Jax to me.

A mischievous smile tugs at my lips and the sizzling of magic jumps back and forth between my fingertips.

Jax chuckles once, looking at me with a knowledgeable grin, but when he glances away, his face becomes occupied as if in deep thought.

Huh... I wonder what that's about...

A loud sound resembling a squeal that a young pig may make when racing toward a trough of fresh slop pierces the air, and I turn to see Leum jumping in excitement, his chest rapidly sucking in and expelling air.

I can't help a grin at his feverish elation, *I guess he finally put two and two together.*

"You, YOU!" he points at me, beaming, "YOU DID THAT!"

THE COUNTDOWN...20 HOURS LEFT

Time 13:00

"Uh-huh," I say amused.

"YOU ACTUALLY HAVE POWERS!!"

"Yep."

"But... that makes you like a... a GENIE!" He stops jumping and runs up to me, "Wait... can you grant wishes!?"

A snort tumbles from my nose, followed by a bout of genuine laughter, "No," I say, "I think if I could grant wishes, I would still have Sakura."

An uncomfortable silence follows my words--words that I didn't even intend to say.

"I'm sorry about Sakura, Kay-"

"It's fine. There's no time to grieve right now," I interrupt Leum quickly.

Another moment of silence stretches out uncomfortably, before Leum tentatively asks, "So it was you who made that earthquake this morning, wasn't it?"

"Yeah," I reply quietly, "but-"

"But it was DIRTY amazing, that's what it was!" exclaims Leum, looking around at us as if we are not awed enough, "Jax, isn't that incredible!"

"It is," he says looking at me intently, "it really is."

Not noticing Jax's serious tone, Leum barrels on, regaining his frenetic attitude, "so what else can you do?"

I rise up from the ground, stretching my arms over my head quickly, spreading my feet shoulder-width apart so I'm as stable as I can be. Air rushes in through my nose, and I exhale it out slowly, focusing on the simple act to clear my mind. After all, I need extreme focus for what I'm going to do next.

A sly grin urges my lips up at the insanity of this situation, and excitement hops around in my stomach. I've been so busy the last month, focusing on Sakura and the rebellion that I never even tested out my powers. I guess I'll figure out just how much I can do now.

Closing my eyes, I breathe in one last time, truly honing my thoughts on the very molecules of air that swish past my lips as I exhale, that brush against my skin, that sit on my shoulders. I focus, then after a minute, I can actually feel the presence of every air molecule in the room, tapping against furniture and whizzing around.

Carefully, I open my eyes. Glistening threads of blue and gold fill my vision, strung across the entire room like tinsel on a Christmas tree. However, the strands are finer than a web of a spider and are inextricably interwoven, thousands of times, as they string from one object to the next.

As I focus more intently on the lines composed of what appears to be pure, shimmering light, the seemingly random pull of the molecules in the room becomes a steady throbbing, synchronized with the beat of my heart.

The gold strands almost immediately curve toward me, and an odd feeling washes through my body akin to how cold water droplets feel as they slide off of warm skin.

Whispers fill my ears in an ancient language, and yet I seem to understand what they ask; *welcome the power, take in the energy, it is yours.*

And so, I let go of my reservations and open myself up to the threads of energy.

Immediately, gold light shoots toward me from the strands, puddling against my chest right above my heart, before slowly seeping into my skin and filling me with great warmth.

My blood starts to sing, and something within me stirs in excitement.

Energy continues to pour into me, and I inhale satisfied as if I have just consumed a great feast.

Bringing my thoughts back to my goal, I ignore the energy that puddles around me, instead looking for the molecules of air.

Spotting the bluish bronze strands of air, I narrow my vision so that I only see the ones that are directly around me.

With no other idea how to ask them, I think towards the strands: *gather around me closer.*

The bluish threads pulse once as if in acknowledgment and then immediately weave themselves tighter around me.

I gasp in surprise and a little laugh falls from my lips.

Curious I think: *make me fly.*

Faster than I can see, the strands rearrange themselves even tighter around me, especially under my feet, and in a second, I feel my toes leave the ground, supported by the softness of air.

This time a full-out laugh passes my lips. It tumbles into the air that holds me, loud and rich, and as the blue strands raise me higher and higher, I laugh harder in disbelief, a giddy joy washing over me akin to one I used to feel as a child on Christmas eve.

I'm actually FLYING!!

With a thought, I slow to a stop, floating in the air with my arms out to my sides as not to lose balance.

The glistening strands of energy gradually fade away, but I still feel the overall throb of the energy.

As my vision clears, I see both Jax and Leum staring up at me agape.

I guess even flying surprised Jax.

"You are literally a SUPERHERO, " Leum whispers almost as if to himself.

"Okay, I'm not *that* powerful," I respond rolling my eyes.

"Umm yes you are," he says pointedly, looking at my floating figure, "You can control earth, fly and... is there more? Can you control water?"

I scrunch my face in thought, remembering that night after Sakura was captured, when I sat in the rain for hours and felt as if every drop was comforting, the storm above me like a consolatory friend, "Maybe."

THE COUNTDOWN...19 HOURS LEFT

Time 14:00

Leum laughs excitedly and hurries off to the sink in the corner of the room.

Watching him fill up a bowl with water, I carefully try to fold my legs under me. With a little bit of wobbling, I manage to sit criss-crossed in the middle of the air.

Leum just shakes his head with another incredulous laugh as I slowly lower myself to his level, and I can't help but grin.

I guess this is pretty cool.

Instead of directly taking the bowl from him, I concentrate on the water. Soon the glimmering threads come back into my vision, but I quickly let them fade away except for the silvery blue ones of the water.

I focus on the shimmering strands until I feel their pulse line up with mine. This time, instead of whispering, I simply move my right hand, gesturing to the water to rise from the bowl.

In one smooth motion it does, forming a watery sphere in the middle of the air.

Shocked, Leum loses his hold on the glass bowl and it starts to tumble to the ground. Instinctually I reach out my left hand as if to catch it, but instead of my fingers grabbing around the bowl, a gust of air does.

Stunned by my own skill, I barely manage to hold onto the sphere of water long enough to safely deposit it into the bowl, which I float back to land gently in Leum's hands.

Once the bowl is secure, I lower myself the rest of the way to the ground, stretching out my legs to land quietly, the tingling in my shoulders receding to a hum.

"So you control earth, air, water, and … fire, don't you?" Leum asks breathlessly.

I nod.

Silence enters the room as the magnitude of my gift becomes apparent.

This is not just a skill that could come in handy during bar tricks.

This is true power.

THE COUNTDOWN...18 HOURS LEFT

Time 15:00

"I can't believe this," Leum mutters in awe, pacing the room like some little kid with excess energy to spend, "I know a DIRTY SUPERHERO."

"I haven't actually saved anyone yet," I grumble with a smile, sitting relaxedly on the floor. A breeze slides into the room, playing with my hair like the gentle hands of a mother, and I shiver, cold at its feathery touch. Spotting a black sweatshirt next to me, I pull it on, only realizing that it's Jax's once I'm wearing it.

Jax, who, of course, saw me put it on, raises his eyebrows playfully at me.

I just blow him a kiss with a smirk in return, settling happily into the warmth of the oversized item of clothing.

*It's kind of nice to have a boyfriend...*I glance nervously at Jax at the thought...*if that's what we are.*

Leum keeps muttering excitedly to himself, "Can you make snow?! Oh that would be so cool because we could eat snow cones in the summer. But it would be awesome if you can boil water because then we could cook pasta so quickl-"

"Leum, we have to focus," I say rolling my eyes at him.

"But, there are so many cool things you haven't even tried to do yet!"

Amusedly, I reply, "We'll have time to try things out after we finish this revolution."

"Fine," he says, "but promise you'll make me a snow cone in the summer?"

With a laugh, I answer "Sure. But now, we should really go meet with the other hackers we need." Using the map on the table, I thoroughly point out the location of the people that Leum should visit and then those that Jax should meet with.

"Alright, everyone good with where they have to go? I'll be meeting and contacting the last few people I think may help. Remember, don't bring cash on you, that's like asking to be robbed. Instead, offer them the money for the job and when you get back, we'll transfer it to their bank accounts. And make sure you are back here in two hours, these should be quick negotiations! Don't let these guys give you any dirt. Got it?"

"Sounds good, Kayda. I'm going to head out now," Leum says, putting his coat on and walking out the door, "good luck guys!"

As Leum leaves, I quickly send out brusque emails to the hackers who don't have actual addresses, offering them the job.

It shouldn't be long until they reply.

After all, a hacker is almost always online, trying to bring down some online monarchy or regime.

Sending out the last email-using my *dragon* account--I pick up my four knives from where they lay on the windowsill, tucking each and every one into their rightful spots, breathing out a prayer every time one of the four metal blades whispers against my skin: *for strength, for stealth, for protection, for forgiveness.*

As I turn to leave, Jax calls my name, "Can I talk to you for a minute?"

Bemused at the hesitation in his voice, I swing around to face him, curious.

His jaw is relaxed, a large grin pulling at his cheeks, and the gold in his eyes sparks in excitement, but his forehead is scrunched in thought as if he has the greatest news to share but doesn't quite know how to go about it.

Exasperated by his silence which only serves to mount my curiosity, I snap at him, "Spill already!"

With a chuckle, his shoulders relax and he falls into a large chair behind him lazily, "I just wanted to make sure I phra—"

"Get to the POINT. You're killing me with this suspense."

"Fine," he teases, "you can keep your fire to yourself little dragon!"

I just glare at him.

"Alright, don't get mad at me. I couldn't tell you this before because I was under oath—"

"Oath?" I ask bewildered, "What oath, and who forced you to take it?"

"I took an oath to not tell anyone about well…" he gets up to face the window, his defined shoulders tense once again, "my home, and I wasn't forced to take it, I chose to," and then in a soft and amused tone, he mumbles to himself, "actually, I practically begged to go on the journey."

Now, even more confused, I stutter, trying to put words to my thought, "What are you talking about?! Jax, I don't understand what you're getting at. Maybe it's just me, but you're talking like a complete alien!"

He doesn't directly respond to me but instead lets out an aggravating chuckle. "I kind of am an alien!"

I take a demanding step towards Jax, my ignorance flaring to anger as the drops of my patience slowly dribble to a stop, "Jax!"

Upon seeing the look on my face, his easy-going manner flees, replaced with deep seriousness, "Kayda, I'm not from around here."

THE COUNTDOWN...17 HOURS LEFT

Time 16:00

An incredulous laugh sucks the air from my lungs as it bursts out, making my words choppy and thrown in between giggles, "What does that mean!?! Are you saying you're a green alien with little antenna hiding underneath that hair?!" The bizarre thought starts a whole new bout of laughter, and small mirthful tears spring to the corners of my eyes.

What could he even be talking about? "I'm not from around here"!

"I mean," he continues, taking a small step towards me, but at the same time leaning backward, opposing movements, "that this," his finger traces the boundaries of the city on the map "is not... everything."

My feet guide me a reluctant step forward, as a spoonful of unease mixed with a large bucket-full of hope sloshes in my stomach. "You mean—," my eyes meet his wild, passionate ones, and immediately I know that what was unsaid is true.

The air becomes suddenly light, my tongue dry, as the truth of my whole life, my whole world comes crashing down around me. And yet, as I watch the buildings and walls I built over the years, from facts that I had known to be true, tumble into debris, I don't shed a single tear. No, when it all falls down to dust, I smile, a wide, mischievous smile, and breathe in, perhaps, my first full breath in my entire life: my cage has cracked open and now, I am finally able to spread my wings, a dragon free to fly away.

"How? Where? Who?" I walk towards Jax excitedly, the questions popping into my head as abundant as crystals of sugar on a brioche bun.

"I can't really tell you yet... that's not my job."

"Are you kidding! You can't just tell me this and then expect me to not want to know! And what job and journey do you keep talking about anyway?" I demand, a hand resting accusingly on my hip.

Seemingly undaunted by my words, Jax responds, "I came here to find you."

Confounded, I blurt out "Why me?"

"You're a legend, a prophesied leader," I almost interrupt, a scoff already breaking through his words, but he barrels on before I can further stop him, "and I wasn't sure at first that I had found you, but your power, its unmistakable, and the shimmer to your skin...it all fits the prophecy"

He trails off, a moment of silence passing before he continues, "I found you."

The rawness of his last words catches me off guard, and the questions I was ready to ask, melt on the tip of my tongue.

Jax swallows, and then turns his dark eyes on me, "I know my lack of explanation is going to kill you, but you have to trust me when I say, I can't tell you yet. The time will come, but it is not now. Can you trust me?"

I pause at his words, at the carefully hidden hope in his expression, the small intake of air that he is retaining in anticipation. In fact, a laugh bubbles up when I notice the worry etched into his tender smile.

He has no idea.

A few months ago, I wouldn't have risked turning my back on Jax, not sure of what he would do when I wasn't looking. For dirt's sake, a few months ago, I was sure that it would take years for Jax to gain my trust!

But now…

I am hopelessly dependent on him, affected by his every word, waiting on every one of his touches.

I don't just trust Jax, I need Jax.

And that is a much scarier truth.

And so for once, I don't even argue, I just smile and affirm his hopes with one single word because after all, it would be pointless for me to try to resist the one truth within my life of falsehoods, "Yes."

THE COUNTDOWN…16 HOURS LEFT

Time 17:00

Now, away from Jax's presence, the warm blanket of nerves and excitement that always seems to muddle my thoughts when I am around him, lifts, and instantaneously questions start flying into my head as I make my way to my last contact.

What place is he talking about?

What is the prophecy he mentioned?

Why did he say my skin has a shimmer to it?

But the two questions that keep coming back, no matter how many times I try to discard them are:

Did he really mean what he whispered to me as he carried me back to the base?

And…

How would I respond if he said those three words again?

The thoughts send hot prickles down my skin, and I automatically bow my head in shame, although no one can hear them.

For dirt's sake, I am not some star-crossed girl who can't focus on the task at hand! I am a warrior.

I try to prove the statement true by eradicating all thoughts of Jax, but it's useless. He's permanently ingrained in my mind.

Fine...I'm just a warrior who naturally likes to relive happy moments in her life...like her first kiss.

I bite my lip as a sly smile spreads across my face, heat flaring in my cheeks as for probably the one-hundredth time I close my eyes and imagine Jax's soft lips ever so gently pressing against the flutter of my pulse just below my collar bone.

The bliss is short-lived though, for following the vision is a rush of guilt taking the image of a small girl, her hair fanned out as she falls, blood splattered across her chest, bullet wounds violently littering her body.

The vision is so real, so detailed that I cannot help but tear up, trying futilely to reach out and hold her to me.

But just like in reality, I'm too far away.

Too late.

Destined to uselessly watch her die.

But in this vision, when her eyes meet with mine, they are not mirthful, stuck in a laugh, but instead, the corners are creased in horror, her mouth open in shock, halfway to a soundless scream.

But the worst part, my very fear, is the disappointment and hurt that paints her pretty blue eyes.

In this nightmare, she falls feeling unloved.

Unnoticed.

Alone.

And as her broken body finally disappears beyond the wall, I swear I hear her voice whispering in my ear, "Why didn't you save me?"

The vision fades rather quickly, but I can't fully shake the image of her lonely eyes fading in death, blaming me for not being fast enough, smart enough, dedicated enough to save her.

Shudders wrack my body even as her eyes finally disappear, replaced by old buildings and quietly walking people. They stare at me as I shake, as tears plink onto my cheeks, as I fold my hands together and blink up at the sky, whispering "I'm sorry, I'm so sorry, I'm just so so sorry."

After a while though, I stretch my wobbly muscles and rise from the ground. Wiping the tears from my eyes with dirty fingers, smearing the dust and sweat of the city onto my face, I make a promise, which I will spend the rest of my life trying to fulfill, whispering it up to the heavens--for once truly believing that such a place exists--with firm resolve:

"I will make this world worthy of your sacrifice, Sakura. I promise I will make you proud every single day of my life."

THE COUNTDOWN...15 HOURS LEFT

Time 18:00

People swarming the scene like ants.

Hawkers shouting out their goods.

Thieves snatching coins and purses.

Just what I expected.

I deeply inhale the warm and sticky scents of sweat, *pao douce* buns and spices in comfort, trying to wrap myself in the frantic, colorful energy of the evening market, but even all the hustle and bustle can't make me forget. Besides, I made a promise and I intend to keep it.

Slithering through the crowd, I head ever so slightly south, only stopping when I break through to the edge of the mass, finding myself at the start of a long row of quaint little shops.

The air is thinner here, cleaner, crisper as if somehow the shop owners sweep it like they do the street in front of their property.

It is not surprising, though, for I have been here many a time.

But today, the crisp air serves to fill my lungs up confidently.

In the shadows of the orderly buildings, I start to walk.

I don't rush or drag my feet.

I don't tiptoe or stomp.

I don't blend with the shadows, or hide at the edge of the crowd.

No.

For once, I casually stroll, my feet unhurried, my shoulders relaxed, my breaths even.

Down the perfect street, I walk with the perfect gait.

I finally slow to stop once I reach a storefront I thought I would never see again.

Grand red doors stand tall, straightening and fixing their lavish coats under my gaze.

I smile at the flowing golden letters swirled onto the faded red sign which reads *Apothecary* even as a rush of emotions swirl inside me: joy, sorrow, pain, fear, longing.

For a moment, I just glance through the windows at the plants that still cling to the rafters and grow so thickly on the bookshelves, at the towers of books, and the shelves of dusty novels, encyclopedias, and textbooks. I look at the black table covered in vials, the tall ladders affixed to the bookshelves, the little pillow in the corner where I used to spend hours reading and playing games with Sakura. After a minute of reminiscing, I almost turn away.

For me, I've seen enough to find peace.

But it's not about me.

It's about Sakura, about the people who live and die each day struggling for equality.

People who need more than just a glance through the windows.

A pretty jingle of chimes sounds as the door swings shut behind me.

THE COUNTDOWN...14 HOURS LEFT

Time 19:00

I don't make my steps silent as I walk into the store, but instead, I let the thumps and the chimes announce my presence, walking in confidently.

After all, what have I to fear?

As I wait for the store owner to extricate himself from whatever book he is observing in some musty corner, I walk nearer to his desk, glancing at the titles of the books that are strewn all over it: *The Adventures of Pittacus Thindle, The Hope of the People and How to Raise It, War Strategies.* Curiously, I notice that there is one book without a title. Inching closer, I notice that it is not so much a book, but one of Fumihiko's notebooks that I now see he has labeled in small black letters as "A Documentation of--" my attention is diverted by the sound of shuffling footsteps behind me.

An old man with peppered hair and laughing wrinkles around his eyes turns out of one of the rows of bookshelves. His thin arms grasp fervently onto a large stack of books that puffs out a cloud of dust every time he takes a step, causing the old man to let out a great cough.

Once he regains the ability to speak, the man walks towards his desk and gracefully says "Pardon my tardiness, I was just so consumed in an old book that I haven't looked at in a while," he carefully rests the books in his arms on his desk before excitedly continuing on, "It's about the studies of a young archeologi-" the word dies on his tongue as he finally looks up to see who exactly is visiting his store.

A shocked expression settles on his old face, his twinkling golden-brown eyes suddenly filling with sorrow and regret.

Unsure of what to say, I greet him how I used to, although a bit more formally, "Konnichiwa, Fumihiko."

Some of the worry in his expression disappears, but plain shock still holds his mouth slightly open. After a moment he quietly says, "I thought you were never coming back."

"I thought so, too, but it seems our paths have crossed again."

He nods and looks away as I speak as if my response was what he expected.

A moment of silence fills the room, and for the first time I actually feel a tendril of uncomfortableness in Fumihiko's presence.

I'm not sure where we stand.

I now realize that it was not fair of me to blame him for giving up on Sakura. After all, with his simple remedies and my constant care, her body did manage to fight the sickness off by itself. But I still don't believe he should've stopped trying to find a better cure.

So now that I am finally seeing him after all that has happened, I don't know whether to hug him or to yell at him.

He makes the decision for me, rushing around his desk and throwing his arms around me in a flurry.

At first, I stiffen at his touch, surprised by the outward show of affection, but after a moment my boundaries disappear, and I lean into the touch of a man who used to be as close as a father to me.

I missed him.

My arms wrap around the old man, holding his small frame steadier. He seems thinner, frailer, than just a few months ago, and the thought worries me.

Could he be sick?... No, it's probably just old age.

I'm about to ask him if he's getting enough to eat when I feel his body shudder.Terrified that he is about to pass out or throw up, I wrap my hands around his shaking arms so that I can guide him to his seat, but when I pull away, asking, "Fumihiko, are you okay?" I notice the tears streaming down his normally jovial face, the confusion of emotions painting his scrunched-up eyes.

Relieved to see that his health is in no immediate danger, I breathe out a relieved sigh, but almost immediately, my thoughts grow tender as I watch him cry.

I gently shift back into a hug, rubbing his back gently. "What is it Fumihiko?"

He sniffles and a cough shakes his body, but then he responds quietly, his voice sounding small and fearful, ¨I thought you were dead.¨

Reality washes coldly over me as for the second time today, I am reminded of what happened just this morning.

"They announced your name and then I saw them force you up on the wall--I was so far in the crowd I couldn't do anything and then people crowded in front of me so thickly, I couldn't even see you. I only heard--" he pauses, fresh tears falling down his face, "the gunshots and the howls of the people behind me. And when the square cleared there was nothing, just the retreating backs of the Bullets. I thought that I had...lost you."

He grabs me to him harder, as if unsure if I really exist. The action causes me to wince in pain, my shoulder throbbing at the contact.

Oblivious to my discomfort, he pulls back anyway, wiping the tears from his face, putting himself back together as fast as he fell apart, becoming every bit an apothecary and scholar again, questioning what he learned, "But how *did* you escape?"

Softly, I let go of Fumihiko, retreating back towards his desk, my face angled into the darkness. When finally I speak, the words come out so very softly as if I dare not to say them too loud, lest they become reality. "It wasn't me up there… It was," my words fail me and

I turn to Fumihiko, my eyes pleading with him to understand, to spare me the pain of speaking such a horrible truth.

He pulls in a ragged breath, the relief that blossomed in his eyes upon learning of my well-being, empties to a fearful blankness, a look of disconnection, of buried pain.

I barely hear his words when he speaks, “It was her wasn’t it?”

THE COUNTDOWN...13 HOURS LEFT

Time 20:00

The slight raising and lowering of my head is perhaps the most difficult thing I have ever done.

And the expression of plain grief that bleeds onto his face following it, I can only imagine mirrors my own face. Although I bet I look even worse.

A small hard tear dribbles its way down his cheek, taking its careful time to fall to the ground.

We both stare silently, watching it splat against the hardwood floors, its beautiful spherical body destroyed immediately upon impact. A beautiful droplet destined to die.

I stare at its broken little body until my eyes blur too greatly with tears for me to see.

Thin fingers strongly guide my face upwards, so that my reluctant eyes inevitably meet Fumihiko's. He puts a hand on my shoulder, and I can't help but wince. His eyes take it all in, noticing my moment of pain, analyzing my sorrowful face, the tears that pool in my eyes, the slight stoop of my shoulders. A moment of silence passes before

Fumihiko's words fly in brazenly, like the wings of a phoenix battling against a raising storm.

"My brave girl. My strong fighter. You are a true *senshi*." He steps forward slowly, his hand coming to cup my face, his long-calloused index finger ever so softly wiping a tear that manages to fall from my cheek. "Oh my child, you fought for her, didn't you?" He looks purposefully at my shoulder.

I nod. Sucking in air, my breaths become fast and uneven as I am submerged into the icy cold memory of this morning.

Will I ever escape her death?

The soft touch of fingers sketching out a certain pattern against my palm draws my attention away from my grief.

"Your mother and father would be so proud," Fumihiko says slowly, continuing to trace the pattern against my palm, a method he always used to soothe me as a child, "You have fought. You have lost. But even now, injured and in mourning, I see that you have not laid down your arms. So, I am sure when I say that Sakura is only proud to have you as a sister."

At his last words, I heave in a large, shaky, breath, my worst fear finally denied.

Sakura doesn't blame me. She knows I tried. She knows I would never abandon her. That I miss her every second I live knowing that she doesn't.

She knows I love her.

I dry my tears, still my wobbling jaw, and silence my sniffles.

In the quiet of my courage, I listen to the beat of my very much alive heart. Finally, I hear it.

You gave me love and then you were forced to leave, Sakura. But now I realize, your love never went away. You prepared me for this moment, giving me enough love to last a whole lifetime without you, enough to give to others, enough to fight with.

And so I will.

I straighten up, pulling my shoulders back, setting my jaw, an ever-so-small grin daring to pull at the corners of my lips, "Although it was nice seeing you again, I bet you know I didn't just come to see your wrinkly face," Fumihiko laughs at my barb, his eyes sparkling with pride, his lips mouthing *that's my brave little* senshi, "I came because I need your help for the rebellion."

THE COUNTDOWN…12 HOURS LEFT

Time 21:00

"I can't believe you are the head of a rebellion! Do I have to call you something different? Should I be saluting?!" Fumihiko's amused voice and smooth laugh repeat in my head causing a smile to blossom on my face as I quickly walk through the alleyways, heading back to the *Library,* night air gently tickling my face.

The meeting was as successful as it could have been. I recounted all that had happened since I last saw him--which was a lot--and asked him to spread the word around, to get his other scholar friends writing papers about the rebellion and to make the people believe that I, in fact, am not dead. What surprised me was that Fumihiko had already been recording the actions that we in the rebellion had taken in the very journal I had seen on his desk. Immediately, once I had been able to read the title: "A Documentation of the Freedom Thieves", I asked why exactly he had recorded the rebellion.

If any man were to record history before it became history, it would be Fumihiko, but I still wanted to know why.

Flipping the small notebook open, the front of which was embellished with a small bird frantically flapping its wings, chained to the ground, a rising sun behind it, Fumihiko answered without thought, his voice fiery with passion and awe: "What you have achieved so quickly..." he waves his arms in the air, a large grin on his face as he searches for the right words, "It's simply incredible, astonishing, a thing of fairy tales, even! Something as pivotal as this, something that could change our whole city--whether this rebellion fails or not--it *has* altered the future, and therefore, it is by earth, worth writing down!"

I laughed at his excited response and his use of "earth," the polite version of "dirt".

What an old scholar he had become!

But at the same time, his words had warmed my heart. I was always the one giving hope to others, making the motto and symbol of the rebellion that ignited fight in the hearts of the city people.

And so, I always wondered how it would feel if I were not the one heading the rebellion.

If I were still just a simple, poor orphan girl with a younger sister.

Dreaming like the rest of the city for something else, for something better.

How it would've been to hear that change was coming, to be swept up in the excitement and feverish hope.

His simple words had made me feel akin to how I imagine I would've if I were just an ordinary person learning that something extraordinary was coming.

They reminded me of what I started all this for:

Change.

Fumihiko told me that if I don't win this last battle, I will still have achieved my goal.

Well, news like that...the type that confirms a dream coming true...that does something to a person.

It relaxes them.

Appeases them.

Fills them with eternal joy.

Too bad I made another dream at the moment that Jax told me there was more.

To think I could have been peaceful and content now.

A giggle bubbles up my throat as I burst into a run, turning onto the street of the *Library*.

Like I could ever be calm.

THE COUNTDOWN...11 HOURS LEFT

Time 22:00

"Leum! Jax!" I call out, swinging the door open, "Hey!"

Leum turns around when I enter, a nervous smile on his face.

"What's with the face?" I ask, and then teasingly add, "Did one of the hackers beat you up?"

Leum scowls, but my attention is diverted as I glance behind him looking for someone else. I scan the room, "Where's Jax?"

At my words, he starts to pace, his eyes growing a little fearful, "He's gone."

"What do you mean gone?"

"Well I got back before both of you and transferred the designated money to the confirmed hackers. Once I had done that, I decided that I should just look over the plan--you know double check our facts--"

"Yeah okay, so how does this relate to Jax?"

Leum shoots me an annoyed look for interrupting him before continuing on, "Well as I was researching the hand scanner, I realized that if you heat it up too much, the system will fry, and the bank will be permanently locked."

"Okay so I won't heat it up too much!"

"Well, think about it, your Lynk will record your temperature so you'll know when you have reached 1,600 degrees. But to get your hand that hot, you will have to focus all your energy on it, and at that point, your hand will be heating up so fast that you probably couldn't even stop it from getting too hot before it's too late. Such a task requires *immense* control."

"I can do it," I say my voice coming out determined, although on the inside I am not really so confident. After all, I basically just discovered my powers yesterday.

"Well Jax didn't want you to worry about it, so he left to go to his place where he said he had something that would help you concentrate your power."

"What?!"

Leum backs away from me, his hands fidgeting with his shirt. He looks nervous.

And rightfully so.

"'How could you have LET HIM GO?!!"

"He-he insisted… saying you needed--"

"I DON'T CARE."

"But-"

"You do realize that Jax has been sleeping here for months because his house is being watched 24/7 by the DIRTY POLICE! He was a criminal to the government before me and look at what they did to Sakura--who they thought was me! Do you remember what happened this morning?!"

He swallows and nods his head frantically, curling into himself, trying to hide away from my anger and despair.

"THEY KILLED HER. SHE'S," my voice fades away, sorrow causing it to die down to barely a whisper. "She's dead Leum. She's dead! And I can't lose two people I lo--" I stop myself realizing what I was about to say, smoothing over my words. "I just can't lose two people in one day!"

I run to the table, grabbing my backpack where I left it. Quickly I make sure all my knives have not moved from their positions.

“I’m sorry Kayda,” Leum whispers, “I didn’t realize how dangerous it was for him.”

I turn around and walk right up to him, our eyes meeting--mine wild, his ashamed. “I understand, okay? But we can’t change the past. He’s already out there now--alone. And he needs my help if he’s going to get out of this. Alright? So can you please tell me which way he went?”

Without hesitation he replies, “Left, in the direction of the south wall.”

Before Leum even finishes the sentence, I’m running out the door. Faintly, I hear him call out, “What should I do?”

“Wish me luck,” I yell back.

I’ll be needing it all.

THE COUNTDOWN...10 HOURS LEFT

Time 23:00

I run through the darkened streets. A gust of wind sweeps mourningly across the buildings' roofs, and the normal chatter of the city's nightlife is non-existent as a cold chill drives even the liveliest of spirits into their beds.

And yet, I ignore the sensation, blasting through the somber mood like a knife through water.

Wind streaks by me and turns back to propel me forward, sending me running forward as fast as possible without my feet completely leaving the ground.

Unfortunately, I decided that flying would be too noticeable.

Besides, the familiar pounding of my feet against the rough asphalt road calms my nerves.

As I run, my breaths measured and even, I think of all the possible solutions I could be sprinting into:

Jax could be perfectly safe or

He could already be caught or

Policeman could be chasing after him or

He could be hurt...

The list goes on and on, but too soon my thoughts lead me to the fearful truth that Jax might not escape, that I might have to say goodbye...a thought that both almost kills my heart in sorrow and jump-starts it in panic...I can't lose him, but what would I say to him if he had to go?

You're insane!... Why would you go back to your house when you knew it was being guarded?... How could you do that to me?... I need you...You know I can't live without you... I lov-

I'm running so fast, my thoughts wheeling around trying to figure out what I would say, that I don't see the guy until he's slamming into me. We collide, and I stumble back into the nearest alleyway at the force of the hit.

Even before I fully regain my balance, I assume a fighting stance, cursing annoyedly, "Why do random strangers always have to knock into me?"

The strange runner turns with a large grin, the golden flecks in his green eyes glowing mischievously: "Hey, darling, I'd love to talk and all, but I didn't slam you into a wall for nothing. There are people chasing me."

Immediately, relief washes over my body releasing some of the tension in my shoulders. With a laugh, I wrap my arms around him, squeezing tight. My words muffled in his shirt, I tease, "You know, you used to be a lot more annoying."

Jax chuckles, but pulls me farther into the alleyway, glancing carefully around us.

Noticing his vigilance, as if he is looking for pursuers, I automatically stiffen up, heightening my senses: "How long do we have?"

"Five, six minutes if we're lucky," he says his grin fading.

"Alright, then we have to come up with a plan," I say shifting, about to take inventory of what's in my backpack, but Jax stops me, a hand resting on my arm.

"It's too late-"

"It's never too late-"

"Kayda, they are dispatching officers throughout the entire city as we speak, searching street by street for me. There's only a matter of time before they get me or find the *Library,* and I can't let them do that."

"But we can-"

"Please don't make this harder than it is. I'm already so glad that you're here...I thought," he looks away for a moment, his right hand drifting up to run through his hair, "I thought I would have to leave without seeing you."

"Jax, we can't give up-"

"And I'm not Kayda. I'm doing this so you can succeed--"

"I won't do it without you," I say stubbornly, annoyed that he can't see the mistake he is making.

"Oh but you will. It'll be amazing...you'll free the people, straighten out the city, but I won't be there."

"Yes YOU WILL," I say between clenched teeth, trying and failing to move his body toward the fire stairwell on the side of the building.

"Kayda, I wouldn't leave you unless I had to, okay?" he says softly, taking my hand is his, "And I must. For your own good. They won't stop until they find me, and the longer I let them look, means there's more of a chance that they will find you, too, so please just let me have this moment. You know I'll leave whether you approve or not."

The pleading look in his eyes, combined with his determined words crumbles my resolve, and I sink into his arms.

"But I need you," I whisper against his chest.

He shakes his head proudly, "No you don't."

I cling to his shirt, tears welling in my eyes, sucking in quick and shallow breaths: "I can't lose two people in one day. It's not fair."

Jax's arms tighten around me, and one of his hands comes to gently caress my head, the strokes slow and calming, "I know. It's not fair. This world isn't fair. Someone like you should never have to lose so many people. But I know that you're strong. You won't just live on, you'll change the world for the better. I believe in you, Kayda. You can do this"

I sniffle, looking up at Jax's beautiful face in despair, a sob escaping my mouth "But you can't leave me. You can't die. You promised me that you would always be there for me!"

He wipes the tears from my cheeks tenderly and lifts his mouth in a thin smile, "Who said I was gonna die? I've still got some tricks up my sleeve. After all, I did tell you that this city was not all that there is."

My eyes widen in hope, and I search his eyes for any sign that he is lying, but I only find warmth and sorrow.

In the distance, a siren wails.

Immediately, Jax lets go of me and procures a pair of gloves from his jacket, quickly handing it to me, "These will help you control your power."

A small broken laugh passes my lips as I finger the seemingly normal gloves, "This is what you're dying for."

"Not dying," he corrects, reaching behind his neck and unclipping the small silver chain that is always there.

He presses it into my hand and looks directly into my eyes. "Squeeze this necklace three times and concentrate only on where you want to go, and it will bring you there. Only use it when you absolutely have to because it will only work once, okay?"

I shake my head, trying to shove it back into Jax's hand, "You need it more than I do. You could use it to get home!"

His eyes tighten and he looks down for a moment, regaining his composure, but he continues to refuse the necklace, "Don't worry about me little dragon. I can take care of myself."

"So can I," I say thrusting the silver chain at him.

His eyes soften and he lets his lip wobble, "Well then, it is my death wish that you take it."

Annoyed, I tuck the gloves in my backpack and let Jax clip the necklace around my neck, whispering, mockingly to him, "I thought you weren't gonna die."

"Maybe not," he whispers against my neck, causing a shiver to scurry down my skin, "But I knew if I said it was my last wish that you would do it. Oh how much you care for me," he teases, placing his hand on my cheek.

A siren wails again, this time louder.

I start to turn towards the opening of the alleyway, but Jax gently shifts my face back towards his.

He stares at me for a moment, tracing a finger gently along my lips, down my nose, and over the scar on my left cheek, as if trying to ingrain the image of me into his mind.

It's funny because I do the same, focusing on every detail of his beautiful face--the angelic curve of his lips, the hard line of his jaw, the length of his dark eyelashes, the way the four gold flecks in his right eye and the five ones in his left shine as he looks at me. I soak it all in, and after a moment, I can't bare the truth that he is leaving me.

Perhaps forever.

But then he leans in, erasing the space between us, and all thoughts leave my mind.

We become one and the same.

Our hearts beating together.

Pure emotion and longing.

His lips move holily against mine, wrapping peace around me like a blanket.

My fingers slide into his hair, and I draw him closer.

Our mouths are gentle, our thoughts fevered as all our pain, anguish, longing, and affection is poured into this one kiss.

Perhaps it lasts for only a moment, but I live in the bliss as if it spans over an eternity.

Jax whispers three words against my lips that I will never forget, his voice gravelly and deep, his warm hand perfectly cupping my cheek, his scent of pine and spices deliciously wrapping around me: "*I love you.*"

An incredible warmth spreads through me, flaring my heart to fire. I burn at the sound of the three words, love making my soul glow brighter than magic ever could.

And I can't help but think that maybe this is my happy ending. This impossible moment birthed in a time of loss.

It's not exactly how I imagined it would be. But it is true that I have never been happier than I am now--in this alleyway, at the edge of falling apart, as time ticks towards midnight on the day my sister died.

Isn't it funny how the world works?

Finally, Jax's lips leave mine, and he steps towards the entrance of the alleyway, gesturing for me to climb a building and disappear to never see him again.

I intend to tell him how I feel, but for some reason the wrong three words come out of my mouth: "Is this goodbye?"

He turns back towards me, outlined in starlight like some angel from the old tales, and looks at me with his iconic mischievous grin: "Oh my little dragon, this is just the beginning of our story."

THE COUNTDOWN...9 HOURS LEFT

Time 00:00

Roofs away from where I left Jax, I stop running, my legs refusing to carry me any farther away from the person I'm supposed to abandon.

A person whose absence already tears at me only a few minutes after I left him.

I desperately miss the touch of his fingers caressing my hair, the heat of his lips against my own, the distinct scent of him.

I moan, resting my face in my hands.

If I can't spend a minute without missing Jax now, how am I ever going to just let him go?

Especially without ever telling him how I feel...

A siren wails loudly nearby.

I can't.

Picking my head up, a wild smile stretches across my face, and I turn around, facing once again in the direction of the alleyway I left Jax in.

The flashing red and blue lights of several police cars heading towards the south wall are just visible beyond the tops of the buildings around me.

I don't hesitate.

I run.

At the edge of every building, I use my power to drift over the gaps.

An untamed pounding beats against my ribs as I run over the buildings, drawing ever closer to my destination.

My legs stretch farther every time, my strides lengthening with hope.

Jax's words repeat in my head: *It's too late.*

Well I sure do hope he was wrong and that I can still save him.

Finally, I reach the building closest to the south wall, crouching behind the roof's lip.

My breath catches in my lungs as I make out Jax's strong figure standing on top of the wall.

Only two Bullets stand at its base preparing to fire this time.

But two is still more than enough.

They'll kill him just as fast as eight Bullets would.

Fear cracks through me like a bolt of lightning, and my mind threatens to shut itself down, unprepared to deal with more loss than it already has today.

How is he planning on getting out of this?

Prayerful words fall from my lips in desperation.

My hands shake.

My eyes close.

But my heart still beats on.

I feel its frantic thumping, its dance of hope, pounding out in my chest, trying to tell me not to give up.

Not to forsake the one truth in my life.

The one thing that has always kept me together from the day my parents died until this very moment, watching Jax stand on that wall all alone.

Love.

For many years it saved me.

But now, it must save Jax.

I stand up, no longer hidden by the building's lip, and I yell out the most unadorned, beautiful words I have ever spoken, the sound of them fracturing into millions of pieces and tucking themselves into every moment of time, becoming an unchangeable truth: "I love you Jax."

And in those words, I give Jax the gift of a million years, of a thousand lives, of a peace past death, for in love, one lives forever.

THE COUNTDOWN…8 HOURS LEFT

Time 1:00

Jax's gaze locks with mine, and his beautiful rich laugh reaches my ears: "Took you long enough," he mouths, and then, without warning, he steps back into the void beyond the wall.

Just like that, without bullets, without pain, he's gone.

Disappeared.

Perhaps for forever.

THE COUNTDOWN...7 HOURS LEFT

Time 2:00

"The hackers are all in?" I inquire, swinging my backpack onto my shoulders and heading for the door.

"Yep, we've already started attacking the security system," Leum mutters in response, not even sparing me a glance, his fingers typing away furiously at his computer's keys, "It should be down in about thirty minutes."

"Alright good," I say and then add, "Forever or never."

Finally looking up, he reverently echoes back the words, "Forever or never," and then after a slight pause, he murmurs, "For Sakura."

"For Jax," I gently whisper back.

The door of the bank yawns widely before me, massive white columns framing its shining black door. In large, proud, gold letters above the entrance, it is written, "We are proud to protect your possessions."

A cold wind curls around my neck, spurring me into action.

Hurrying up to the door, I quickly pick the lock. It's quite a simple one, and the door yawns open sleepily when I turn the knob, not even uttering a squeak in defiance.

I'm in, I think and my Lynk automatically sends the message to Leum through our private comm line.

Softly closing the door behind me, I stare at the inside of the empty bank. Outrageously high ceilings, white shining paint, delicately carved wood furniture…just fancy enough to please rich guests and yet lavish enough to ignite greed in the hearts of those less fortunate.

Therefore, I'm not surprised to spot the locks around each valuable item in the room, tethering it to the bank's pristine green marble floor. A taunting laugh thrown in the faces of the poor.

Oh how torturous a visit to this bank must be for anyone on my side of the city…I bet that was its intent, I muse darkly.

Striding forward, my feet sink into the plush dark carpet that leads to the main front desk. Its charcoal tassels shift uncomfortably under my feet as if it knows that I'm not supposed to be here.

Well, hopefully I won't be here long.

Past the seating area, past the front desk, past the employees' lounge, I finally spot a beefy white door, built up like a blockade, a small hand scanner ingrained in its center. This must be it.

As I approach closer, scrutinizing the structure, I notice with unease, the unmistakable glow to the white stone, the impossible unblemished smoothness of it. My stomach tightens like a fist when I take a step closer, my legs already weakening.

It's made of the same material as the cells in police headquarters.

This is going to be tricky.

Taking a few steps back, the sickening pull of the door leaves me. Experimentally, I take one step forward. Immediately, my stomach swirls nauseously.

Stepping back once again the sickness leaves me, and I ponder the meaning of this.

It's as if the door has a force field around it. If I'm far enough away, it doesn't affect me. But the closer I get, the stronger its attacks on me are.

Mulling this over, I decide that I'll just have to heat my hand up outside of its force field, and then try my best to run to the scanner, which I'm starting to realize, might just be impossible.

It's worth a try though.

Automatically, I close my eyes, breathing in deeply, expelling all thoughts until my mind is the empty beach of a forgotten island, only the waters of awareness lapping at the silence.

When all is at peace in my mind, I pick out certain memories, fiery angry ones, full of anguish and despair: when my parents didn't return home, when Fumihiko told me he couldn't find a cure, when the first bullet hit Sakura, when Jax stepped off the wall. I gather them together, and like seeds I plant them into the sands of the still beach, detached from the emotions, but siphoning off the passion and energy of each memory.

Sucking the heat from the room, gathering it into my gloved palm, I feed the seeds of energy, turning the heat into an outright conflagration.

I feel the flames seep into my skin, disappearing into my veins as the temperature in my hand rises, and the dark glove that Jax gave me somehow manages to tame the wild joy of my magic, helping my hand heat up steadily.

After a few seconds a buzz sounds in my ear, my Lynk's warning that I've reached 1,600 degrees in my hand.

Exhaling, I let go of the energy that flies at me from all over the room, breaking most of my connections to the heat surrounding me, only keeping a few that will help me maintain my temperature.

And then I open my eyes.

The world is swathed in red and gold. Shimmering like a sun on the border of exploding.

Dark vermillion orbs of heat mix with energy spheres the color of a damask rose.

And weaving them all together like stars caught in a great constellation, are shimmering strands of gold, so elegant in their finery that one would assume they are created of nothing other than strands of hair from an angel's holy head--the life connecting all things together.

The beauty of it all catches my breath.

I'm reluctant to blink and let it all fall away, but I do in order to better focus on the task at hand.

I glance at my right gloved hand, smiling mischievously as heat waves flow visibly from its surface.

Leum, how long until the system is down?-- I'm ready to burn this scanner to Hell.

The system should fall in six and a half minutes so just make sure the hand scanner is carefully deactivated before then, k? Good luck.

Let's hope I won't need it, I send back, and then I run with full force forward, using a large gust of wind to propel me straight towards the door. I break through its forcefield, nausea immediately cutting through my stomach, pain piercing my skin like thousands of daggers.

As the space between the door and my body decreases, the agony increases tenfold, slowing my body so greatly that by the time my hand is a few inches from the scanner, I am sluggishly crawling towards it.

Waves of pain crash against my head rendering my thoughts splintered like wrecked ships. Sweat drips down into my hair, and my arms quiver dragging me forward.

Soon my wind dies out and it's all I can do to maintain the heat in my hand and sluggishly slide closer to the door.

Every second is torture, and they drag out, each becoming an eternity. If only I could press my hand against that scanner.

A warm liquid drips from my nose, sliding into my mouth, bitter with the bite of iron.

Blood.

I struggle to move forward one last inch, my muscles spazzing, my heart almost stopping, but finally by the work of a miracle, my hand presses against the scanner.

Immediately upon contact, a pain greater than another steals up through my arm, biting its way down my spine, ripping a deathly scream from my throat.

I long to pull my hand away, but I force myself to keep it firmly pressed against the scanner.

I feel the door draw at my energy, gobbling it up like how a child might inhale cookies--without restraint and with no knowledge of when to stop. Seconds pass by, blood continues to drip down my face, and pain steels into my lungs, emptying them of air. My heart beat slows to half its normal speed, and yet my hand remains pressed against the scanner.

After thirty seconds, my vision gives away and I slump against the white stone, but I no longer feel pain at its contact, my mind so far detached from reality, my senses so terribly clouded with a thick fog.

Against my will, my fingers waver and start to slip, but just as my hand totally leaves the scanner, the screen malfunctions and flashes two words in neon blocky letters, "**System Deactivated**."

Letting my hand shakily drop to the ground, I let go of all the heat, and with my last reserve of energy, I summon a wind that pushes me away from the door's forcefield.

Crumbling to the ground, the pain leaves me trembling-- just a pile of skin and bones.

I almost pass out, but a steady stream of energy is being pulled from around the room by my gloves. They seem to be amplifying the weak power I have left to give back some of the energy that was stolen from me. It's brilliant.

I almost laugh in irony, *these stupid gloves that Jax gave his life for actually ended up saving me,* but instead, as weak as I still am, only a somber sigh whistles between my teeth.

Already though, I feel stronger.

Air fills my lungs.

My heart beat speeds up.

Blood ceases to drip from my nose.

I did it.

Made it just in time like always ;) The system is crashing in three… two… one…

I breathe in nervously, my fingers crossed, as I await the outcome.

We're in.

I let my breath go in excitement and more than a little bit of shock. Perhaps I never thought the plan would go as perfectly as it did: It's over. We did it!! We won.

Not so fast. The hackers and I still have to deploy the code that will take the same percentage of total wealth from all large money accounts and evenly distribute it among the rest of the people--

Could you just let me relax for once!

Nope. And if you've forgotten, you need to give the most amazing speech in history to convince the people of this city to rebel against all they have known for their entire lives before the customary 24-hour celebrations of the police end. In fact, Fumihiko and the hackers spread the word that the meeting would be at 3:00 a.m. on the left side of the lake, which is in...about two minutes.

Is that all?

Yep.

Such an easy task, I send sarcastically.

That's the spirit.

THE COUNTDOWN…6 HOURS LEFT

Time 3:00

The stars twinkle in the firmament, dressing in their brightest gowns, preparing the most splendid of feasts. They hurry about, making the last final touches, before all settling into their seats. For the first time in a thousand years, every star turns its eyes away from whatever planet or civilization it had been previously following, and collectively, the mighty stars, guards of the heavens, settle their gazes on one girl as she runs towards a lake, in one small city, on just one of the thousands of planets they watch every day.

Chittering in excitement, the stars whisper to each other, "It's soon. Oh, it's soon now."

THE COUNTDOWN...5 HOURS LEFT

Time 4:00

The crowd is frightening. People swarming the scene in hundreds. They flood the area beside the lake, packing together in small groups to huddle under the streetlights like packs of penguins--pre-A.R.T birds--squawking in excitement.

Clouds disperse to reveal clear skies and extra bright stars, gleaming like diamonds in the night. Their light eradicates the last puddles of solid darkness around the people, swathing the grouping in a pool of rich light as if Heaven itself is showing approval.

Hurrying towards the edge of the lake, I spot a small raised wooden structure just at the water's edge, placed there so people can better enjoy the scenic view. Immediately, I make a beeline for it, planning to use it as the location for my speech.

Shoving my way through the crowd, I pick up snippets of conversations, "How is the leader still alive, we saw her get executed!"... "This better not be a sham, the whole city needs a rebellion--and a successful one at that--more than ever!"... "I heard that the rebellion's leader is not actually a human, but an angel that was injured in battle and fell to earth..."

A few of the wilder ones make me chuckle, but through the parts of conversations that I hear, I realize that the people have a ton of hope, but just as much doubt.

In other words, I have to give a dirty good speech!

A tendril of nervousness stirs awake in my stomach, but I ignore it as best as I can, continuing to slip through the mass of constantly moving bodies.

Finally, I part through the last throng of people blocking the wooden platform, striding into crisp, refreshing air.

Seeing a few people seated on the platform, I climb the stairs to the top quickly, and politely start to ask them to leave, but just as I utter the words "Can you," all their faces turn towards me and in less than a second, the man closest to me, young with an easy-going smile, lets out a gasp, his eyes widening in recognition.

"It's true," he whispers breathlessly, his smile stretching to twice its original size, "you're alive… "

Without waiting for a response, he turns and hurriedly rushes to the steps, urging his colleagues to descend before him.

Confused they cry out, "Who is it?" clamoring for a peak of me over the young man's shoulder, curious who had the authority to make them leave their spot.

Continuing to force his colleagues off the structure, he answers proudly, "She's the one who's going to save us all," and then turning he winks at me before he and his friends disappear into the crowd, as if saying, "Now you *really* better save us all."

His hopeful expression and the faith he automatically put in me, sends my heart into a panicked gallop, clomping out a nervous beat, and I almost collapse into a puddle in apprehension.

It's not just him who I can't let down, it's everyone at this meeting, everyone in the city.

They all need me, and expect me to be this untouchable hero, a savior fated to rescue them from their oppression.

And now, I'm realizing that in order to win this fight for freedom, I'm going to have to win over the faith of the people, and their trust and support.

And to do that I'm going to need to not only live up to the reputation they've built for me, I'm going to have to be far better than it.

My breaths speed up and I gasp for air, my head becoming light and my fingers shaking uncontrollably.

I don't know If I can do this.

In my panic, I search the crowd for a familiar face, an anchor, but all I see are the expectant faces of more and more people whose lives are in my hands, whose weight sits unbearably heavy on my shoulders.

My anxiety mounts, stealing my breath, and I turn around looking for an escape, my eyes lighting on the steps that lead down to the ground.

I could so easily slip away into the crowd, hide in the Library and disappear there for weeks. Nobody would know what happened to me. Nobody except that one guy would really know I was ever here. The rest of them would just go back to believing that I had really died yesterday. It would be so easy...

I take a step forward.

I'm sorry I let you down, I whisper thinking of that young man, *but I can't save you. It's best if I just leave now, live a quiet life...*

And then what? A voice whispers in my thoughts.

I would get a modest job, earn enough to just get by.

Could you really do that? Leave these people behind and live satisfied with the unfairness of life in this city?

Of course I can. After all, I did it for years!

You sure about that?

I struggle to answer, my thoughts utterly divided, half of me vehemently screaming 'yes' and the other half of me fighting to make my lips form the word 'no'.

Could you live knowing that you have disappointed your friends, the entire city? That you broke your promise to your sister?

Horror spreads through my mind at the words, a sense of unease finally breaking through my wild thoughts, and I feel something inside of me trying to claw its way back up into my mind: could it possibly be my courage?

Could you live knowing that you disappointed me, little dragon? Whispers the voice, as it grows deeper and huskier, taking on a slightly mischievous tone. The voice of someone I love.

At the sound, my doubt flies away, total clarity splashing over my head like a bucket full of ice-cold water:

I will NEVER EVER disappoint the people I love.

That's my girl, whispers the voice proudly, morphing into the memory of Jax talking to me in the alleyway, ***"I know that you're strong. You won't just live on, you'll change the world for the better. I believe in you, Kayda. You can do it."***

Yes, I think in response, *I can.*

Pulling my shoulders back and lifting my head defiantly, I raise my gaze to the crowd, no longer feeling burdened by the countless number of people who stand before me. Instead, at the sight, a feeling of warmth spreads throughout my body, lending strength to my limbs and mind: *these are my people and I will save them.*

Opening my mouth, I declare, my voice strong and even, "I am Kayda Kobayashi, leader of the Freedom Thieves and of the rebellion. I fight in the name of all that I lost and in the memory of all those I love. I fight in the name of every person who has felt the anguish of an empty stomach or tasted the tears of despair. I fight for you!" I exclaim fervently, my voice thick with passion, and then after a pause of silence, I continue on confidently, "And so, I think it is about time that we STEAL OUR FREEDOM BACK!"

As I speak, I whip up wind, blowing my words across the entire sea of people, amplifying my voice so that it crashes over them like mighty waves, sounding like the voice of an untouchable hero, like the declaration of a savior, like the promise of a small girl standing before a crowd of hopeful people--a small girl who has already lost her sister and a friend, to keep her promise, and yet by some sort of miracle, she is still willing to move the heavens and far more, just to make her words come true.

THE COUNTDOWN...4 HOURS LEFT

Time 5:00

Silence.

My words are followed by utter silence, the thunderous crashes of my voice fading away to whispers in the air like a retreating storm.

But all I hear is the absence of everything, the sound of a world put on pause.

It sits heavy in my ears, the lack of noise, like a bundle of wool pressed right up against my eardrums.

And with the quiet comes the cold hands of solitude, the brush of sadness, the caress of suffering, but right when the moment would become too long, letting the silence in forever, I see people's arms raise, hands weave together, hundreds of in-flight birds forming.

A sign of protest against the enemy who thrives in the quiet of its victims.

A symbol of fight against *being* that oppressed victim too fearful to speak a word.

A signal that the people of this city will no longer let themselves be ruled by silence.

No, it is time we rebel.

The interminable moment ends.

The world explodes into a chaos of sound.

People shout into the air, yelling to the skies, vociferating their fury, their pain, their passion, screaming in answer to my declaration, "YES, YES, YES!"

THE COUNTDOWN...3 HOURS LEFT

Time 6:00

The cheers quiet, and I take advantage of the moment, starting my speech by doing what I know best, what is ingrained in my being, written in my blood:

I tell a story.

"I once confronted one of my best friends--in fact, it was the man who first asked me to get up and fight for what was mine--saying *I still don't get what makes you think we can do something that experienced spies and soldiers probably can't even do. These people we're going up against, they have money, they have resources, and compared to them, we're just a bunch of rats with dreams."*

A hush falls over the clearing. Reality settling in.

"I had thought at the time that he was asking me to start a suicide mission. A war that would be defeated before we even had a chance to fight. Like most of you, I doubted my own ability, turning away from the chance of freedom so I could avoid the chance of failure. Well, for all of you who once felt like me, I am here to do for you what he once did for me. I am here to make you believe!

"The rich may have money and resources, but we have dreams,

we have hope, we have motivation!" I let my words hang in the air, before continuing on, my eyes, fervently glowing, resting heavily on the crowd, "Let me make clear that victory doesn't come with troops who wear untouched pristine uniforms! NO, it comes with a group of soldiers who wear dirtied and worn clothes; soldiers who carry their hopes and hearts on their sleeves, even though they've been trod on again and again."

Cheers and howls rise up from the crowd in agreement.

"This is NOT a war to be fought by trained spies, agents, and soldiers. NO, this is a war for the common people, FOR US; the thieves, the criminals, the merchants who bellow out their goods from dawn to dusk. This is a fight for righteousness, and only the people who've been oppressed and beaten down too many times to count know what that really means.

"And by that, I mean that EVERY SINGLE one of you should know what I mean!"

"AM I RIGHT?" I holler demandingly out at the sea of people.

They knock against each other, pushing and shoving in their excitement. Men and women and children all yell and holler and clap, the whole crowd wreathing with a vehement spirit, calling out "YES."

"Are you the worn soldiers who still carry their hopes and hearts on their sleeves?"

Again, they scream in unison, "YES!"

"Are you the dreamers that I need? The street rats, the thieves, the criminals, the merchants, that will WIN THIS WAR through pure will? Well, ARE YOU?"

"YES, YES, YES!"

"THEN LET THIS REBELLION BEGIN!" Police cars stream out from the headquarters on the opposite side of the lake, sirens blaring, lights flashing.

My words don't even falter.

"And to those who still doubt us--to the cowards, to the rich, to the police who laugh at us thinking, 'They are trying to achieve what is impossible'--We must respond "If we don't go for the impossible, then WHO ELSE WILL?"

People who were alarmed by the sudden movement of the police, are drawn back into firm resolve at my words. They look up at me expectantly, once again dedicated soldiers to the cause, waiting for my signal that will start the battle.

And so as the police cars drive closer, seconds away from the gathering, we don't move, but instead stand strong. Light outlines every person, smoothing away the wrinkles, lightening the scars, turning the dirt on each shirt to a bedazzling sparkle.

In this moment, we are not animals of dirt and grime and sorrow. No, as sound fades away in concentration, as breaths become even and measured, as hearts sink into a steady driving rhythm, we become soldiers of light, of sun, of hope, shining like flames against the darkness around us, our crude knives and weapons now gloryful blades burning with the heat of our passion.

We are sharp and dangerous in our hope. We are steel and unmovable in our patience.

We are warriors of the sun, destined to sunder the night into pieces small as dust, to drown those flakes in our light, to watch them shrivel and become nothing.

We are now an infinitely burning fire, and no longer will we be snuffed out like mere candles.

Watch Us Burn!

"IT'S TIME! This fight starts as ours and it will end as ours! For the past, for the present, for the future, we fight TODAY!

And with those words, the doors of the police cars fly open, the crowds surge forward--the fight that has been put off for decades, has finally begun.

THE COUNTDOWN...2 HOURS LEFT

Time 7:00

Chaos breaks out, scuffles and fights happening all over as women and men catapult themselves at the officers, grappling with all their strength: bony arms punching and scrabbling at hard uniforms.

A few of the policemen fall down in the crowd and are immediately restrained, held down by multiple people, as the rest of the crowd surges forward searching for their next target. Children yell words of encouragement, running back and forth at the edge of the fight, patting backs in praise, handing out stones they find to fighters.

For a second, it seems as if we hold the dominance in the fight, slowly but surely pushing the officers back. That is until the first gun goes off.

It goes almost unnoticed at first, the sound of the gun so quiet that it doesn't even pierce the roar of battle. But when the bullet hits its victim square in the chest, burying deep into his heart, a keening wail rises from his lips and floats over all the crowd like a phantom.

It echoes ghostly, the sound so raw and lost, like the cry of an innocent, struggling to comprehend the blood gushing from his chest, the shortening of his breaths, the dimming of his vision. Confused why Death took him before it was his time.

For a moment the battle stops, everyone looking at the young man, probably only a year or two older than me, cradled by a sobbing woman who must be his mother, closes his eyes for the last time, a tear still rolling slowly down his cheek, to splat to the ground, mixing with the puddle of his blood.

Every one of us has seen death before or has been very close to it, but the passing of this young man is different. It sits sour in the air, curdling in our stomachs like something rotten. The skies dim to a livid purple, throwing the police in darkness; the stars, too, sense the wrongness of this moment, feel the thickness of the air, like mouthfuls of ash.

He should not have died.

He should have lived for another half a century or more.

And yet his chest is still. He will never suck in another breath.

All because of *them*.

Collectively the thoughts of my people ignite in rage, their vision becoming lined in red.

They stand up, looking away from the young man, but his crumpled body is imprinted on their eyes, burned into the way they grit their teeth, shown in the fingers they hold in fists. They will fight like animals, give everything they have, and yet I look around worried.

Will it be enough?

It takes one bullet to kill a man.

So how many bullets are in each gun?

How many guns are on each policeman?

My stomach tightens.

I can't let my people be slaughtered. I pull up my gloves.

I need to help.

A sliver of sun parts from the sky, falling down to alight on the barrel of a gun, a gun that is fixed on the grieving mother that cradles her son's dead body. I watch as a finger presses down on the trigger, as a bullet flies out with startling speed.

A bullet of the same make and model that shot me in the shoulder, that killed my sister, that was meant to kill Jax.

This is where the cycle ends.

I raise my hand.

Focusing on the air around the bullet, streaks of gold become visible, connecting bluish-bronze strands of air.

My concentration focuses and all sound fades away.

I can do this.

The bullet speeds towards the woman, heading straight for her heart like it did for her son. Her brown hair flutters in the wind, her fingers still clutching the bloody shirt of the corpse next to her. She should be dead in less than a second, laying splayed on the ground in a puddle of mixed blood.

But I won't let that happen.

Gritting my teeth, I pull at the air strands, tightly knitting them together in a cup under the bullet with my mind. With a surge of determination, I send a focused gust of air right at the little cup, and an inch away from the woman's chest, the bullet shifts, shivers as if uncomfortable, and then at the last minute, entirely alters its course, heading straight up into the sky and then plinking harmlessly into the lake.

Immediate exhilaration floods my veins, setting my magic humming pleasantly through my body.

Cocking my head with a grin, I can't help the crazy laugh that burbles past my lips and bounces into the air.

My hands buzzing, my heart thumping, all I can think is:

This is what I was born for.

THE END

Time 8:00

All eyes are on me. The rebels, the police. The stars, God.

But I don't stop.

I'm way past doubt.

Triggers are pulled, bullets speed toward me, but it all just aids me in my mission.

I call to the metal of every bullet, using air to push them from their guns, feeling each small orb as they shift and shimmy, flying past me to plink into the lake.

One after another, they sink into the depths of the water, creating light, little chimes as they meet with the lake's surface, sighs of content to finally being laid to rest.

I don't stop until I feel that every single gun is empty, and then on a whim, I snatch all the guns with hands of wind and toss them into the water as well. Then with gusts of air, I carefully extract the crude weapons and farming tools of the rebels, making a great pile behind me.

I am sick of fighting. Of weapons. Of death.

We can finish this battle another way.

Slowly I walk down the steps of the platform. The crowd of rebels parts for me, some people bowing their heads as I walk past, others watching me with slight distrust, glancing nervously at my hands, and a few even dare to whisper "She has magic!" or "She's alien!"

They don't know what I am anymore. What I can do.

I am unpredictable.

And it's smart that they fear me.

After all, a prideful smile touches my lips, *I did just disarm hundreds of people with a wave of my hand.*

My black boots hit the ground confidently, small puffs of dust lazily circling them, and rising to drift onto my black pants that stretch and tense, perfectly fitted so that I can move as fast as possible. My charcoal shirt is tight, my midnight jacket flexible so that I can climb and fight unrestrained. Everything is fitted and orderly and neat, except my hair, which whips in my own wind, wild and unrestrained. It tumbles long down my back, dark and free.

The strands glow silver blue as I stop in a beam of starlight.

I have halted in the strip of land that separates the police from the rebels.

Saying nothing, I watch both sides as they watch me.

I wonder how I must look to them.

Clothed in all black, hair flying in the wind.

Dangerous, powerful...beautiful.

For sure, they no longer think of me as their perfect savior or a celestial being that fell from the heavens to deliver them from their pain.

No, but those who really change the world, almost never are.

I imagine that now, shining in the sun, all in black, I would look more like a dark angel.

A fitting title.

For I will save my people, but it was a dark path, the one that led to this light.

I have lost much.

And I am no longer innocent.

But I am still here.

I have not given up.

And so I glance one last time at the message Leum sent me during the fight earlier: The money is transferred. I'm on my way to see you SAVE THIS DIRTY CITY!

With a small smile now on my lips, I start to speak: "I once asked myself a question. A simple question in many ways. One that had only two possible answers: yes or no. And when I answered it that day, I knew that if I said no, then I would never do it, and if I said yes, then I would be doing it forever. Therefore, the two possible answers were really not yes or no but forever or never. The question I asked myself was: 'Should I fight for this city, for the beginning of something right, for the end of everything wrong?' And as you can guess, I chose *forever*.

"That day I promised I would fight until my death, or until I could no longer raise a fist or utter a word," I stare out at the crowd, my voice unflinching, ringing out across them and over the lake like a solemn prayer.

"And that is why we are here. For years this city has been ruled by a council of the seven richest people in the city. They made taxes. They controlled the police. They oversaw our work. In other words, they stole, they cheated, they lied."

I pause looking in the eyes of the officers around me. Daring them to stare into the gaze of the person who will bring about their demise.

"The cycle ends today! As you all fought each other, my team and I managed to hack and break into the bank." The eyes of the officers bulge in surprise and some of them exchange uneasy glances as if just realizing that this fight is real. On the other hand, the rebels start to cheer and whoop in excitement. "As we speak, money is being redistributed so that those who have nothing, will now have enough to eat and buy necessary items!"

Screams of jubilation and triumph drown out my words for a second, and I pause before continuing on calmly, an excited smile starting to stretch across my face as I witness the euphoria caused by my words.

"No longer does the government hold our money. Therefore, no longer does the government hold power. It's over!"

The rebels stream forward, clapping and jumping in joy.

"If you surrender now," I address the policemen, "we will show you mercy as we rebuild this city anew."

None of them move, although some whisper to each other, trying to figure out if what I said could be true.

"I assure you that it is best you give in now. After all, you have no weapons. And you have no clue as to what I can do." I raise my hands in a false threat.

Immediately, one officer kneels and raises his arms, deciding that pride is not worth the possibility that I am telling the truth. Within seconds, the rest of the policemen follow his lead.

"Good choice! You made that easy!" I chirp happily, moving my gaze to the celebrating rebels.

With a clap, amplified across the crowd with wind, I gain all their attention, and immediately silence descends over the area.

"Now hold off your celebrating! We still have to create a whole new government and rebuild this city! So in the next few days while we figure this all out, I will be standing in as a makeshift leader. If anybody has a problem with that, speak now."

A cat meows in an alleyway, pots clink in someone's kitchen, the stars smile, but no one in the crowd utters a word.

"Well then," I remark surprised, "We will be holding meetings here by the lake at 8 a.m. every day for the next week or more to discuss the future of this city. Every family is welcomed to send in one member as a representative…" and finding nothing else essential to tell them, I just raise my hand in the symbol of a flying bird, and as the crowd follows my example, hundreds of birds flying free, I etch the bird symbol in the sky with fire, pulling water from the lake to form the word "Forever."

I watch as the crowd gasps and laughs in surprise, pointing at the fire and water in awe. In moments, young rebels start running into the streets with glee, shouting out to those who stayed in their houses that the fight is over and that we won.

The police slowly retreat, heading back into their cars, leaving quietly in defeat.

As I watch it all, a great feeling of victory washes through my veins, and warms my limbs, but even as a content smile stretches across my face, I can't ignore the small twinge in my heart.

I did it, I made you proud today didn't I? I think to Sakura.

I freed the people, started to straighten out the city just like you said I would, I think to Jax.

A small girl comes and throws herself on me in a hug, whispering 'thank you' before her mother comes and takes her away with an apology.

But even as I reply 'you're welcome' with a grin, I can't help but think to myself: *Then why do I feel unsatisfied?*

24

THE BEGINNING

My feet swing gently as I sit, tickled by a warm wind. A few weeks after The Redemption--the name given to the battle that gained the city people freedom--the chill that had sat in the streets for months, suddenly left. Some said that the cold had been caused by sadness and that after The Redemption, nobody had room for it in their hearts anymore. Others claimed that the Dragon had went about warming the streets with her love and fire. And of course the reasonable people, just said that summer was bound to come.

I'm not sure what I believe, but I am enjoying the warm weather.

The snow cone in my hand drips onto the stone beside me, and after taking one last bite, I melt it into a puddle with a thought, heating my hands to evaporate any sticky residue.

An amused smile touches my face as I recall handing Leum a snow cone this morning. He was thrilled that I had remembered his request, and thought it was just the coolest thing ever that I had made snow in the summer. His unburdened laughter upon receiving it was better than any goodbye.

My grin wanes as the memory fades away, and I stand up, brushing the dirt from my shorts.

The city looks small before me as I stand on the top of the wall swathed in fog. From what I can see, trucks and volunteers are knocking down old buildings as I watch, while sturdy ones are being built up with cranes and scaffolds.

It almost looks like a living thing, the city. A battered old creature that is finally being tended to. And if I close my eyes, I can almost hear its heartbeat.

Ta dum ta dum ta dum

The rhythm is slow and a bit uneven, but it gives me hope.

I believe that the city will get better. Not immediately, I know. But in time it will.

After all, just in the last two weeks, through daily meetings, the city people and I managed to create a whole new democratic government. Hundreds of people had asked me to lead, but I refused every time. I've already done my part.

In the end though, the young man who had recognized me when I climbed the wooden platform, was chosen to work out the last details and kinks of the governmental system. Apparently, he had been a great supporter of the rebellion and was known too many to be a genuinely kind man.

Anyway, I already have a good feeling about him from the first time we met. I believe he'll do a good job of guiding the people into a great new era and help them rebuild this city into something different.

Something better than it ever was.

And although I look fondly on the change that has taken ahold of the city and its people, it also brings me a certain amount of melancholy to see the old theatre get knocked down and Li Jin's repainted.

The city I grew up in, the buildings I know by heart ... it's all fading away.

The place I've always called home is becoming something of the past.

And Kayda Kobayashi has started to vanish with it.

She is stuck in the fading wallpaper of her mother's bedroom, in the books of Fumihiko's shop, in the last laugh of her sister.

And now in her place, I stand, with nothing else to call myself but the nickname my people insist on addressing me by, the Dragon.

I am no longer a person, but a legend, a myth, a tale told before bed. I am the wings in the shadows, the warmth in the night. I am the broken chain, the granted wish.

I am finally free and yet I have not tried to leave my cage, test the boundaries.

But as the last bits of the old city fade, as the final remnants of Kayda Kobayashi disappear, I more and more have the feeling that I no longer belong here.

This city, this battle, was just leading to the start, for in this moment I am sure that my story has only just begun.

And so I know now that it's time to move on.

I lift my backpack up from the wall, swinging it onto my back. All it holds is the blanket of stories my mom made for me, the desert painting I stole, the gloves Jax gave me, a bundle of food and water, and an old picture of my family. My knives are strapped in their places like always: *For strength, for stealth, for protection, for forgiveness.*

I have all I need to live.

All I need to never forget.

I take a small step backwards, my foot resting at the edge of the wall.

Looking up, I soak in the image of the city I can see past the fog--the lake, the fancy buildings in the distance, the squat and crumbling ones in front of me, all tinged in a dusky violet, the sun a few minutes away from relinquishing its role to the stars.

Grasping Jax's small silver chain in my hand, I whisper to the place that has been my home for the last sixteen years, *goodbye*.

My foot reaches back and finds air, and by the laws of gravity, I start to fall.

Vanishing into the mist.

Perhaps for *forever*.

ACKNOWLEDGMENTS

Writing a book has not been easy, not just for me, but for my family and friends who have supported me through the whole endeavor; Writing the entirety of a book by fourteen takes a lot of focus and a lot of hours, and a lot of drives to the library (so thank you to my drivers, snack-makers, and sideline coaches). I want to especially thank my mother for always fueling my passion for writing and for not only pushing me to pursue my dreams, but for helping me make them substantial. I want to thank Bridget who was with me every step of the way, helping to bring Kayda to life (linkala ka sa). Thank you, Anna and Sarah, for catching all the double spaces and making sure it was somewhat realistic even when my imagination took off. Thank you, Chloé, for being the best older sister ever, reading it as I wrote it, and always supporting me. Thank you, Nick, for being one of my first readers; I hope you also pursue your dream of writing. And I want to give a big thank you to Dee Ernst, who made the publishing of this book possible. And most importantly, thank you for reading this :) What is a book's purpose, if not to be read?

Made in the USA
Monee, IL
29 January 2020

20956960R00162